'I loved this book! As a parent of two autistic people myself, I can assure the would be readers that the life described by Denis Deasy in this entertaining tale is spot on!'

'Against all the odds, love and positivity comes shining through in this touching and ultimately uplifting snapshot of a life less ordinary.'

'Funny, sad, honest and most importantly well written. This is a stunning first novel about the challenges raising a child with autism through the eyes of a father. I can't recommend this book highly enough.'

'This book is one of the best I have read, the honesty, love, laughter and tears all captured in one brilliant read.'

'A wonderful book beautifully written, covers a whole series of emotions, I recommend you read this book if you do nothing else.'

'It is full of honesty, humour but most of all love and respect with seemingly getting little in return. Everyone should read this book, whether touched by autism or not. It would help to make us all more tolerant and accepting of those that are a little bit different.'

I'm Sorry,
MY SON'S AUTISTIC

Denis Deasy

Grosvenor House
Publishing Limited

The right of Denis Deasy to be identified as the author of this
work has been asserted in accordance with Section 78
of the Copyright, Designs and Patents Act 1988

The book cover is copyright to Denis Deasy
Denis Deasy on Twitter: @DeasyDenis

This book is published by
Grosvenor House Publishing Ltd
Link House
140 The Broadway, Tolworth, Surrey, KT6 7HT.
www.grosvenorhousepublishing.co.uk

This book is a work of fiction. Any resemblance to
people or events, past or present, is purely coincidental.

A CIP record for this book
is available from the British Library

ISBN 978-1-78623-638-8

To Joanmarie, Denis, James and to all my
extended family and friends
(I think that covers everyone).

Acknowledgement

There are several people who have helped me in writing this book. My thanks to Cliff McNish and Noreen Keane for spotting my seemingly obvious mistakes. I am also extremely grateful to Sean Poole, Tony Prouse, Joanna Rees and my wife, Joanmarie, who have all read my book at least twice. Your advice and guidance has been invaluable.

PRICELESS

'Fuck off, can't you see I'm busy?'

'I beg your pardon?'

'You heard me, now fuck off.'

Harry's mentor, Jon, quickly steps in.

'I'm sorry madam, Harry has just started today. He's autistic.'

'That's as maybe, but his attitude is totally unacceptable. I was only asking where I can get paper towels.'

'Just go away; you're blocking my view of the KitKats,' Harry demands.

'He's uncontrollable. How can you employ such an individual? '

'Again, I apologise, but he *does* have special needs,' Jon re-iterates, before leading the lady to the paper towels aisle.

Harry's first day at our local supermarket, *PriceLess*, hasn't got off to a good start.

Harry's daily encounters with members of the public can be a rollercoaster of emotions. They are usually confused and often hurt by Harry's comments, and I can understand that, as it's not something that they would experience too often; if at all. However, I do get frustrated and sometimes angry, when even after Harry's situation is explained to them they still seem pissed off.

At the same time I also get upset with Harry for instigating these situations. I frequently warn him to think twice before saying such hurtful remarks. However, up to now it hasn't had any effect. It does get me down explaining about Harry to strangers on a daily basis.

'Why were you so rude to that lady?' I ask my son.

'I'm trying to sort these stinky cheeses into the correct order, and she was disturbing me.'

'Harry, part of your job is to help the customers.'

'Fuck them; they're all a bunch of losers; with weird hair.'

I don't remember this alternative customer services approach being discussed at his induction course.

Harry is my sixteen-year-old son and about a month ago I visited *PriceLess* to discuss the possibility of employment for him. Harry attended an interview about ten days later and Steve, the store manager, asked him why he wanted to work at *PriceLess*, to which Harry replied 'I need the dosh to buy more *Thomas The Tank Engine* DVDs, and with all the food in this place I'll be able to have some great lunches.'

Steve tried to stress the importance of customer services, stating that all the staff must always be polite and helpful to the customers. Harry just smirked and said, 'Yeah, right.' Despite this, Harry got the job. It was one of the most proudest moments of my life. I've always had doubts about Harry's employment prospects, but *PriceLess* does have a reputation for employing special needs people. After this morning they may be revising this policy.

I was able to be with Harry at both the interview and the induction course.

'This is boring shit,' Harry proclaimed after watching a work health and safety video earlier this morning.

'Can I watch a James Bond DVD instead?' he asked Steve, who smiled sheepishly in return.

As this is Harry's first day I'm also allowed to spend the day with him, to give Jon and co a crash course on the world of autism.

'I'm sorry about that. Harry can be a bit full-on,' I say to Jon, upon his return.

'She was a bit shocked, but when I gave her a ten pound gift voucher she seemed much happier.'

I hope that the end of day totals for gift vouchers doesn't exceed Harry's daily wages.

'Harry, if a customer asks you a question just tell them politely to come to me, or another member of staff, 'Jon says, 'is that OK?'

'If they interrupt me again they're going to get a black eye.'

Jon has a bewildered and slightly desperate expression as he looks at me for reassurance.

'He doesn't mean that,' I smile back.

'So, how's it all going?' Steve asks as he walks towards us.

Jon and me look at each other, but it's Harry who replies first.

'Apart from those wankers,' Harry says, pointing at the customers nearby, 'this place is the dog's bollocks.'

'Good to hear.' Steve nervously looks around to see if anyone else heard Harry's rather forthright comments.

'I don't like the ceiling. It's too high. Can it be brought down by seven feet and eight inches?'

'That's a bit difficult.'

'But you're the manager of this joint. Sort it out.'

'Ok, Harry, we can discuss this later. Why don't you carry on with the cheeses?' I intervene.

'Can't you make the cheeses smell better? They're vile,' Harry asks Steve.

Steve just grins, and quietly walks away.

All first day employees must do a stint on the till. Although this is part of the 'throwing you in at the deep end' philosophy that *PriceLess* encourage, I did remind Steve that it was a huge risk to put Harry in that position.

'He'll be closely monitored, so don't worry, it'll be fine,' he responded confidently.

At the induction course Harry did some training on the till and managed OK, so I have no fears about that, it's just those damn customers.

Jon and I stand alongside Harry as he serves the first few customers without any problems. Jon is then called away to deal with another issue, but reassures me that he won't be long.

The next customer is an elderly man. He hands Harry a bottle of red wine.

'Have you got any ID?' Harry asks.

'What for?'

'To prove you're over eighteen of course.'

'I'm seventy-nine years old mate.'

'I need to see your ID and I'm not your mate. I've never seen you before.'

A group of teenagers in line start giggling.

'I'm sorry sir but this is Harry's first day and he's autistic,' I add.

'Why on earth would he be put in this position when he clearly can't do this job?'

'He certainly *can* do this job, he just needs some guidance,' I reply rather too loudly.

'He needs a hell of a lot of guidance if you ask me. Can I speak to the manager?'

4

Steve arrives shortly afterwards.

'Can I help you sir?'

'Yeah, this boy refused to serve me unless I produce ID. Why do you employ such people?'

'You still haven't given me your ID, you old fart,' Harry chips in.

The elderly man looks stunned, while the teenagers cannot stop laughing.

Steve attempts to take the bottle off Harry, but my son is refusing to let it go. Steve then goes to the beers, wines and spirits section and picks up another wine bottle and hands it to the man, free of charge. The man is still shaking his head as he leaves the store.

'I think we'll take Harry off the till for now,' a more subdued Steve remarks upon his return.

'I did try to warn you,' I feel like saying to him, but why kick a man when he's down?

There was only one further incident, when Harry decided to get about half a dozen items for lunch (a KitKat, crisps, Thomas The Tank Engine magazine, etc) but as I was waiting in the checkout queue, Harry just walked out of the supermarket while crunching on his salt and vinegar crisps. Of course this set off the alarm. A security staff member immediately chased after Harry. After a few minutes of questioning, he realised the situation for what it was, and Harry returned to the store to pay for his goods.

'This is ridiculous. I should have everything for free.'

'It doesn't work like that, Harry.'

'What a bunch of greedy bastards.'

Whenever a customer approached Harry, both myself and Jon literally ran towards them to answer their query, before Harry got a chance to reply.

'You're very enthusiastic,' one customer told us.

His job at *PriceLess* is only on Saturdays. If he gets through the probation period (the local bookies are offering very low odds on this!) then his contract will be reviewed, with the hope of working more hours. But one small step at a time.

Harry is sixteen years old. He has Asperger Syndrome, which is the milder form of autism. He also has ADHD (Attention Deficient Hyperactivity Disorder). He has to take Ritalin medication every day, which helps calm him down.

Harry's mother is Laura. I met her in a pub at Waterloo on Christmas Eve, nineteen ninety-eight. I was out having a drink with my postmen colleagues when I noticed her. She looked stunning in a beautiful red dress and I mentioned this to my co-worker, Alan, who promptly told her as much. Laura came over and introduced herself and we started dating soon afterwards. We had a lot of common interests – a love of music, theatre and Italian food. Our wedding day in July two thousand and two was, and still is, the happiest day of my life. We planned to have at least two children but Harry's diagnosis changed everything. His strange behaviours at such an early age and his ability to go night after night with such little sleep took its toll on us and consequently my relationship with Laura suffered. I remember going to work most days on only one or two hours sleep. If Harry was awake either Laura or me had to be up with him. It got to the point where Laura stayed up most weekdays as she said that I needed my rest for work. He was constantly hitting both of us, and showed no interaction with anyone. When he was two years old he started to smear his excrement all around the house and this continued until he was toilet trained at four. I had difficulty coping with everything, but Laura simply collapsed under the strain and had a breakdown when Harry was four years old. Although it was one of the most difficult decisions of my life I had no choice but to take full custody of Harry. Laura was in no fit state to look after him for any period of time. We eventually divorced five years ago. However, eventually her mental health improved and she made a full recovery, but she's never got over the guilt of not being there for Harry. Would we still be together if Harry was a 'normal' child? I'd like to think so, but who knows?

Because of some of Harry's behaviours, we saw a child psychologist just before his third birthday who concluded that Harry just had learning difficulties. He was officially diagnosed as autistic two days before his fourth birthday.

As we're ready to leave, Steve approaches us.

'Have you got a few minutes to spare?' he asks.

Oh dear, this doesn't bode well, as he leads us to his pokey office at the back of the supermarket.

'Please don't worry, this is just a routine chat that I always do after any new employee's first day. It's just to get some feedback, and identify any issues,' Steve says as we enter his office.

'Well, Harry, how do you feel after your first day at work?'

'I feel like having a shit.'

'What, now?' Steve asks.

'Yep.'

Steve looks over at me, a little lost for words.

'Where's the crapper?'

'OK, Harry, there's no need for that language,' I say.

Steve looks somewhat perplexed. I'm pretty confident that this first day review isn't the norm.

He gives Harry directions to the toilet, and we wait ten minutes before his return.

'That's better, although that yellow toilet paper is ridiculous. What the hell's going on there? You should always get white. I liked the sink though.'

'Ok, that's enough about the toilet facilities,' I tell my son.

'As I said before, this is just a quick appraisal on your first day, Harry. Did you enjoy it?' Steve asks.

'Where's my dosh?'

'I'm sorry?'

'My money. I worked my bollocks off out there.'

'We pay you every four weeks, so the next pay day will be Friday the twenty-third of August.'

'Piss off.'

'Harry, you've got to stop talking to Steve like that.'

'But he's a con artist.'

'That's the rules for everyone, Harry,' I say. 'Don't worry, Steve, I'll give him some money today to keep him quiet.'

'Are you letting him get away with it?' Harry asks me while pointing at Steve.

'Harry, just drop it, OK?'

Steve now looks totally disorientated.

'My apologies, Steve. I think Harry's just a bit overwhelmed.'

That's a lie and doesn't make any sense whatsoever. Steve isn't the only befuddled person in the room.

'Perhaps we can continue this on your next shift? But the overall feedback I got was good, although we need to work on a couple of robust comments you made, and a little more training on the sales of alcohol.'

That semi-positive endorsement makes me feel a little better.

'Thanks for your understanding, Steve. I know that Harry's very different from the rest of your staff, so I really appreciate your patience,' I say.

Steve smiles and nods towards me.

'Harry, is there anything you want to say to Steve?'

'Yeah, I don't like your belt, it's too brown.'

'What colour should it be?'

'Any colour apart from brown.'

Another Harry conversation comes to an abrupt end.

We leave shortly afterwards. I'm pleased that overall Harry did OK today, but the big worry is his interaction with the customers. As the store is full of shoppers throughout the day, this will be an on-going problem. Jon cannot stay by Harry's side every minute of every day, so the chances that Harry will let rip again are extremely high. Having said all of that, I'm relieved that his first working day is over.

I'm not sure what his wages will be, but, as promised, I hand over a twenty pound note to my son for his days' work. Although Harry does have a bank account, letting him loose with the pin number would not be a wise move.

'Wow, that's amazing. I'm going to buy a Thomas DVD and twelve packets of Starbursts,' Harry proclaims.

'That's too many Starbursts.'

'OK, eleven packets of Starbursts and a packet of Love Hearts. Shall we go to the police about the robber?' Harry asks.

'What robber?'

'Steve, of course.'

'Harry, let me explain again. All the staff gets paid every four weeks. This has nothing to do with Steve, OK?'

Harry doesn't look convinced. My mobile rings before I can explain further; it's Laura.

'How did he get on?' she asks.

'Well, he did tell a lady customer to fuck off.'

'Oh my God, how did she take it?'

'A little startled, but they managed to smooth things over with a gift voucher. Apart from that, he did well.'

'Why does he keep on insulting people?'

'I don't know. I kept on telling him to be nice to the customers. It's a worry.'

'Can't they keep him away from the customers?'

'Maybe there're some jobs behind the scenes, but he was hired to stack shelves and serve the public.'

'I'm not confident about this.'

You and me both.

'They're all very supportive. Let's hope that continues'.

I'll mention the ID incident to her later.

'Have you packed Harry's clothes yet?' she asks.

'No, I'll start tomorrow.'

Harry is going to a residential schooling placement in three days' time. The house is in Hastings, which is about an hour and forty-five minutes' drive from us. The thought of Harry living away from me frequently brings me to tears. I feel so guilty. It's such an emotional time for us all. Harry doesn't want to go, but I hope that once he settles in he'll be fine. The plan is for Harry to stay there from Sunday night to Friday morning, and we'll have him back for the weekends.

'Can I pop over tomorrow evening? I want to see Harry.'

'Of course.'

'Will it be OK with Kerry?'

'Yeah, no problem.'

Kerry and her son, Niall, are living with me and Harry. Niall and Harry were in the same class. I'd bump into Kerry at school events and birthday parties and got to know her quite well. She's divorced from Danny, who hasn't been the most supportive of fathers, so she's virtually bringing up Niall on her own. She has that wonderful Irish warm, friendly manner about her, and, despite everything, she has a great sense of humour. We lost touch until I bumped into her while out shopping about nine months ago. We started dating shortly afterwards and four weeks ago Kerry and Niall moved in with us. Niall is severely autistic and completely non-verbal. It's been quite a change in routine for us all.

'I can't believe that I'm so rich,' Harry exclaims on our walk home.

'You'll get twenty pounds again next week if you stay at *PriceLess*, but if you continue to swear at the shoppers you may lose your job, and then there'll be no more money.'

'But they deserve it, the little shits.'

I'm too tired to argue with Harry right now.

'I'm going to send Bernadette three and a half packets of Starbursts in the post.'

'Why don't you just give them to her when you see her tomorrow?'

'Nah, they taste much better when you post them.'

Bernadette is Harry's girl friend, as opposed to girlfriend. She was also in Harry's class. Bernadette also has Asperger Syndrome. It's a lovely, sweet relationship. When they go out together they are always chaperoned by either myself, Laura or Bernadette's mother, Alice.

'Where would you like to go with Bernadette tomorrow?'

'Peckham,' Harry replies without hesitation.

'What's in Peckham?'

'I like the traffic lights there.'

I would have thought that once you've seen one set of traffic lights...

'OK, apart from the traffic lights, what else do you want to do in Peckham?'

'Nothing. I'm just going take photos of the traffic lights, especially when they change colour, and also when the cars stop at the lights.'

'Will Bernadette enjoy this as well?'

'She's going to love it.'

That's a cheap date.

'What do you like the best about Bernadette?'

'She always washes her hands after going to the toilet.'

NEVER REGIONS

We arrive at our house and Kerry gives me a hug as I enter the hallway.

'Well, how did he do?'

I explain the customer incident; Harry thinking that he can eat anything in the store at no personal cost, the ID issue, and his assumption that Steve is a con artist and a robber.

'Sounds like a typical Harry day,' she says.

'They asked if I could come along again next Saturday. I really want this to be a success.'

Niall strides into the kitchen and heads straight over to me. As he's close to me, I immediately recognise that glazed look in his eyes.

'Niall, shall we go to the sweet shop?' I ask, mainly as a diversionary tactic, although I know from past experience that this is a waste of time.

Niall is looking at the rather delicate area between my legs.

'What about some chocolate ice cream? That's your favourite,' I plead, attempting to keep him at arm's length, but he forcefully pushes both my arms away.

Kerry steps in but he brushes her aside with ease.

'Get my cricket box,' I shout to Harry.

Niall is still focused on my nether regions. I try to hold him off but it's pointless. He's much taller and stronger than me. With all his might he punches my testicles, which causes me to fall back against the wall, completely out of breath, but he hasn't finished yet. Despite Kerry attempting to hold him back he manages to punch me again where it hurts the most, with even more force. I collapse onto the floor. I look up and see Niall standing over me, holding his hand out, presumably to apologise.

Kerry attempts to usher him away from me, but he shakes his head, still holding his hand out to me. I manage to get to my knees and gently shake his hand.

Kerry hands him his Action Man and leads him into the living-room. I hear him stride up and down, making grunting noises to himself.

Harry then rushes into the kitchen and throws me my cricket box. Better late than never.

I'm still out of breath when Kerry re-enters the kitchen.

'Oh, David, I'm so sorry. I just don't know how to stop this behaviour.'

Niall has whacked me in my testicles before, but since we've been living together he's doing it several times daily. We saw a psychologist recently about this, and he said that it's not a sexual action, it's severe OCD behaviour. He could be just so easily hitting my arm or leg, and this will still satisfy his OCD cravings. He simply has to go through with his punch, and nothing will stop him from doing so. This is always the same greeting when he first sees me every day, and it continues from there.

His face has a hypnotic expression just before he's about to punch me. Immediately after he fulfils his OCD needs, he always wants to shake my hand, as if he has come out of a trance.

I have resorted to wearing a cricket box whenever I'm with Niall, and this helps, but it's extremely uncomfortable and causes severe irritation. At the weekends I'm wearing it from morning to night.

'I should've had my cricket box on before coming into the house. I was distracted with talking about Harry.'

'Still, it can't carry on like this.'

I stagger to my feet and immediately undress to put on my jock strap and cricket box.

'Kerry, I knew all about Niall before you moved in. This isn't a surprise.'

What I didn't know though was the sheer volume and intensity of these assaults. However, Niall simply can't help himself.

There is a link between autism and OCD. Sufferers from OCD constantly feel high levels of anxiety and their ritualistic behaviours reduce these anxieties. However, generally they do not enjoy their routine compulsions and do feel an over-riding sense of urgency to perform these actions in case something bad happens.

I lay awake at night thinking about Niall, and wondering what the hell is going through his mind. Kerry worries about him twenty-four hours a day. I try my best to relieve some of that stress, but it's not easy for me too. Niall is a very complicated boy, and difficult to read. I'm finding it extremely challenging dealing with *both* Harry and Niall. In a couple of days' time Harry will be at the residential home from Monday to Friday, so hopefully that will ease the pressure.

I know first-hand the impact of having an autistic child has on a relationship. Laura and I had a strong marriage before Harry, but as Harry's autistic behaviours kicked in, combined with the endless sleepless nights (which continue to the present day), it began to affect our relationship. Initially it was just snippy arguments, which we rarely had before, which developed into intense, shouting disagreements. Something had to give, and it was Laura's health and eventually our marriage. I read somewhere that if you have one autistic child the divorce rate is eighty per cent. This fact is definitely reflected in my own autistic circle of friends.

My divorce shattered me and made me extremely wary of female relationships, especially given the Harry baggage. Kerry is my first serious relationship since my divorce.

'What are you thinking about?' Kerry asks me, almost as if she can read my mind.

'Nothing, really.'

'Any regrets about us moving in?'

'Why do you say that?' I ask, as if I don't know the answer.

'Niall has raised the stress levels in this household, which were already high to begin with,' Kerry replies.

'Look, I'm not going to lie, it's been tough. Do I like getting punched in my nuts every day? Do I sometimes fear entering my own house when I know that I've forgotten to wear my cricket box? Yes, of course. What person wouldn't? But we'll work through it, we have to.'

'I realise it's been so difficult for you, but any future that we have together *has* to include Niall,' she replies.

'I just want to be honest with you.'

Kerry nods and then walks into the kitchen. She returns with a bottle of red and two glasses.

'I think you're in need of a glass or two,' she says.

'Are you implying I'm an alcoholic?' I reply smiling.

'Not yet, but my son is definitely pushing you in that direction,' Kerry says as she pours me a glass.

'What's on the box?' she asks.

'The usual – *Pointless*, *The Chase*, etc, but there's a premier league game on in ten minutes.'

'I think I'll do the laundry.'

'OK, *Pointless* it is. It's only Spurs anyway.'

'Any plans for tomorrow?' Kerry asks.

'Harry wants to go to Peckham with Bernadette tomorrow to look at the traffic lights,' I say.

'Sounds exciting,' she replies with a slightly sarcastic tone.

'We could go for a coffee and some shopping after, if you want?'

'Yeah, Niall will like that.'

Harry walks into the kitchen.

'Are you going to take off your trousers and underpants, and get your willy out before dinner?' he asks me.

'What are you talking about?'

'Are you going to bonk each other?'

'Harry, that's very personal. Don't ask me about that again, OK?'

'Robert told me that his mum makes groaning noises when she's doing that bonking stuff, so he always rushes into the bedroom to make sure she's ok.'

'And was she?' I ask, although a little afraid of the answer.

'She tells Robert that she has a pain in her groin, but it'll go away soon. Does the bloody bonking hurt you as well?' he asks Kerry.

'Can we drop this subject, Harry? Now what do you want for dinner?' I ask, trying to distract him. I must have yet another sex education chat with him, because he clearly hasn't grasped the concept.

'Steak, chips and beans, with the steak well done. And some garlic bread on the side. Niall will have chicken wings and his own chips as well. Get cracking.'

There are no grey areas as far as food is concerned.

'Kerry, you're a shit cook, so just let Dad get on with it, OK?'

'Harry, if you're rude to Kerry one more time, you're not going to get any dinner.'

'Come on, Dad, even you've got to admit that she's really crap at cooking.'

'No, Kerry's an excellent cook. Your problem is that she makes different dinners to mine, and you don't like change.'

Harry looks confused.

'If she makes my dinner, I'll just give it to Figaro, and I'll eat four KitKats instead.'

Figaro is our cat. I'm not sure whether Figaro would like the chips and beans, and I think she prefers her steak medium rare.

Kerry looks at me and smiles, but the smile is weak. I can tell that she's a little hurt by Harry's comments.

As always, Niall is standing right beside me as I prepare the meal, constantly staring at the oven. Every few minutes he presses his fingers to his lips and makes a grunting noise, which is the Makaton sign for food. Makaton is a language programme, using signs and symbols to help people communicate. Although I tell him it won't be long, he gets increasingly frustrated and head-butts my elbow a few times. Cooking a meal in this household is always extremely pressurised.

'That was average,' Harry remarks, after finishing his meal. 'You're better than mum and Kerry, but you must improve.'

Thank you, Marco Pierre White.

There is one bean left on my plate, but Niall quickly grabs it.

'Hey, I wanted that.' Harry says to Niall, but Niall just swallows the bean and makes his way to the garden, clutching his ever present Spider-Man toy.

I watch Niall as he paces up and down the garden, following the same route. He's done this so often that it now looks like a footpath. He then stops to stare up at the sky for a couple of minutes. I look up myself, expecting to see a plane or a bird, but there are only clouds.

'When's Niall going back to where he came from?'

'He isn't going anywhere. Kerry and Niall are living with us now.'

'But that's preposterous. They're ruining my life.'

'Why?'

'They eat too slowly.'

'OK, Harry, why don't you get ready for bed?'

'And your tits are way too big. Can't you change them?' Harry asks Kerry.

Kerry puts her arm across her chest. She looks embarrassed.

'Harry, that's enough. Now you apologise to Kerry.'

'I'll only apologise after she gets a new pair of knockers, that don't stick out too much,' Harry replies, before dashing upstairs.

Harry does seem obsessed with breasts. Then again is he any different from the average sixteen-year-old boy?

Kerry looks out to the garden, where she sees Niall throwing a potted plant over our neighbour's fence. Richard, our neighbour, will be so pleased.

Kerry just shakes her head, and for once doesn't reprimand her son.

'It's OK,' I say, 'I'll pop over to Richard and get it back.'

'What's left of it,' is Kerry's muted response.

'I'm sorry about Harry. Let me have another word with him.'

'Don't worry,' she replies glumly.

Even though she has a severely autistic son it doesn't automatically make her immune from some of Harry's cruel comments. Living with Harry can be a tough gig.

I go upstairs to see Harry. He's watching a *My Little Pony, Friendship Is Magic* DVD in his bedroom.

'Dad, you've got to watch this. Twilight doesn't like Starlight making friends with Trixie, because she knows that Trixie is going to double-cross her.'

I don't understand a word of that. My guess is there are not too many sixteen-year-old boys watching a *My Little Pony, Friendship Is Magic* DVD.

'I don't know how many times I have to keep on telling you, Harry, but you mustn't be so rude to Kerry.'

'What you do mean?'

'You told her that she couldn't cook, and that her breasts were too big.'

'And what's the matter with that?'

Empathy is not high on Harry's agenda, which from my experience is the norm in the autistic world. Last year I decided to take a five day break in Cork. Laura had taken some time off work to take care of Harry. She was looking forward to spending some quality time with him and I was excited about going away on my own. Just before I booked the flight I told Harry that my return flight was due to land at Heathrow at nine-thirty at night and I wouldn't be picking him up until eleven. Harry told me that this was like 'shitting on my head' and told me to cancel the trip. This is because Harry likes to go to bed early (when he actually goes to sleep is another matter). I tried telling my son that I've never been away on my own before and I needed a break but he just shrugged his shoulders and told me 'ring up the pilot to let him know that you won't be on that plane.' Laura offered to keep him for the night, but he wanted to come home. So despite all the protests from family and friends I didn't go. Laura told me that I should have been stronger and maybe she has a point, but Harry would have made her life hell for five days and that's why I decided not to go.

'All I'm saying is just be nice to Kerry,' I reiterate.

'I want to go to bed in seven minutes,' came the reply.

Precisely seven minutes later I'm lying in bed with my son. I've been sleeping with Harry most nights since he was a baby. Harry goes to his residential placement in three days' time, so this will no longer happen. It'll feel strange going to bed without him.

I'm getting older and finding it increasingly difficult coping with Harry, so I know that going to the residential home is the only long-term solution for him, as well as for me and Laura. Should anything happen to Laura or me where would that leave Harry?

Having said all of that it'll break my heart to see him go.

My friends have been telling me that it'll free up so much time, and I'll be able to socialise more, but right now I can't see any positive outcome for me; only worry.

'I don't like it when the Streatham sky is dark.'

'Why's that?'

'It's just stupid. Can't those Government clowns change that?'

'No, that's just the way the universe is.'

'That's ludicrous.'

'Are you afraid of the dark?'

'I just can't see the clouds. I love the clouds, they're funny.'

Does Harry share my worry about going to bed on his own? He hasn't said as such, but that's the first time I've heard him make such a comment.

In the few months that Kerry and Niall have been with us, Kerry and I have never gone to bed together at the normal time (whatever normal means in this household). I always go to bed with Harry, and Kerry with Niall. We both inevitably fall asleep, waiting in vain for our respective child to go to sleep. If I wake up first, I go in to get Kerry, and vice versa. It's a strange existence having half conversations with each other at three o'clock in the morning.

'Mummy's coming over tomorrow,' I say to my son.

'What for?'

'To see you, of course.'

'Is she bringing that leprechaun man again?'

'If you referring to Sean, then no, and before you ask, no he hasn't got a weird voice, he speaks with an Irish accent, OK?'

There are many groundhog conversations with Harry, and Sean, with his Irish background, is one of them.

'Anyway, did you enjoy your first day at work?'

'Yeah, I love working in a building that has twenty-two Bounties and thirteen Curly Wurlys.'

'Did you like your work colleagues?'

'They're OK. Jon's ears are too big and his eyebrows are out of shape. Steve's shoes make too much noise when he walks and he's a con...'

'Artist, yes, you've told me before.'

At two-thirty-eight I wake up, still in Harry's bed, and of course Harry is nowhere to be seen. I rush downstairs to find him watching a Thomas The Tank Engine DVD, drinking coke and finishing off a Mars bar.

Like a lot of autistic children, Harry is obsessed about Thomas The Tank Engine. There have been many explanations given for this, but for me the one that makes most sense is that in the videos, if Thomas is cross then that expression is static for a length of time, when he is happy, the cross Thomas train is replaced by a happy Thomas train. Autistic children (and adults) seem to identify with these static facial expressions.

'How many times have I told you about eating sweets in the middle of the night? It's got to stop.'

'I read on the internet that Starbursts used to be called Opal Fruits,' Harry replies.

'I don't give a fuck about Starbursts. Now go to bed,' I say, although I'm not sure how much sleep he'll get with all that sugar intake.

Harry is about to take another bite of his Mars bar, when I grab it off him and throw it into the bin.

'No more sweets, OK?'

'But my life's shit without a Mars bar.'

'You've had half of it already, so that means that your life is only half shit.'

Harry looks sadly at the kitchen bin before reluctantly making his way to his bedroom.

How will the Hastings residential staff cope with his nightly antics? In just a few days I shall find out.

TRAFFIC LIGHTS

I wake up in my own bed and see a tall figure in the dark looming over me.

Initially I'm frightened until I realise it's Niall. However before I've a chance to gather my thoughts he punches me again in my testicles. As I'm not wearing my cricket box, the pain is excruciating. A succession of expletives follow, which wakes up Kerry.

'What the hell's going on?' she asks.

Again I'm too out of breath to reply.

'Are you OK?'

'Actually, now you ask, I have to say I've felt better,' would have been my response if I could speak.

Harry rushes into the bedroom.

'Has Niall destroyed your knackers again?' he inquires, while smiling.

Somehow I can't see the humorous side in all of this.

'Agh, agh, agh,' Niall shouts, while offering me his hand.

I'm always baffled at how he could be so violent one minute and seemingly so apologetic the next. I manage to shake his hand and with that he literally skips out of the room; job done.

Kerry rushes out after him and I hear her telling him off. Sometimes I think there's little point of doing this, but I admire her persistence. If she was dealing with a normal child you'd think that sooner or later the penny would drop, but Niall's OCD is so ingrained that it's much more complex.

I glance at the alarm clock; it's three-forty-two.

'Why is Danny DeVito only four foot and ten inches, and has no hair?' Harry asks.

'I'm not sure, maybe his parents...'

'And Greg Davies is six foot and eight inches and has loads of hair. I just don't understand,' my son adds.

'I'll get back to you on that, Harry.'

'I told Fiona that she looks like Danny DeVito.'

Fiona is my sister. I'm not sure she'll be too happy with that comparison.

'OK, Harry, it's time to go to bed.'

'There's no point.'

'Yes, there is, it's only quarter to four.'

'I want to go to Aldershot after our trip to Peckham.'

'What's in Aldershot?'

'Charity shops.'

'There are loads of charity shops in Streatham.'

'But they're all hopeless.'

I'm not sure what the Aldershot connection is here, as we've never been there. I do have some strange conversations with Harry, but the night time/early morning ones take some beating.

'Go to bed, I'll be with you shortly.'

'Aldershot, Aldershot, here we come, Aldershot here we come,' Harry sings as he leaves my bedroom.

I can't remember making any promises on that.

'How are you?' Kerry asks, while gently rubbing my shoulder.

'I'll survive.'

'He's never done that during the night.'

'I'll just have to wear a cricket box to bed, that's all,' I say.

'That's not good.'

'What else do you suggest?'

'I don't know. I just don't know…'

Kerry wearily makes her way to Niall's bedroom, and a few minutes later I'm in bed with Harry.

The rest of the morning passes without any further incident and at midday I ring the doorbell of Bernadette's house and Bernadette's mum, Alice, opens the door.

'Hi, come in,' she says.

I look over at Kerry, who's in her car with Niall. She nods in encouragement. She obviously doesn't want to bring Niall in.

'I won't be long,' I say to her.

'Hello, Harry,' Bernadette says with a straight face.

'Hello,' Harry replies, equally nonplussed.

That's not the most enthusiastic greeting that I've ever seen.

'Harry's dad, I don't like your knees today. They're too wobbly.'

'I'm afraid they're the only ones I've got.'

'And you have too many hairs on your legs. I can get rid of them if you like.'

'No, thanks.'

When I put on my shorts this morning I didn't know that my knees and legs would be under such close scrutiny.

'Coffee?' Alice asks.

'No, thanks. We'd better get going.'

Alice recently got divorced from Francis, and, as much as I sympathise with her, I don't want to get involved in another lengthy discussion about it all, as she goes into far too much detail, particularly on the rather peculiar sexual needs of her ex-husband.

'How's it going with Kerry?' she asks.

'If I'm honest, it's proving difficult having both Niall and Harry together,' I answer, surprised by my own truthfulness.

'Hopefully that'll improve once Harry's gone.'

Just her saying that gives me a knot in my stomach. I don't want him to go to Hastings; I need him to live with me forever.

Bringing up Harry has dominated my life, which is not unusual for a parent to say. However, because of Laura's breakdown I've had sole custody of Harry since he was eleven years old. I go to bed when Harry goes to bed, and wake up when he wakes up. Laura helps out as much as she can, but the bulk of the parental responsibility is down to me.

Sometimes, in a quiet moment, I reflect on the impact this has had on me. In the morning I make his breakfast, iron his clothes, supervise his bath and drive him to school. I then leave work early to pick him up from school and continue my working day from home. I cook his meals and always go to bed with him. We're attached at the hip and I wouldn't have it any other way. It's pointless to put into words how much I love my son. I'm going to miss him so much.

'Have you been in any relationship since…?' I ask. I can't even say the word divorce, as understandably her feelings are still extremely raw.

'It's a catch twenty-two situation. It'll take a really special guy, who has no autistic connections, to take on Bernadette, and even if I find one who has a special needs child, it'll still be so difficult, as you're finding out.'

'I'm sorry, I didn't mean...' She adds.

'It's OK, don't worry. Having Niall staying with us has been tough, even though I'm supposed to be more clued up about autism than the average guy in the street.'

Bernadette comes rushing into the living-room.

'Harry told me that Niall smashed your balls apart. That's amazing.'

How come nearly everyone, apart from me, seems to be delighted that my testicles got a bashing this morning?

'OK, Bernadette, can you get ready now please?' Alice tells her daughter.

Thirty minutes later we're driving through Peckham.

'Is this the traffic lights that you want?' I ask.

'Get the fuck out of here, they're absolutely useless,' Bernadette quickly replies.

'They're on Queens Road, Daddy. I gave you the directions last week. Take the second left and then it's first on your right. Do you want me to drive?'

'That's ok, I think I can manage.'

'Can you?'

Because of his disability Harry will never have a driving licence; however he's constantly asking if he could drive the car to the shops as, he says, 'I can't be bothered to walk.' On a few occasions he's taken the keys and situated himself in the driver's seat, but I've always caught him in time. I don't think he would've known how to start the car, but I really didn't want to find out.

We eventually arrive at the infamous traffic lights.

'So what now?' I inquire.

'Harry's dad, you are a clueless moron,' Bernadette tells me.

Harry nods in agreement.

'Why do you say that?'

'These are the best traffic lights in the United Kingdom. They were built in nineteen-fifty-four and change from red to amber to green.'

I'm obviously missing the significance, but I don't pursue it.

'I hate to desert the sinking ship, but this isn't Niall's thing. I'll see you in an hour or so,' Kerry tells me.

'Get out while you can,' I reply, before giving her a hug.

'That's the thirty-second change from red to amber and also the thirty-second change from amber to green,' Bernadette tells Harry.

'That's just fantastic,' Harry replies.

'On the first red there were eight cars waiting, and seven people crossed the road, on the second red there were only six cars waiting and five people crossed the road, and on the third red there were eleven cars waiting and nine people crossed the road...'

'Ok, Bernadette, I can see that you've got it all documented. Can we discuss this later?' Or perhaps never?

'You're such a party pooper,' Harry responds.

This isn't like any party that I've ever been to before.

I've been watching the lights change for over an hour, and to be honest this hasn't been the most stimulating hour of my life, but I had to be alert as we're standing on the edge of the pavement and both Harry and Bernadette are not too clued up on road safety.

We've had some mystifying looks from strangers, as Harry and Bernadette cheer every time the lights turn red.

'That bastard is really pissed off now,' Bernadette laughs while pointing at a driver who had just come to a screeching halt at a red light. He's obviously in a hurry, and didn't look too happy at stopping. His mood probably hasn't improved after witnessing Bernadette's gloating. I'm relieved when the lights turn to green.

I'm pleased to see Kerry and Niall approaching us, however Niall is hitting his head with his fist, which isn't a good sign, and just before they reach us Niall rushes over to a teenager, grabs his arm and gently head-butts his shoulder. Kerry and I dash towards them and attempt to prise Niall away, but when we get there he's licking the teenager's shoulder.

'What the fuck's is going on?' the teenager shouts.

'I'm sorry, he's autistic. It's his way of saying hello.'

'Fuck off,' the teenager then elbows Niall in the face.

'Hey, watch it, he can't help it.'

'I don't give a fuck,' he replies, before running away.

I start to chase after him, but Kerry pulls me back.

'Please, David, it's not worth it.'

Niall is even more furious now, and continues to bang his head. He'll probably have a few bruises in the morning, some of his own making and some not.

It takes Kerry another ten minutes or so before she calms Niall down.

'What got him annoyed in the first place?' I ask.

'I've no idea. He had his pick and mix at WH Smiths, and his sweets at Marks, so we hit all the stores that he likes.'

'I can't believe that arsehole hit Niall, even after we told him about his autism,' I say.

'Yeah, I know. I understand why he got startled when Niall approached him, cos that's a bit scary, but having seen us trying to hold Niall back you'd thought that he would grasp that something wasn't quite right,' Kerry responds.

I look over at Niall, and he's now smiling.

'I think that you should review his OCD medicine; it's obviously not working.'

'Yes, yes, I know,' Kerry replies irritably.

We both guide Niall into Kerry's car, mindful of another such attack to an unsuspecting member of the public.

'It's probably best that I take him home now,' Kerry tells me.

Shortly afterwards Kerry drives away. She looks sullen, while Niall is still smiling.

'That was just great. That boy's elbow really cracked Niall's head,' Harry informs me.

'So you're pleased that Niall got hurt?'

'He deserved it.'

'No he didn't.'

'He shouldn't be going up to people. That's stupid.'

'But he has OCD, and can't help it.'

'Course he can.'

This conversation is going around in circles. Harry applauded Niall for crushing my testicles, yet disapproves of a much less harmful attack on a stranger.

'Are we finished with the traffic lights now?' I ask, keen to terminate this conversation.

'I don't know why you hate traffic lights so much,' Bernadette replies.

'I don't, but can we do something else now?'

'I can tell you're lying, but there's another amazing set of traffic lights in Newcastle. Can we go there tomorrow?'

'Ask your mum.'

And ask her to take you as well.

Finally we agree that the next port of call is Waterstones.

For nearly an hour I'm sitting on a chair that was designed for a three-year-old in the children's section of Waterstones listening to Harry narrating the latest Thomas The Tank Engine book to Bernadette.

'Wow, Thomas is incredible,' Bernadette tells Harry.

'Yeah, he's the best thing in my life, that's for sure,' Harry replies.

Thanks. I wonder if I even make the number two slot?

'Ok, are we ready to head home? Mummy will be coming soon.'

They both get up immediately and follow me out of the store. We walk for few minutes before a man in uniform stops us.

'Excuse me, can you follow me back into the store please?' he asks us, while holding up a security badge.

'What's all this about?' I reply.

'I'd prefer to discuss this back at the store.'

In a small room at the back of Waterstones, the security man asks me to put the contents of my holdall onto a desk. They include three cans of coke, a packet of peanuts, a half packet of Gingernut biscuits and the latest Lisa Jewell book. That's me in the clear, but I'm getting increasingly anxious about the contents of Harry's bag. As Harry turns his bag upside down on the desk the contents include the Streatham telephone directory (he never goes anywhere without it), a couple of *My Little Pony* DVDs and a rather new looking Thomas The Tank Engine book. The security guy picks up the book.

'You didn't pay for this, did you?' he asks Harry.

'No, and what's it got to do with you?'

'So you admit you stole it?'

'Of course; I love Thomas.'

'Just wait here, I'm going to get the manager.'

With that he disappears, leaving us with another stern looking security guy standing by the door.

'What the hell did you do that for?' I shout at my son.

'I just want that book, that's all. What's the problem?'

'If you wanted it, just tell me and I'll buy it for you. You don't steal.'

'But sometimes when I ask for a book you say no.'

'Harry's right. He wanted the *Three Cheers For Thomas* book on Tuesday September the nineteenth two thousand and seventeen and you refused, so what do you expect?' Bernadette chips in.

The manager arrives shortly afterwards. She introduces herself as Jane.

'And this is my son, Harry. He's autistic and while I'm not condoning the fact that he stole the book, he's not aware that it's a crime, and this is the first time that he's stolen anything.'

'No it's not, I've stolen four Thomas books from Waterstones before – on Saturday November the eleventh, two thousand and seventeen, on Saturday January the sixth, two thousand and eighteen, on Friday September the seventh, two thousand and eighteen and on Friday July the fifth this year; that's all.'

Jane looks accusingly at me.

'That's the first I've heard of this,' I say, holding my hands up.

I don't think she believes me, but it's the truth. I'm mortified. This is now looking very serious.

'What colour knickers do you wear?' Harry asks Jane.

Well that's broken the ice.

'What did you say?'

'I said what colour knickers do you wear? My guess is yellow. Am I right?'

Jane looks stunned, so I intervene.

'I'm sorry about that. He has no filter.'

'Are you going to answer Harry's question? It's very rude to ignore him,' Bernadette chips in.

'She's autistic as well,' I add.

Jane closes her eyes and takes a deep breath.

'Bob, can I have a minute?' she asks the security guy. They leave the room.

'Don't you ever steal anything again; do you hear me?' I shout at Harry.

'But I love Thomas.'

'That's irrelevant. If you want a book just ask me, OK?'

'But sometimes you…'

'Yes, I know, refuse to buy you a book. Harry I've bought you hundreds of books. I don't have to get you a book every time we go shopping.'

'There you go again.'

'You're in a lot of trouble now. The police could be involved.'

'Wow, that's great. Can you take a photo of me and one of the pigs please?'

A few minutes later Jane and Bob come back into the room.

'Harry, my guess is that you'll be able to tell me the titles of all books that you've stolen and their prices. Am I right?'

'Of course, they are...'

'Hold on. Your dad will pay for all of these books, and I'll let you off this time, but you must promise me that you'll never steal from this store again, or any other store come to that.'

'But, it's just fun stealing Thomas books.'

Jane looks over at me.

'Rest assured he won't be stealing any more books from now on. Please accept my apologies and thanks for being so understanding.'

Jane smiles for the first time since we met. I meant what I said.

I wonder if Waterstones will now install extra security cameras around the Thomas The Tank Engine book section?

That shopping trip has just cost me thirty-four pounds and ninety-five pence, but it could've been a hell of a lot worse.

I pay for the five books. We're accompanied out of the store by Jane and Bob, but just before leaving Harry turns around.

'You still haven't answered my question about your knickers. Are they yellow?' Harry asks.

Before he gets a reply I usher Harry out of the store, but I did manage to catch Bob smiling behind Jane's back.

KNICKERS

I drop Bernadette off at her mum's. Her parting words were 'don't forget about the Newcastle traffic lights tomorrow'. I attempted to explain that it was too far to go, but she didn't seem interested in the details and just dashed off. I shall phone Alice later.

Now comes the hard bit – telling Laura about this latest incident in Harry's life. Laura will probably be at my house now, so it won't be long before she hears this wonderful news. She's already depressed about Harry going away, and this is definitely not going to improve her state of mind.

When I arrive home Laura is in the garden with Kerry. They're drinking wine, and look in a relaxed mood. That'll soon change.

Whenever an incident like this happens, Laura tends to point the finger of blame; usually at me. Although this could have had very serious consequences, I'm more inclined to let Harry know where he went wrong and move on from there, however, Laura will worry constantly about this and bring it up in conversations years from now.

I feel awkward at the thought of having this type of serious discussion with Laura in Kerry's company. Although I don't have any secrets from Kerry it still doesn't feel right.

I find it strange seeing my ex-wife and partner together, although they had known each other before I started going out with Kerry. Kerry does sometimes feel a little awkward around Laura, which I understand, given the history between us. I'm not sure what Laura's thoughts are, but the fact that she's been with Sean for a while has obviously eased the situation.

'Come join us,' Laura calls out.

However, before I have a chance to utter one word, Harry rushes into the garden.

'I didn't get to meet the old bill in the end, or find out about that slapper's knickers,' my son blurts out.

Oh well, that explains everything. There's no need to expand. I can have that glass of wine now.

'What's he talking about?' Laura asks me.

'Harry stole a Thomas book in Waterstones. We were caught by security as we left the store. We had a meeting with the store manager and it transpires that Harry has stolen another four books over the last couple of years.'

Laura closes her eyes and shakes her head. 'So what happened then?'

'The manager kindly took his disability into consideration and let us off. I paid for all the books though.'

'Harry, come here,' Laura shouts.

'Hi ya mum, what's up?'

'If you ever steal any books again you won't get any pocket money for two months. Am I making myself clear?'

'Mum, cool your jets. I thought you liked Thomas? You always read his books to me.'

'That's not the point. You can't steal. It's against the law.'

'But Thomas is a good engine. He's always helping Henry and James when they're in trouble.'

I'm trying to understand why Harry thinks that it's alright to steal books. OK, I get the idea that he's obsessed with Thomas and that's the driving force behind his actions, but despite his disability Laura and me have always tried to teach him right from wrong. He obviously hasn't grasped the seriousness of his actions, which is worrying.

'Laura, let's leave it for now. We'll have to be more vigilant whenever we're in a book store with him.'

'Didn't you see him put the book in his bag?'

'Give me some credit, please? Just leave it, OK? I've dealt with it.'

I must admit I did have my eyes closed for various spells during Harry's Thomas narration, as it wasn't quite up to the standard of Richard Burton's *War Of The Worlds* recital. Harry must have used this window of opportunity to go about his business. I decide against telling Laura this small nugget of information.

Kerry refills Laura's glass and pours one for me.

'I think David's right. If we keep a close eye on Harry in these situations I think it'll be OK. I mean there's always an adult with him, right?'

'Yes, but in the last few months he's really trying to be more independent. He wants to go on trains journeys by himself, and go to the shops on his own etc. We've tried to suppress this although it's the only way forward for him in the long-term, but now this complicates everything,' Laura replies.

'Meaning that'll give him the opportunity to steal more?' Kerry asks.

Laura nods.

'He'll be OK, please don't worry,' Kerry adds.

'Speaking of train journeys, Harry wants to go to Aldershot tomorrow,' I add.

'What the hell's in Aldershot?' Laura inquires.

'Excellent charity shops apparently.'

Laura and Kerry look at each other, both a little confused.

'Anyway I thought that I'd go with him on the train, but sit a few seats away to make him feel that he's on his own.'

'Sounds like a plan. What do you think, Laura?' Kerry asks.

'I suppose it's a sensible approach,' Laura replies, although she doesn't sound too convinced.

A few minutes of silence ensues. We all take some much needed sips of wine, while deep in our own thoughts.

Niall then lies down on the patio and goes through his usual OCD routine, which involves licking and spitting on the ground, lying sideways and bumping up and down while holding his crotch. Throughout this routine he makes constant grunting noises. He's been doing this same ritual for as long as I've known him. His public performances are exclusively reserved for Sainsbury's (no other supermarket) and WH Smiths. This does get some curious looks from strangers, a lot of whom rather insensitively stand a couple of feet away from him, just staring. I used to tell them to 'take a photo, it'll last longer,' but I'm used to this now.

'I think it's time for bed,' Kerry says, as she empties her wine glass.

'Please don't worry too much about Harry, he'll be fine,' Kerry reassures Laura, before she heads off for what surely will be another sleepless night.

Laura smiles and pours herself another glass of wine.

'That was sweet of her to say that. How's everything with you and Kerry?'

'It's a big adjustment having Niall here. I can't deny it. Harry's made some brutal comments to her. It's all put a strain on our relationship.'

'I'm sorry to hear that.'

'The lack of sleep is another issue. It puts us both on edge.'

Laura bows her head. I can tell from her expression that she feels guilty that she can't help more, but her living situation is not ideal for Harry. Laura lives with Sean and his two teenage children, Timothy and Mary.

'Did you arrange to stay overnight with Harry on Friday?' Laura asks.

Friday is Harry's first overnight stay at his residential placement.

'Yes, but they weren't happy about it. They seem confident that they can deal with anything that Harry throws at them, but I managed to persuade them that it'll be in their interests if I'm there on the first night.'

'Do you think they'll let me stay too?'

'I don't see why not. I'll ask tomorrow.'

'Yes, please.'

'How's Sean? I haven't seen him for a while.'

'He's been really busy at work lately. I don't usually see him until late.'

'Are Timothy and Mary OK?'

'I suppose so. They keep themselves to themselves.'

'Harry hasn't stayed there for a while. Presumably it's still a problem?'

'With Sean out a lot there's usually an atmosphere when Harry stays. Harry's always liable to say something, which they react to, especially when Sean's not around. So I'd rather avoid that for now.'

Laura takes another sip of her wine before speaking again.

'Has Harry said why he seems reluctant to stay at my flat?' Laura asks.

'Not really. Well he does complain about the colour of the tiles in the bathroom and that the water in the bath taps comes out too slowly, but that's about it. Why do you ask?'

'I know that it's difficult at Sean's, but I'm always offering for him to stay at my place, but he just tells me that he can't be arsed.'

'I don't think it's anything to be concerned about, but I'll have a word with him.'

Laura still has a worried expression.

'Is anything wrong?' I ask.

She hesitates before replying.

'Do you think that he resents me because I wasn't there for him when he was growing up?'

'No, I don't think so.'

'It must have affected him; it must have...'

'What happened was completely out of your control. Please stop beating yourself up for it. You're better now and you give him all your time; that's what counts.'

She nods but I can tell she's not convinced.

'I don't think he's forgotten that I let him down...'

'Laura, it's all OK. You always get a bit melancholy after a couple of glasses of wine.'

Laura gives me a weak smile, but doesn't reply.

As Laura's over the limit I call for a cab.

'Thanks for your company tonight and please tell Kerry I appreciate her kind words,' she says as she gets into her cab.

'I know that today wasn't good, but at least we dodged a bullet,' I reply.

Laura nods as she puts her seat belt on, but just before the taxi pulls away she unwinds the car window.

'What did Harry say about knickers?' she asks.

CLEVER BASTARDS

'How long do you think this will last?' I ask Kerry.

'Judging by all his other OCD rituals, I'd say at least a year, probably much more.'

I attempt not to look too disheartened, but the truth is I'm feeling depressed. It's one thing being attacked during the day by Niall, but to be woken up at three in the morning with him punching my testicles is another matter. This happened again this morning and he kept hitting the cricket box from all angles, as he couldn't feel the sensation of my balls. At least this time I was protected. However the side effect of wearing the cricket box for lengthy periods, apart from being extremely uncomfortable, is that it has given me infections in my testicles. Last week I went to the doctors about this. He prescribed a cream and advised me to ditch the cricket box, but that's impossible right now.

Harry was lying alongside me in bed this morning when Niall attacked me. He just laughed and turned over.

'Coffee?' Kerry asks.

I glance at the alarm clock; it's one minute past four, but we're too wound up to go back to sleep now.

'Yeah, why not?'

At four-fifteen we're joined by Harry, who is holding an A4 sized envelope addressed to The Prime Minister, 10 Downing Street.

'What's in it?' I ask my son.

'Some drawings and a letter.'

'Why would you be sending drawings to the Prime Minister?'

'He needs cheering up.'

'Can I have a look?'

'Of course, you're going to love it.'

Harry never seals the envelope flap, as I now have to examine all of his letters. This stems back to when he wrote to our local police station and enclosed a drawing of three policemen covered in excrement, with the heading 'Streatham pigs are shit. Get rid of them.' Needless to say we got a visit from the local constabulary a few days later. They eventually understood our situation, but not before I was quizzed.

'Why do you think we're shit?' was their opening question to both me and Harry. Ironically, after their visit, Harry now loves the Streatham pigs.

This time I'm taking no chances.

There are three drawings – one, inevitably, is of Thomas The Tank Engine, and the other two are characters from the *My Little Pony – Friendship Is Magic* program.

'Who are these two?'

'Twilight Sparkle and Pinkie Pie. Why the hell don't you know that? It's about time you started watching the *My Little Pony* DVDs.'

I pick up the letter. It reads as follows:

'I know that you're an old duffer, but you've got to start watching the *Thomas The Tank Engine* and *My*

Little Pony – Friendship Is Magic DVDs. I can send you a couple if you want, but I want them back, OK? Thomas is a fantastic engine and he always helps Henry and James. Twilight Sparkle is a princess who lives at Friendship Rainbow Kingdomcastle. She's lovely and a bit of a looker. Pinkie Pie organises parties for Sugarcube Corner. I've seen you talking to those tossers in the suits and you always look pissed off. When they shout at you just tell them to fuck off. That'll work. When the arseholes get you angry again get the boring fuckers to watch the Thomas and *My Little Pony* DVDs, and you'll all be much happier after that. Anyway, I want Channel Four to show repeats of the Thomas episodes that Ringo Starr was in, so get that sorted. Also, can you make the summers in Streatham hotter? Because at the moment they're just shit. I'm going to have a crap now. See ya.'

'Get rid of the swear words and cut out the bit about having a crap.'

'Why?'

'You don't use swear words when you're writing to the Prime Minister, and he really doesn't need to know when you're going to the toilet.'

Harry looks perplexed.

'Ok, I'll change it this time, but I think it's a mistake. He does want to know what we're all doing.'

I don't recall any political opinion poll that details the toiletry activities of the voters.

Harry makes the changes and I seal the envelope. What the Prime Minister will make of this I dread to think.

Harry is constantly writing to celebrities and cartoon voice actors, the latter of which must be cock-a-hoop to receive fan mail.

My son wanders off to the living-room, where a few minutes later I hear Ringo Starr telling us how Henry crashed into Percy on one of Harry's many Thomas DVDs.

'What are your plans today?' Kerry asks.

'I'm going to see mum.'

'With Harry?'

'Yep.'

'Good luck,' Kerry replies, knowing that it's almost certainly going to be a stressful morning.

My mum has been in a care home for the past nine months. She's always been a heavy smoker and in the last few years this has caused a number of health issues, the worse of which is emphysema. Smoking also killed my father eight years ago. I've always been closer to my father; he was a kind and gentle man. Of course I also love my mother, but she's a harder person and more difficult. She's also frightened of Harry. He often barges into her 'for fun', and hugs her way too tightly when they meet up. So why am I bringing Harry when there is such a health risk to my mother? I just want Harry to see his grandmother, because, without sounding too morbid, I don't think she has too many years left. I've asked the home if any of the helpers could be by her side during our visit for protection. They understood, as they've met Harry previously; need I say more?

By midday we're on our way to see my mum. Harry is in the passenger seat of my car reading the two thousand and eight Streatham A-Z telephone directory. He's kept every directory for the past eleven years and often carries an old edition with him. When I ask him why, he just says, 'it brings back memories.' If the author of this 'publication' ever did a book signing Harry would be the first in the queue.

After my early alarm call, courtesy of Niall, I'm feeling tired. Niall did attack me several more times later, but instead he focused on pinching my arms, face and neck. He also does this to Kerry, but not with the same intensity. I've managed to find a way to protect my testicles, well, most of the time, but how do I guard the rest of my body? Again, after each attack comes an immediate apology. It's actually a relief to be away from Niall for a while, and I hate myself for thinking that.

We're met at the care home by three helpers, who swiftly escort us to mum's room. Some of the staff and residents glance over at us, almost as if we're celebrities. Well, I suppose Harry is in this neck of the woods.

Even though it's only a couple of weeks since I last saw mum, I'm taken aback at how frail she looks. I'm beginning to regret bringing Harry.

'How are you keeping?' I say, giving her a gentle hug.

'I'm not long for this world.'

That's an uplifting start to the conversation.

'Harry was keen to come along,' I remark.

'No I wasn't. Just look at this place, it's shit. All the people look like zombies.'

'He doesn't mean that,' I intervene.

Actually he does.

'Grandma, you look pathetic. How old are you now? I reckon you must be at least one hundred and four. Am I right?'

'Harry's got a quirky sense of humour,' I say, looking around at the team of people surrounding my mum. I don't think they believe me, and by the look of mum's expression I know that she certainly doesn't.

'I'm serious. Just look at the state of her,' Harry re-iterates.

'Harry, didn't your father ever teach you not to be rude to people?' my mum asks.

'I'm not being rude. You look like a lump of turd.'

'One of these days you're going to say the wrong thing to the wrong person, and then you'll be in trouble,' mum says with a tenderness that I didn't expect.

'I don't know what you're banging on about. Have you lost the plot again?'

'Your father will explain.'

'I'm bored. Can we split this joint?'

'I can take him out to the foyer,' one of the helpers remarks. 'Don't worry, I'll take good care of him.'

'Harry, be good to your mum and dad, and look after yourself,' mum says, as Harry is walking away, accompanied by his bodyguard.

Harry either doesn't hear or chooses to ignore her.

I notice some tears rolling down my mother's face. She immediately dabs her eyes with a tissue.

'Are you OK?' I ask.

I wait a good sixty seconds before she replies.

'Are you going to marry that Irish woman, or not?'

That melancholy mood didn't last long.

'Her name is Kerry.'

'You haven't answered my question.'

'It's too early to decide the future.'

'And you're going to bring up her boy as well? He's even worse than Harry. He'll skin you alive. I'm only thinking of you. I see you struggle with Harry. How will you cope bringing up another one?'

She does have a point, but I don't acknowledge it. I then realise that the three helpers standing beside mum are still here, listening to our conversation.

'Do you mind? Harry's gone now.'

They nod, but seem disappointed to leave.

'I just worry about you, David. You've been through enough.'

That's about the first time that she's ever acknowledged the difficulties in my life. I'm surprised at her openness.

I don't think she's ever grasped the concept of autism; she always thinks that Harry is just a naughty kid and I should have disciplined him more. She's told me this on numerous occasions; almost blaming me for Harry's situation.

'There's no need to be concerned. Harry starts his home placement tomorrow, and that'll free up more time for me.'

I sound as if I'm looking forward to it. I'm not.

'Have they any idea what they're letting themselves in for?'

That sounds more like my mum, and for once I'm glad.

'They tell me they've seen it all before.'

'I doubt it.'

'I better go and see what Harry's up to.'

'Take care of him, David. He needs your help.'

Mum's feistiness (for want of a better word) is still there, but I've rarely seen her compassionate side.

Mum and Dad came from a generation where hugs and kisses were not the done thing. My father was a gentle guy, with a lovely sense of humour. Mum was always a much tougher and moodier person. I rarely saw my parents argue, but maybe that was more down to Dad, who seemed to overlook a lot of mum's faults. Even as a youngster I could tell they loved each other and on Saturdays they would often open up a bottle or two of Guinness and listen to traditional Irish music. They would sometimes have a dance together; I wish I could've videoed those moments.

The affection she showed to my father was rarely shared with Fiona or me.

Mum's never really recovered from my father's death and neither have I.

Mum slowly walks towards me and gives me a gentle hug. This sign of affection worries me. It's almost like she's trying to make amends, while she can.

Just before I leave the room I turn around and see her get her tissue out again. She looks sad and afraid. Before I leave her today I'm going to have a chat with the management to get a health update on her.

As I approach the foyer, I stop dead in my tracks as I see Harry sitting at the piano, surrounded by a group of elderly men and women, the youngest of whom is probably around seventy-five. Harry is singing the Ian Dury and the Blockheads song, *there ain't half been some clever bastards*. Everyone is joining in with the chorus, literally shouting the word BASTARDS. At least this genre of music makes a change from the resident pianist, who tends to stick with Barry Manilow, Neil Sedaka and Kenny Rogers.

I record the last couple of minutes on my iPhone. This will make an amusing anecdote to add to the never ending Harry stories.

'Now, can I tell you about the day I pissed on my dad's head when he was sleeping?' Harry announces to his newly acquired fans.

Only one person laughs at this, the others look at Harry and each other in total confusion.

'OK, Harry, it's time to go now,' I say, breaking up his one man show.

I really don't want to be reminded of that particular incident.

'Am I getting paid for this?' Harry asks his audience.

'I can give you one of my polo's,' one of Harry's newly acquired fans shouts back.

'That'll do.'

Just before leaving the home I had a chat with the manager, who seems to think that mum's suffering from depression. He promised to keep an eye on her. During the car journey back I kept thinking how sad and weak she looked.

As we're approaching home my mobile rings. It's Ray from work.

'David, I'm sorry to contact you when you're on holiday, but we've got a big problem with the new Barclays credit screens, and they're going crazy. Can you pop in for a bit? I'll pay you overtime at the weekend rate.'

'OK, but I'll have to bring Harry with me.'

'That's great. Thanks, David, I really appreciate it.'

IT CROWD

I was made redundant from Homely Insurance four years ago, but luckily I managed to secure another job within a couple of months. I work for an IT consulting company called Strategy IT. They develop software for various companies, one of which is Barclays.

As I recently developed some software for Barclays, I'm about the only person who knows how it all hangs together, and that's why they contacted me. It's far from ideal, but unfortunately that's the nature of the beast.

Kerry is meeting her mother this afternoon, so I've no alternative but to bring Harry with me.

'Harry, let me tell you right now, there are a lot of young women who work here, so I don't want you saying anything about their breasts, or asking what colour knickers they wear. Do I make myself clear?' I say, as we enter the office building.

'I'm clear and you're definitely clear,' was Harry's confusing response.

My IT colleagues are a strange bunch. Ask them a question about computers and they will wax lyrical about hard drives as if they're recalling their greatest love-making experience, but get them off the subject of computers and they're clueless. If I attempt to talk about the latest premier league results or a television hit show, it's met with blank stares, almost as if they're from another planet, which in a way they are.

'Good morning' and 'good night' are virtually my only interactions with most of my colleagues.

This is the first time that I've brought Harry to my office, so I'm a little nervous.

We take the lift to the third floor and straight into Ray's office.

Ray is in his mid-thirties, single and devoted to his job. He's a good guy and has always been very understanding when I needed to leave work early because of issues with my son.

'Ray, this is Harry.'

'I'm very pleased to meet you, Harry.'

Ray offers his hand to my son, who promptly ignores it.

'On Wednesday March the twenty-first, two thousand and eighteen my dad told my mum that you were a prick for making him stay late, because he was supposed to be going to watch Arsenal play. He also said that you're a fucking simpleton.'

A few moments of silence follows Harry's rather incriminating announcement.

'I didn't say that. Harry does tend to make things up,' I respond, smiling at my boss, but his expression tells him he doesn't believe me.

'Harry, from what David has told me, you seem to have a great memory for dates. Do you know when David first started working here?' Ray asks.

'That's easy. It was Monday September the seventh, two thousand and fifteen.'

Ray checks this on his laptop.

'That's correct, I'm impressed.'

Perhaps I was a tad wrong in my earlier assessment of Ray. With his subtle line of questioning I think he'd make a great lawyer, which is probably what I need right now.

An embarrassing silence follows. It seems I'm banged to rights.

'I better crack on,' I say.

Ray nods, but his grateful mood has somewhat disappeared.

I start working on the Barclays problem, while Harry sits at the desk opposite me.

'And how are you today?' Mark, a colleague, asks Harry.

As far as I'm aware, Mark doesn't know anything about Harry's autism. We rarely discuss anything personal at work. It's computer talk or nothing.

Harry doesn't acknowledge Mark, and continues to read his Streatham telephone directory.

'What's that you're reading?' Mark asks.

'You're fat,' comes the reply.

'Sorry, what did you say?'

'You look like a fat fuck.'

'Harry, that's enough,' I tell my son.

'But he'll never be able to screw any of these babes with that belly,' Harry says, pointing at the various women nearby.

'Harry, stop it.'

'I'll prove it. Excuse me, what's your name?' Harry asks a woman walking past his desk.

'Lucy.'

'I've heard of you. Dad told Kerry that you're the office tart. He said that you'll shag anything that moves.'

Lucy looks startled, which is hardly surprising.

'Would you shag that?' Harrys asks, pointing at Mark, or more specifically at Mark's stomach.

Lucy looks accusingly at me, and starts to walk away.

'You've got a lovely arse. Is that why all the men want to give you their willies?' Harry shouts at Lucy.

Suddenly the keyboard typing stops as everyone looks up to find the source of that statement. A number of them even stand up to get a better view.

I really have to fix this IT issue as soon as possible because if I stay in this building much longer I won't have a job to come back to next week. I spend the next ten minutes explaining to Mark about Harry's autism, and then attempt to convince Lucy that I didn't say she was a tart. Listening to her rather frank sexual recollections on a regular basis, it's obvious that she tends to sleep with anyone who makes eye contact with her, so Harry's proclamation rings true, which of course means I've been found guilty yet again. I never say these personal things when Harry's in the room, but he's always nearby. He has damn good hearing and an excellent memory.

'I thought I told you not to say anything rude to the women.'

'You said don't talk about their breasts or knickers, and I didn't.'

'OK, don't talk about their breasts, knickers, bottom, legs, feet, arms, fingers, face, ears, eyes or hair. In fact don't talk about anything to do with their bodies, and that includes the men as well,' I say rather too loudly. Our IT audience are still tuned in.

'I was being nice to Lucy.'

'No, you weren't.'

'Her arse is just fantastic. I thought she'd be pleased to hear about that.'

'It's best that you concentrate on reading the telephone directory now, and try not to talk to anyone, OK?'

Harry looks confused, but shrugs his shoulders and continues to read about all the residents in Streatham who possessed a telephone in two thousand and eight.

An hour or so later I manage to resolve all the IT issues and then pop into Ray's office.

'All done,' I say, trying to keep our conversation as brief as possible.

'David, thanks for sorting that out, and I'm sorry for disturbing your holiday,' Ray replies.

'No, it's me who should apologise for earlier.'

'Don't think twice about it. You have a tough life. I really don't know how you cope with everything. Today's been quite an eye-opener for me.'

'Do you like Boycie?' Harry asks Ray.

'Sorry, who's that?'

'You're kidding me, right?'

Ray glances at me with a perplexed expression.

'Harry's talking about the Boycie character in *Only Fools and Horses*.'

'Oh, I see. It's been a while since I last saw an episode, but yeah he was good.'

'It's on TV Gold every day, so there's no excuse for not watching it. Boycie's amazing. John Challis is the actor that plays Boycie, and he was born on August the sixteenth nineteen forty two. I think he should be the next James Bond.'

Somehow I don't think the Bond producers have Boycie as their number one choice. But what do I know?

'And how many times a year do you cut your toenails?'

'I'm not sure…'

'You do seem a bit of an idiot.'

'Ok, that's enough, I think we better get going. Sorry about that.'

'Don't worry. Enjoy the rest of your day. Did you like coming to your dad's workplace, Harry?' Ray asks.

Harry just walks out of the office, without responding to Ray.

'Ring me if you have any more issues, and please extend my apologies to Lucy.'

'I think she was a bit shocked at first, but she'll be fine.'

'Why were you so rude to Ray?' I ask my son as we leave the building.

'I can't believe he doesn't watch *Only Fools and Horses*. It doesn't make any sense.'

Harry is quiet in the car journey home. There's no talk about Lucy's posterior, or any commentary on the many traffic lights that we stopped at.

'Where are you going?' Harry asks, as we approach my house.

'Home of course. I'm dying for a cuppa.'

Although a couple of whiskies would be preferable right now.

'There's no time, we've got to go to Aldershot. Remember you promised.'

Did I?

'We're going all the way to Aldershot just to visit some charity shops?'

'They have the best Cancer Research and Oxfam shops in the world.'

'Why are they so special?'

'They have books, and they're always in the alphabetical order by the author.'

Aren't they all?

When Harry gets a bee in his bonnet there's no stopping him. As he'll pester me about this until I'm ninety-eight years old, I decide to give in. However, I fully expect these Aldershot charity shops to be exactly the same as the ones a couple of hundred yards away.

'OK, OK, we'll go by train.'

'It's the only way to travel,' my son replies.

ALDERSHOT

Following on from my conversation with Laura and Kerry last night about Harry's independence, I decide that now is a good a time as any to implement my theory. I'm going to sit a few seats away from Harry on the train, giving him a level of freedom. This trip will hopefully be a positive experience all round.

We get on a train at Streatham Common station. Harry takes a seat near one of the doors, and I sit a few feet away at the back of the carriage, but I can clearly see him. I warn Harry not to talk to himself.

'But I like video talk,' is his reply.

As we're approaching Clapham Junction station my mobile rings; it's Ray.

'David, really sorry to bother you again, but Barclays want to talk to us about some of the new screens. I don't think it's a major issue, but would it be possible to speak to them just to keep them happy?'

'Do you know what screens they're talking about?'

'Yeah, it's the loan and transaction ones. Is that OK?'

I look up and see the train doors closing at Clapham Junction station.

'Oh fuck,' I shout.

I jump out of my seat and can see Harry walking along the platform. I press the button to open the doors but the train is already moving. I bang on the window to get his attention, but he's walking with a purpose, and before long I can no longer see him. I ring his mobile several times, but he doesn't answer, which isn't unusual. A lot of times he has it on silent for some reason. The train is now well on its way to Victoria.

'Fuck, fuck, fuck,' I scream again.

'Is everything OK?' I can faintly hear Ray ask.

'Harry's gone,' I reply, as tears roll down my face.

'What do you mean?'

'I was too busy fucking talking to you. I didn't see him get off at Clapham Junction.'

'Stop the train.'

'No point. We're on our way to Victoria.'

'Then call the police.'

I try ringing Harry again, but there's still no answer, which gets me even more worried. As the train pulls into Victoria station I'm left with no option but to dial 999.

I give the police all the details, trying desperately to remember what Harry was wearing this morning, even though I ironed all his clothes and laid them all out for him. They told me to meet them at the ticket office at Clapham Junction station, so I jump on the next train out.

Fifteen minutes later I'm back at Clapham Junction. As I approach the ticket office I'm desperately hoping that Harry will be waiting for me, but all I see is a policeman deep in conversation on his walkie talkie.

'We've stopped the Aldershot train and a couple of policemen are going through it right now,' he informs me.

He must be on that train. Harry is constantly looking at all the various train schedules on the internet, so he must have worked out the connecting Aldershot train in advance; surely?

Why did he go there alone? Why didn't he try to contact me when he discovered I didn't get off the train?

The sound of someone speaking on the walkie talkie interrupts my thoughts. I cannot hear clearly what the chap at the other end is saying.

I'm feeling sick to my stomach.

'I'm afraid your son isn't on that train,' the policemen inform me.

'He must be. Tell them to check again.'

'They've been through the whole train twice. He's definitely not on it.'

'Then he must be still here.'

'We're currently searching the station, but we haven't found him yet.'

'Then where the hell is he?' I shout at the policeman.

'Don't worry, sir, we'll find him. It's only been twenty minutes since he got off that train. We know he's not going to Aldershot and it doesn't look like he's here. Did he express an interest in going anywhere else?'

I'm racking my brain to think if he said anything recently that might give me a clue, but Aldershot is the only place he talked about visiting. To be honest I just can't think straight right now.

'What shops does he like? He could still be around here.'

'Are there any book stores nearby?'

'Yes, there's one just outside the station.'

I immediately start running through the commuters and reach the book store within a couple of minutes. I look around, but can only see an elderly man.

'I'm looking for my son. He's sixteen, dark hair, five foot eight, and wearing a light blue jacket. Has he been in here just now?' I ask the lady behind the counter.

'I think so. A teenage boy was looking at the younger children's books a short time ago. I thought it was a little odd, given his age.'

That must be Harry.

'When did he leave?'

'About ten minutes ago.'

The policeman, who was standing right behind me, relays this new piece of information on his walkie talkie.

'We'll have more officers out there looking very shortly. He can't be far.'

I'm encouraged that Harry was just here, but I'm still scared to death. I try ringing his mobile again, but this time it's a dead line. Has his battery run out?

'Can you think where else he'd go?'

'A DVD store.'

'There's one a few minutes from here. Let's go.'

Just as we're leaving the policeman stops, as someone is contacting him on the walkie talkie.

'OK, OK, we're heading over there now.'

'What's happened?'

'They've found him, but it looks like he's been mugged.'

'Is he hurt?'

'I don't know. He's not far away. Let's go.'

The policeman breaks into a trot, and as I jog alongside him I start to cry. How could this have happened? He was only in the book store a few minutes ago.

As we enter a side street I can see Harry with a couple of policemen. I rush towards them as fast as I can.

Harry is holding a tissue, which has blood on it, as he has a nasty cut above his right eye.

I hold onto him as tightly as I can.

'Sir, can we just have a chat with Harry please?' another policeman asks.

I eventually let go.

'So from what you've told us three boys approached you, pushed you to the ground and kicked you a few times, before stealing your phone. Is that correct?'

'If only I had Blossom, Bubbles and Buttercup with me, we would've beaten those shits up until they were dead,' Harry angrily replies.

'Are they your friends?'

'Yes, they're my best friends.'

'They are characters from the cartoon *Powerpuff Girls*,' I say to the policemen.

They nod, but clearly don't understand.

'And can you tell me what these boys looked like?'

'They look like a bunch of fuckers. I wanted to kick their balls up in the air.'

Although the police officers were aware of Harry's autism, I give them more background and explain that it's a waste of time continuing with their questioning.

They reluctantly agree, but not before making the point of saying that given Harry's autism I should have been more vigilant. Of course they're right, but it makes me feel extremely guilty for letting Harry down. Because of my neglect Harry was mugged; it's as simple as that.

They take down all my details and explain to me that a passer-by saw what happened and rang the police straight away, but the boys dashed off with Harry's phone before the police arrived. They got what they came for.

I thank the three police officers for their amazingly swift response to the situation. For once the mention of Harry's autism helped considerably.

'How are you feeling?' I ask my son as we head back to Clapham Junction station.

'Every time we come back into London I'm going to bring a hammer with me in case those shitters attack me again. I'm going to crush their skulls into little pieces.'

'Don't worry, you won't see them again. Did you say anything to them?'

'No, I was talking about Rosie the lavender tank engine when they beat the shit out of me.'

'You were talking to yourself?'

'Yes.'

'I've told you a million times not to do that when you're outside.'

'The men and women on the streets love it.'

The boys who attacked him obviously picked up that he was special needs, and therefore was easy pickings. The bastards.

Unlike most sixteen-year-olds Harry is the complete opposite of street wise, and that's worrying.

'Why didn't you contact me after you got off the train?'

'I just thought that you couldn't be arsed to go to Aldershot.'

'And why didn't you answer your phone either?'

Harry just shrugs his shoulders.

'Hurry up; we're going to miss the eight minutes past two train to Aldershot.'

'You still want to go?'

'Of course, it's going to be amazing.'

Although Harry seemed quite angry when we first met up, overall he doesn't seem too affected by the traumatic experience. However, I take him into the disabled toilet at Clapham Junction station to examine his injuries, and apart from the graze above his eye and a slight bruise on his leg, physically he seems OK, so I decide as he's desperate to go to Aldershot, then we shall go.

Much to Harry's annoyance we miss the eight minutes past two train, but end up on the two-thirty-three.

This time I sit next to my son.

As there is no one else in our carriage, now is as good a time as any to ring Laura.

'How's Aldershot?' Laura asks straight away.

'Harry got mugged,' I quickly reply. There's no room for small talk.

'Oh my God, is he OK?'

'He's got a cut just above his eye, but he did take a beating.'

'Should we take him to the hospital?'

'I don't think so. I've checked him out; he looks OK.'

'Did you get hurt?'

'No, I wasn't with him. He got off the train at Clapham Junction and the door shut on me. He went walking around the streets looking for his usual shops. Three boys approached him, nicked his phone and gave him a bit of a kicking. Luckily a man saw it and phoned the police. They dashed off straight away. It could've been worse.'

'How the hell did you let him off the train alone?'

'I got a phone call from work. I was distracted.'

'I can't believe this.'

'I know it's my fault, but there's nothing you can say that'll make me feel worse than I do right now.'

'I just can't see how you could've let him get off the train without noticing. I can't get my head around that.'

'And you've never made mistakes with him?' I respond.

'Of course, but I haven't left him on his own in the middle of London.'

'I take back what I've just said, you've made me feel even more guilty; thanks for that.'

'Can you put Harry on?'

Harry comes to the phone.

'How are you feeling?' Laura asks Harry.

'Those bastards beat the crap out of me before I had the chance to tear their eyeballs out.'

'Are you still in pain?'

'Nah, I'm much stronger than Harry Hill.'

I'm not sure if I feel re-assured by that.

'OK, you take care of yourself and just stay close to Dad, OK?'

'Those pricks didn't want me to go to Aldershot, but I'll show them,' Harry replies, before handing the phone back to me.

'He seems OK, but I'm going to pop over shortly to see him,' Laura tells me.

'Come later; we're on our way to Aldershot.'

'After all that's happened you're still going?'

'Yeah, he's desperate to go. Don't worry I'll be by his side the whole time; rest assured on that.'

'Please, please take care of him, David, and let me know when you're on your way back.'

Of course Laura was angry and upset, I would be if the situation was reversed, but there's a part of me that really wants to let rip when she reads me the riot act. I looked after Harry for such a long time when she wasn't well, so rightly or wrongly I feel she should cut me some slack.

Thirty minutes later we're in the Cancer Research shop in Aldershot, and Harry's very excited.

'This is the best place that I've ever been to,' Harry proclaims.

I glance around the shop. It's full of the usual collection of clothes, books and DVDs, and to me it looks exactly the same as any other charity shop.

My son approaches the counter.

'Excuse me, have you got *Thomas and Friends: The Great Race* DVD?'

'I'm afraid not.'

'What about *Thomas and Friends*: *Together on the Tracks*?'

'I don't think we've any Thomas DVDs.'

'Are you a bit of a bastard?'

'I'm sorry?'

'Why do you hate Thomas so much; he's lovely and you're a bald arsehole, who doesn't give a fuck.'

The middle-aged man, with a receding hairline, is speechless.

'Please accept my apologies, my son's autistic.'

'Come on, let's get out of this shithole,' Harry tells me, as he storms out of the shop.

'I'm never going to Aldershot again,' Harry says, as we make our way to the train station.

Every cloud…

An hour later we're back at the house, and Laura's waiting for us. She also examines Harry's body and apart from the slight injuries that I've mentioned, she's happy that there's nothing else to worry about.

'From now on, please stay with Harry on any public transport journey, OK?' She tells me.

'Yes, yes, alright, I'm aware of my responsibilities,' I reply irritably, although I'm the guilty party here.

'I just can't believe that he was attacked.'

'He's vulnerable out there; I don't think that's ever going to change.'

Laura wipes away more tears. Perhaps I shouldn't have said that. Not good timing.

'I'll just try to be more vigilant from now on. What more can I say?' I add.

'I dread to think what could've happened if that witness hadn't intervened. Why didn't he even think of contacting you when he was alone at Clapham Junction?'

'I don't know. I guess we'll have to keep onto him about it. We've got to hope that sooner or later the penny will drop.'

She spends the next hour or so trying to converse with Harry, but all he's interested in talking about is the latest episode of *My Little Pony*.

During this time I contact Barclays. I'm a bit abrupt with them as indirectly they're responsible for the train incident, but they don't seem to notice as I resolve all their issues.

Laura still looks anxious when she gets into her car.

'I'll be over at midday tomorrow,' she tells me.

Harry moves into his new 'home' tomorrow.

'OK, you take care.'

I give Laura a kiss on the cheek and she gives me a weak smile in return before driving off.

A short time later Kerry goes to bed with Niall, and I do the same with Harry.

'How are you feeling?' I ask my bed companion.

'Aldershot is a suitcase full of shit.'

'What about you? Are you OK?'

Harry doesn't respond.

'Are you looking forward to going to the Hastings house tomorrow?'

'Is it a prison?'

'No, it's a lovely place. We went there last month; remember? It's by the seaside.'

'How many minutes am I going to be there?'

'You're staying there from tomorrow until Friday morning, and I'll pick you up then to take you home.'

'So I'm there for five fucking days?'

'Yes, I've told you about this before.'

'And that's it for two thousand and nineteen?'

'No, it's five days a week, every week.'

'That's ridiculous.'

'The staff and the children are all really friendly. You're going to love it.'

'But the sea is too loud. Can the prison staff make all that water a bit quieter?'

'OK, Harry, let's try to get some sleep now. Tomorrow's going to be a busy day.'

Harry continues to stare at the ceiling. I've no idea what he's thinking and I'm afraid to ask. His prison references have upset me, and I don't think that either one of us will get much sleep tonight.

SPEAKERS CORNER

It's three fifty-seven in the morning and I'm sitting in my garden smoking a cigarette. I used to smoke fairly regularly, but seeing first-hand the damage it inflicted on my parents' health made me eventually quit. However, in stressful times I succumb.

Yesterday's traumatic event has shaken me, and combined with the prospect of Harry moving out today has meant that I've had very little sleep.

I still can't believe that I was irresponsible enough to allow Harry off the train on his own, and left to walk the streets unaccompanied. Until yesterday Harry has never gone anywhere without me, Laura, or a carer by his side.

Apart from promising to bring a hammer with him on his next trip to London, he seems to be relatively unaffected by the mugging incident, but who knows what he's really thinking?

And now the day that I have been dreading has arrived. How will Harry manage being away from me and Laura? And how the hell will I cope?

The new sleeping arrangement is just one change that he'll have to get used to. I've been sharing a bed with Harry for the past sixteen years. Although this situation is far from ideal, I just don't know how Harry will adjust to going to bed on his own. Believe me I've tried to instigate this many times down the years; without success. I'm aware that it's in Harry's long-term interest to be sleeping independently, but I just cannot bear the thought of my son being alone at night while I'm sixty miles away.

My friends have told me that I'll have so much more freedom to go out socially, but all I'm concerned about right now is how this will affect Harry.

'Can I have a fag?' my son asks, as he steps into the garden.

'No, you can't. Why don't you go back up to bed?'

'Beds are for losers. Anyway, where has Harry Hill's hair gone? Is he going to get it back?'

'I'm not sure.'

'He's got the same name as me, but I've got lots of hair and he hasn't got any.'

This is a typical early morning Harry conversation. The reason most people struggle to sleep at night is because they're usually worried about something; like their health, the state of their marriage, paying bills etc. Harry stays awake at night thinking about Harry Hill's hair.

'Why don't you try and get some sleep?'

'Sleep is wasting my time. I've had enough of it.'

Harry pulls up a chair and sits next to me.

'Is there solitary confinement in the Hastings prison?'

'I keep telling you, it's not a prison. It's a fun place. You're going to love it there. Of course there's no solitary confinement.'

At least I hope not.

'Can I bring my eighteen Thomas DVDs with me?'

'Of course you can. In fact I'll buy you a couple more today.'

'Ok, that's cool.'

I'm not above a bit of bribery. Whatever it takes.

A short time later Niall and Kerry join us for breakfast. There's no sleeping in until midday in this household.

'How do you feel?' Kerry asks me.

'Depressed and nervous.'

'I know it can't be easy, but it's for the best.'

'Yeah, that's what everyone keeps telling me.'

Niall walks over to me and instead of punching my testicles he bites my hair and then leaves with a chunk of hair still in his mouth. He then carefully places it in the rubbish bin. That was extremely painful. I haven't got too much hair to spare and what I do have is quite precious to me. I must say that Niall is getting quite inventive in his physical attacks.

'That's enough, Niall; please leave David alone,' Kerry shouts at her son.

However Niall doesn't look up at Kerry and just hands her the Rice Krispies box, as he's ready for breakfast.

'Sorry, David; you've really taken a beating lately.'

'Do you think he blames me for you moving here? He seems more agitated since he's been here.'

'No, I don't think he's bothered about that.'

'Does he resent me taking Danny's place?'

'No. On the rare times that he meets Danny, he doesn't seem in the least bit excited. I just don't know why he's been so aggressive towards you.'

'Hopefully it'll fizzle out,' I say, although right now I don't believe it will. It's been quite an experience living with Niall. He's such a complex character and very difficult to read. How Kerry has dealt with these behaviours for so many years I just do not know.

'Let's go somewhere today. It'll take our mind off things,' Kerry says.

'OK. Any ideas?'

'What about going swimming?'

'I don't think that's a good idea right now.'

'What do you mean?'

'There's too much flesh around for Niall to grab. It's too risky.'

Kerry nods, silently acknowledging that Niall could approach the other swimmers. Because of the lack of clothing on display we could be entering into dangerous territory. Niall's OCD behaviour has gone up a level or two recently, so it's best to play it safe right now.

'I'm sorry to bring that up,' I say.

'Don't be silly. You're right. I shouldn't have suggested it.'

Now it's Kerry's turn to look sad. Niall loves swimming and it's great exercise for him. It also expels some of that pent up energy, but for now he cannot be put in that situation.

Harry rushes into the kitchen.

'I've just spoken to Bernadette and...'

'Hold on. It's only quarter past four. You didn't wake her up, did you?'

'No, she rang me.'

There's no need for alarm clocks in the autistic world.

'She said that before I'm locked up in the penitentiary we should go to that Speakers' Corner place in Hyde Park. She looked it up on YouTube and said that the crowd get really angry and swear all the time. I wanna do that, and afterwards you can buy me those Thomas DVDs.'

Me and Kerry glance at each other and smile.

'You know what, Harry, that's a great idea. Tell her I'll pick her up at around ten and we'll drive up from there. I'll text her mum, just to make sure it's OK.'

By mid-morning I'm negotiating my way through London traffic. Kerry is alongside me at the front of the car while Harry, Niall and Bernadette are cramped in the back seats.

'Dad, are you going to marry that Irish bird?' my son asks me.

'Kerry is right here; don't be so rude.'

'Well, are you going to marry her?' Harry says, flicking his thumb in Kerry's direction.

'We haven't been going out that long, so it's a bit early to be asking that question.'

Out of my peripheral vision I see that Kerry is looking down. I sense that she's as embarrassed as me.

'You're an old geezer, so you better make your mind up quick. If you don't want her why don't you try one of the American chicks; they're a lot more fun, and they always have nice teeth.'

'Yeah, the yanks are just great. They make brilliant films and they can ride horses much better than the English, who are just shit at it,' Bernadette chips in.

So the message is clear – dump Kerry and bag an American lady because they have good teeth and can ride a horse.

'It's quite clear Harry doesn't want me here long-term,' Kerry quietly tells me.

'Please don't take his comments too seriously.'

'But he's constantly putting me down; what do you expect?'

'Don't worry, I'll speak to him later.'

Kerry stares out of the car window. She's obviously hurt by Harry and Bernadette's remarks. Harry can be quite insensitive in his observations, but that's the nature of the beast.

'American woman smile better than the Brits, and they have nice socks too,' Harry adds.

'OK, can we drop this subject please?'

'When did you get your last haircut, Mister McCarthy?' Bernadette asks.

'Maybe a couple of months ago.'

'What's the exact date?'

'I can't remember.'

Bernadette shakes her head and tuts.

'It's beginning to grow over your ears. If you don't get it cut soon you won't be able to hear anything.'

Given the conversation in the last ten minutes that may not be a bad thing.

'OK, good point. I'll get a haircut tomorrow.'

'About time. Make sure you text me afterwards.'

As we're getting closer to central London the traffic is almost at a standstill. Niall is getting increasingly frustrated and pinches Harry a couple of times in the face.

'Fuck off, or I'll tear your teeth out.'

'OK, calm down. There's no need to swear,' I tell my son.

Travelling in the car with Harry and Niall is like trying to keep control on a couple of naughty five-year-olds. It's always extremely stressful. I search through my CD collection and put on a Nat King Cole CD. This immediately distracts Niall as he calmly nods along to the soothing music. Thanks, Nat, I owe you one.

I spend ages looking for a place to park. A couple of disabled parking spaces were occupied by cars who weren't displaying the disabled blue badge. This is a pet hate of mine, so much so that I always take a photo of the car and email this to the local council for them to take the appropriate action. Westminster Council can expect a couple more photos later this afternoon. I manage to find a parking space about a ten minute walk from the park.

As soon as we enter the park, Niall pulls away from us and runs at great speed. Kerry and me attempt to keep up with him, but that's impossible. From a distance I can see him approach an elderly man with a walking stick. Niall starts to lick the man's shoulder and then spits on it. The man looks scared and confused. Then Niall starts to head-butt his arm quite forcefully, which causes the man to fall over. Niall then kneels down next to him and continues his head-banging routine.

It takes all my strength to pull Niall away from the man, who is now looking shocked and breathless.

Kerry then ushers Niall away from the scene, although I can see that Niall's eyes are totally focused on the man. He definitely hasn't completed his OCD ritual, but that's not going to happen. I don't think that the man can survive another 'attack'.

'I'm so sorry. The boy's autistic, he just can't help it. Let me help you up.'

'The only help I need right now is for someone to call the police.'

'Is that necessary?'

'I've just been assaulted.'

'But he can't control his actions. Niall's very severely autistic. He can't even speak.'

'Should he be out and about if he's going to be attacking people? That can't be right.'

'So you want us to lock him up and throw away the key?' I reply.

The man looks over at Niall, who is standing next to Kerry, about a hundred feet away from us. The man is still breathing quite heavily, but he offers me his hand and I pull him up.

'Do you need to go to the hospital?' I ask.

'No, I'll be OK, just a bit shaken.' The man continues to stare at Niall.

'Did you say he's autistic?'

I nod my reply.

'If I go over there will he beat me up again?'

'No, we'll make sure he doesn't,' I reply, somewhat surprised and confused by his question.

We wait a few minutes and then slowly walk towards Kerry and Niall. I've no idea what the man is going to do or say.

Kerry has a firm grip on her son, and I'm blocking Niall from getting too close. Years of experience dealing with the mum/Harry encounters has stood me in good stead.

'I can't apologise enough,' Kerry says.

'There's no need. I overreacted. I didn't realise...'

'It's a normal response.'

Niall is still staring at the man's arm.

'Now are you going to give me a hug?' the man asks Niall.

'Are you sure you're OK with this?' Kerry asks.

'Of course.'

The man puts his arms around Niall, who in return gently head-butts his shoulder a couple of times. Niall smiles for the first time today.

'I can't thank you enough for your understanding. It's rare to see.'

'It's the least I can do. You must have a very stressful life, why should I add to it?'

Kerry smiles back at the man.

'I better be on my way.'

'Are you sure you're OK?'

'I'm fine. Don't worry.'

'Take care, Niall. Be good to your mum and dad,' the man says, offering his hand.

Niall ignores the handshake offer, but gently rubs the man's arm as a form of apology. The man smiles and gingerly walks away.

'That was amazing. Why can't everyone else react like that?' I say.

Kerry looks like she's about to cry, as she continues to stare at the man.

'Anyway we'd better get going, Harry and Bernadette are miles ahead of us.'

Kerry holds Niall's hand as we start walking. She looks relieved as it could have escalated into a serious incident, if it wasn't for the man's kindness. I walk on the other side of Niall, as extra precaution.

We reach Speakers' Corner without any further incident.

Harry and Bernadette are listening to a man talking about the history of stamps.

'Emails are the flavour of the month, but they're so impersonal. What could be better than receiving a hand written letter, with a beautiful stamp proudly attached to it? Do you know that the first ever stamp was called the Penny Black and was first issued on the first of May eighteen-forty? Rowland Hill is credited in making this possible. The guy was just amazing. In February eighteen-forty-one the stamps were then printed in red because the cancellation marks were hard to read.'

Amazingly there is a huge crowd listening to this less than stimulating topic. I thought Speakers' Corner usually had lively debates about subjects that people feel passionate about, but I just can't see that happening here.

'How many stamps are there in the Streatham Post Office?' Harry shouts out.

'What do you mean?'

'How many stamps do those Post Office counter people have in their stamp books in Streatham?'

'I've no idea.'

'Them you're a goddamn fraud.'

The stamp speaker and his audience stare at Harry in total confusion. I quickly take my son away from the situation. I do not want to get on the bad side of these stamp collector types. They can be right bastards.

'But I like stamps,' Harry protests.

Who doesn't?

'I don't like the self-adhesive stamps though, they're just ludicrous. They were first used in America in nineteen seventy-four and in Great Britain on Tuesday the ninetieth of October nineteen ninety-three. I'll like to execute the person who invented those stamps.'

'Yeah, hanging would be great,' Bernadette chips in.

That's all a bit harsh.

'What do you think of the self-adhesive stamps?' Bernadette asks me.

'They're OK.'

'Mister McCarthy, I don't want to be rude, but you're full of shit.'

The subject of stamps is obviously more controversial that I first thought.

Thankfully we walk away from the stamp debate and take in some of the other discussions. There's one man talking about Hitler. He's saying that Hitler wasn't all that bad, and insisting that his image would be vastly improved if he had had a half decent PR agent. As we're walking away he did admit that Hitler made a few mistakes, but then said 'don't we all?' Needless to say this did get a heated response. There are a couple of the usual discussions about how shit the government is, but we stop at a man talking about the history of trains. He must have known that we were coming.

'Trains are just fantastic, aren't they?' the speaker enthusiastically announces.

'You bet they are, you son of a bitch,' replies Harry.

Once again everyone turns around to locate the source of that comment, but the speaker is unperturbed.

'I live in Leatherhead and every day I board onto a South Western Railway train. They took over from South West Trains on the twentieth of August two thousand and seventeen. Anyway the first South West Trains train left Twickenham on the fourth of February nineteen ninety-six, the final destination was Waterloo. South Western Railway trains leave from Waterloo and travel to south west London, Surrey, Hampshire and Dorset. How great is that?'

'They're the fucking best,' shouts Bernadette.

This is turning into a pantomime. A number of people glance at us; do they think Harry and Bernadette are taking the piss?

'South Western Railway operates one thousand and seventy trains per day.'

'Please don't respond this time,' I plead with Harry and Bernadette. For once they comply.

'They also have quiet zones, where you can't use your mobile or play loud music. What a considerate gesture.'

'That's a load of bollocks,' screams Harry.

'What do you mean?'

'I just love playing *Living Doll* really loud, so you better not stop me or I'll kick you up the arse.'

The train audience start laughing, which is our cue to leave.

It's a well-known fact that many of the speakers here are eccentrics, and that's part of the attraction. Eccentric or otherwise, both the stamp and train speakers are drawing big crowds, although the Hitler chap still seems to be the number one attraction.

'I think it's time to head back,' I say to Harry and Bernadette.

'But I like it here. Those speakers have loads of hair coming out of their ears, ' Bernadette tells me.

That's the least of their problems.

Throughout all of this Kerry and Niall are sitting on the grass a safe distance away. Shortly afterwards we all visit the HMV store and as promised I buy Harry his Thomas DVDs. We then walk back to the car.

Despite the Niall incident and Harry's outbursts, this trip was a welcome distraction. For a couple of hours it took my mind off Hastings.

HASTINGS

Thirty minutes later we arrive at Bernadette's house.

'Don't let those bastards torture you and make sure that your cell has sky blue walls,' Bernadette tells Harry as she gets out of the car.

'If those pricks try to beat me up I'll set fire to their eyebrows.'

'Don't forget to text me every four minutes past the hour.'

'You better believe it.'

They then do the fist bump handshake that they've probably seen in countless American films.   Alice glances at me and smiles. She then looks down at the floor and I notice a tear rolling down her cheek. Most parents wouldn't react to such a simple gesture but everything is magnified when you're a parent of a special needs child.

Boyfriend/girlfriend relationships are rare in the autistic world, and although Harry probably doesn't consider Bernadette his girlfriend they do have a very special relationship. I cannot tell you how happy I am for them both.

We arrive home shortly afterwards and Laura is already in the kitchen making a cup of tea.

'How's Harry?' she asks.

'He's OK, but he keeps on saying that he's going to the Hastings jail.'

Laura shakes her head. Perhaps I shouldn't have mentioned that.

'We're doing the right thing, aren't we?' she asks.

'Yeah, but it isn't easy.'

We gather all of Harry's belongings and thirty minutes later we're Hastings bound.

As expected the atmosphere is subdued. Harry is watching an episode of Harry Hill's Tea-Time on his portable DVD player and notably he isn't laughing.

'How's it going with you and Sean?' I ask Laura.

She turns around to glance at Harry before replying.

'Not good.'

'Sorry to hear that.'

'I know that he's been working really long hours these past few months, but when we're together he seems so distant. Something's not right,' Laura replies, all the time glancing in the rear view mirror.

'Have you talked to him about it?'

'Yeah, but he just says he's tired and there's nothing to worry about. It's just not working out. I'm thinking of moving back to the flat.'

'Wow, it's that serious?'

Laura nods.

'Does Sean know your intentions?'

'No, but I'll tell him tomorrow.'

'How do you think he'll react?'

'About six months ago he would've pleaded with me to stay, but now I'm not so sure.'

'What about Timothy and Mary?'

'I think they'll be pleased, although we don't talk much to each other. When I first moved into Sean's I made a real effort to get to know them, but all I got was one word answers, so I gave up.'

'I really hope that it all works out for you; Sean's a good guy.'

'Thanks, David.'

'How much longer before we get to Hastings?' Harry asks, which is unusual as he normally has every road mapped out well in advance of any car journey.

'About an hour.'

'Fuck that. Is Hastings still in England?'

'Yes, Harry, it's by the seaside.'

'Is the sea full of shit, or is it blue like in Italy?'

'It's blueish.'

'Do they have sky TV in that shithole?'

'Yes, I did check on that.'

'What's the hair colour of all the wardens?'

'They're not wardens; they're just members of staff who'll look after you.'

'Yeah, right; what colour is their hair?'

'Emily has blonde hair, Philip has grey hair, Terry has brown...'

'That's too many different colours. What the hell's going on?'

These are the types of questions I get asked on a daily basis.

'How's the Harry Hill show?' I inquire, desperately trying to distract Harry from the hair colour debate.

'He likes pens.'

'That's nice.'

'I do as well, but I think Harry likes them even more than me.'

The rest of the journey passes quietly. Harry is engrossed in his DVDs, and Laura seems preoccupied

– no doubt thinking about her pending split from Sean and of course Harry's imminent residential stay.

An hour later we arrive at Harry's new 'home.' It's a nice modern building about a five minute walk from the beach. As we're getting out of the car, Philip, the manager of the home, comes out to greet us.

'Hello, Harry, how are you today?'

'Why aren't you bald?'

'I'm sorry?'

'Your face looks decrepit, but you've still got hair.'

'It's just great that you've got a sense of humour. I think we're going to get along just fine,' Philip replies, smiling at Harry.

Harry looks confused; humour really isn't his thing.

'Let me show you around the home and introduce you to some of the staff.'

Although we've been here twice before I'm still impressed by the facilities and the grounds. We first drop Harry's stuff off in his bedroom, which is spacious and has an en suite bathroom.

'What do you think of your room?' I ask Harry.

'There are too many flowers on the wallpaper. It makes my eyes go crazy.'

'But look at the sea, it's beautiful,' I say, as we view the seafront from his bedroom window.

'I don't like the sea, it's too noisy and the waves scare me.'

'Come on, let's meet some of your housemates,' Philip cheerfully announces.

We walk into a large living-room. There are three boys and three carers sitting around. They are all either watching TV or playing on their ipad.

'Who are you?' Harry asks one of the boys.

'I'm Jeff. I was born on the seventh of September two thousand and one and my dad is dead. When were you born?'

'On the eighth of July two thousand and three.'

'That's a Tuesday.'

'Correct.'

The boy then focuses his attention back to the TV. It looks like the conversation has come to an end. Social niceties are not a priority.

Philip guides Harry to the next housemate.

'And who the hell are you?' Harry asks.

'What size are your shoes?' the boy replies.

'Eight.'

'That's alright then. My name is Chris.'

'Do you know Chris Evans?'

'No'.

'Me neither. Do you like Chris Evans?'

'No.'

'Why?'

'I don't like the colour of his hair. It used to be all ginger and now it's ginger and grey. Why does he keep on changing it?'

'Fuck knows. Shall we write to the BBC about it?'

'Great idea.'

That's a more encouraging conversation – bonding over Chris Evans' hair colour.

'Do they have to go to bed at a certain time?' Laura asks Philip.

'Yes, by ten and for security reasons we'll have a couple of staff members in the corridors throughout the night to make sure they don't wander off.'

'Is that what the chairs are for outside all the rooms?'

'Yes, they're for the overnight staff. It's for the residents' safety.'

Laura glances over at me with a concerned expression. Logically I suppose it's reassuring that there's someone on hand in the middle of the night in case there are problems, but it does all feel a bit weird.

'You know that we're staying with him tonight?'

'Yes, I must say that's unusual, but I understand your concerns. I'll get a couple of sleeping bags for you. Let me introduce you to some of the staff.'

We approach the kitchen/dining area and several of the staff are having their lunch.

'This is Kevin; he'll be Harry's main carer.'

'Hi,' Kevin half-heartedly remarks while taking a bite of his sandwich.

'Hello, I'm Harry's father. Good luck with looking after him,' I say, tongue in cheek.

'Why do you say that?'

'Well he can be difficult, but then again if he was normal he wouldn't be here, would he?'

Before responding Kevin takes another bite of his sandwich. We all wait patiently as he meticulously chews on the chicken.

'There's nothing Harry can throw at me that I haven't encountered before,' he eventually remarks.

Despite only just being introduced to Kevin, I've taken an instant dislike to the man. Eating his chicken sandwich was obviously a higher priority than talking to us, and I don't care for his attitude. It's a worry that this guy will be looking after Harry.

We leave Kevin to finish off his sandwich and return to the living-room. Harry is still in conversation with Chris.

'Do you have parents?' Harry asks.

'Yeah, my dad is forty-six and three-quarters, has a beard and doesn't like cricket. Mum is forty-four and a half, paints her finger nails red and dresses like a tart.'

'Are they nice or just idiots?'

'Don't know,' Chris replies.

'Does this joint give you chips?'

'Only on Monday and Wednesday.'

'What size are the chips?' Harry asks.

'Two and three-quarter inches, which is six point nine-eight-five centimetres.'

'Are the wardens arseholes?'

'OK, I think it's time we had a walk around the grounds,' interrupts Philip.

That's a shame as I would have been quite interested to hear Chris' answer to that last question. Although we've already done the whole school tour previously, Philip proudly shows us the vast school complex again. There's even a gym, although I doubt if Harry will set foot in there.

When we arrive back we find the living-room empty. Philip informs us that most of the boys are in their bedrooms, but can hang out in there until ten o'clock, when the lights are turned off and they're not allowed to watch TV or their DVDs. That's going to be a challenge for Harry. One of many I suspect.

As it's just after nine, it seems the only thing left for us to do is to go to bed. As we climb the stairs I notice that one of the staff pulls out his walkie talkie and tells whoever the listener is that 'Harry and the McCarthy family are on their way'. Again Laura and I exchange bemused glances at each other. Anyone would think it's a presidential visit. We're greeted at the top of the stairs by another staff member. I hear him mutter 'received' on his walkie-talkie. He escorts us to the bedroom. I know my memory is not what it was but we were only in the bedroom about an hour ago, so no sat nav was required. I fully appreciate that security has to be tight in an establishment that houses special needs teenagers, but this is way over the top.

We bid goodnight to the two chaps who have overnight corridor duty and enter Harry's bedroom.

'That was strange,' I whisper to Laura.

'And a bit worrying,' she replies.

Two sleeping bags with blankets are laid out on the floor for me and Laura.

'Harry, we're with you tonight, but from tomorrow you'll be on your own and you'll have to have the bedroom lights off by ten. Is that clear?'

'That's ridiculous. I want to watch episodes one, four and six of *Only Fools and Horses*, series three at four minutes past eleven, and I don't want to watch it in the dark cos I won't be able to see the slow motion button on my DVD player.'

'Harry, those are the rules. You've got to turn off the lights at ten and you can't play your DVDs as well,' I reply, thinking why you would want to use the slow motion button while watching *Only Fools And Horses*?

'I told you the wardens were bastards, didn't I?'

I avoid getting into a discussion about the parentage of the staff members and instead I help Harry get ready for bed. By nine-thirty Laura and me are already in our respective sleeping bags. I've turned off the lights in the hope that it'll encourage Harry to settle down, but a few minutes later Harry crawls into the sleeping bag with me, bringing his portable DVD player with him. I'm just too tired to protest.

There's a sense of relief that we've finally arrived here, and with no major incidents. However I'm fully aware that from tomorrow onwards it's going to be far more challenging. Not just for Harry, but also for Laura and me.

I glance over at Laura who is staring at the ceiling. She obviously has a lot on her mind.

It's been a long time since I've shared a bedroom with Laura and it feels a little strange. I wonder if she thinks the same?

Harry is watching an episode of *My Little Pony* and telling me that Josh Harber wrote most of the episodes in series six and should be given an Emmy. He wants to go to California to meet him. Personally I can think of other artists in that neck of the woods that I'd rather get a selfie with, but it's all subjective.

I kiss Harry on his forehead and shortly afterwards I begin to fall to sleep as Harry is telling me that they have filmed two hundred and eighteen episodes of *My Little Pony*, and starts to give me an episode by episode plot summary. This was enough to send me to sleep.

HANDCUFFED

'But I need to have my KitKat and 7Up *now*,' I hear Harry say. I notice that Harry isn't in his bed. A light is shining from the corridor into our bedroom and I soon realise that he's out there talking to one of the staff.

I glance at my watch; it's twenty-five minutes past two. Laura is still asleep so I quietly get up and join my son in the corridor.

'What's going on?' I ask.

'This piece of shit won't let me have my morning snack,' Harry proclaims, pointing at a bemused staff member.

'Harry, that's enough swearing. You know that you're not allowed sweets this early. I've told you a thousand times.'

'I left my KitKat in the fridge last night as there's only thirty-seven days left before it expires. I have to eat it before three o'clock.'

'Why?'

'Because after three it's going to taste like cow's dung.'

Even I don't begin to understand Harry's pretzel logic sometimes.

'I'm sorry about this,' I say to the staff member.

'I must admit this is a first for me,' he replies.

He looks confused; well get used to it. I've had sixteen years of interrupted sleep and this is your job, isn't it? I know that I shouldn't feel so bitter, but maybe I'm just resentful about someone else taking over my responsibilities.

I look beyond this chap and there are two other staff members sitting in their chairs. They don't seem to be taking too much interest in Harry, but I suppose they have their own pupils to look after. It's all a slightly bizarre sight at this time in the morning.

'I'll get you another KitKat later, OK, so let's go to bed now.'

'But I want the fridge KitKat.'

'When I buy you another one I'll put it in the fridge, OK?'

Harry shakes his head and reluctantly follows me back to the bedroom. He frequently gets up in the middle of the night for an early morning snack, and I because I don't always wake up, he has free access to all the goodies in the kitchen; clearly that's not going to happen here.

My sleeping bag, which is designed for one person, now has both Harry and me squashed into it again.

'Doesn't that idiot like KitKats?'

'That's got nothing to do with it. You're not supposed to be eating chocolate in the middle of the night. Now why don't you go back to your own bed?'

'But that's just ridiculous.'

I'm pleased that Laura is still sleeping as she needs the rest, given that she will no doubt be stressed out later when she confronts Sean. She doesn't seem too optimistic about the outcome. After she told me that Sean was arriving home late most nights I did wonder if he was seeing someone else, and I'm sure that same thought has also crossed Laura's mind, although this subject matter is way too sensitive to be discussed between us right now. Without wishing to sound too pessimistic, it looks like their future together doesn't look too secure.

Although I'm physically and mentally tired, I don't feel sleepy. Having Harry next to me, with the sleeping bag bursting at the seams, isn't helping.

Harry is quietly singing Cliff Richard's song *Summer Holiday* to himself. Doesn't everyone do the same at three o'clock in the morning?

I would normally ask him to stop, but it's strangely soothing, even after the eighth rendition.

At around five o'clock Harry eventually falls asleep.

In recent conversations with Laura I've tried to present a positive outlook on Harry's residential stay, but in reality my stomach has been in knots. In the past few weeks my sleeping has been even more erratic than normal, as I'm usually lying in bed worrying about the future.

We looked at a number of residential placements. We really liked a couple of them but were told that Harry wasn't a suitable candidate and in the end it was a choice between this house and one in Norwich. The deciding factor was that this one was that much nearer.

I'm seeing my friend, Ian, tonight for a couple of drinks. I originally arranged to meet up with him to help take my mind off everything, however the way I feel right now won't exactly make me the life and soul of the party. Ian's an old friend from my postman days and is still single. Maybe if Laura splits up with Sean I could play matchmaker? Ian's a good guy and has always had a soft spot for Laura. Will that seem a bit too weird? My mind is racing through all kinds of strange thoughts right now.

I'm desperate for a cigarette and could ask one of the corridor security staff if anyone smokes, but I decide against it. Harry has made numerous prison comments about this place in the last few days and right now I do feel hemmed in, especially with the Secret Service waiting on the other side of our bedroom door.

I manage to slither out of the sleeping bag without waking Harry and climb into his bed. Despite my more comfortable sleeping arrangement, I still can't drift off. It's Monday morning and both Laura and I have taken the day off work. Our plan was to leave Harry's new 'home' as soon as possible, as there seems little point in prolonging the agony. We then hoped to go for a coffee together. I wish now that I hadn't taken the day off because at least being at work would have occupied my mind, although I'm not looking forward to returning to the office, given Harry's behaviour the other day.

Rather than lying in bed I have a shower and then quietly sneak out to the corridor.

'Can I help you?' Harry's security guard asks me.

'I wonder if I could pop downstairs and make myself a cup of tea?' I feel like I'm back at school and have to ask the teacher if I can be excused from class to go to the toilet.

The security guard gets out his infamous walkie-talkie.

'Mister McCarthy wants to visit the kitchen. Are there any staff available in that area?'

'Not sure. I'll get back to you.'

Freedom of movement is clearly not an option in this place, which is somewhat disconcerting.

'Does your son always swear so aggressively?' the security guard asks, as we're waiting for the cup of tea clearance to come through.

'Oh yes. Unfortunately that's part of his everyday speech.'

If you had read his history you would've known that.

'That's something we have to work on.'

'Good luck,' I reply in a sarcastic tone. To be honest that's the least of your worries, but you'll discover everything about Harry soon enough.

A few minutes go past with no further conversation before I break the uncomfortable silence.

'So what time do you finish?'

'When Harry's up, had his shower and breakfast, then I'm off.'

'Do you only work nights?'

'No, two nights and two day shifts.'

Suddenly his walkie-talkie comes alive, interrupting our scintillating conversation.

'Helen's now in the kitchen, so Mister McCarthy is free to come down.'

That's jolly decent of you old chap.

As expected I'm greeted at the bottom of the stairs by yet another walkie-talkie guy, who confirms my arrival to his colleague. When we visited here previously I was totally unaware of this level of security.

In the kitchen I'm greeted by a middle-aged lady.

'Hello, I'm Helen. I believe you'd like a cup of tea?' she says, offering me her hand. It's probably the first friendly gesture I've encountered since our arrival yesterday.

'Yeah, please, if you don't mind. My name's David. Harry's my boy, he came here yesterday.'

'Please take a seat.'

'Do you teach here?' I ask.

'No, I'm just the cook.'

'Have you been here long, if you don't mind me asking?'

'Nearly seven years now.'

I want to ask her more probing questions about the school and the teachers, but I feel it's too soon.

'You look worried,' she says, as she hands me the tea.

'Thanks. I'm anxious for Harry. I'm desperate for him to settle here.'

'Is this the first time he's lived away from you?'

'Yeah. This whole setup is just so different from anything he's experienced before. He keeps on comparing this place to prison,' I say, with a smile.

Helen returns my smile, but noticeably doesn't reassure me. Perhaps I'm reading too much into her lack of response?

'Do you think the children are happy here?' I ask.

She looks at me for what seems like an age before responding.

'Some are, but there are others who definitely aren't,' came the cryptic reply.

Before I had a chance to ask her to elaborate, one of the staff members comes into the kitchen.

'Harry's up. He's asking if you could bathe him.'

'I better go. Thanks very much for the tea, Helen,' I say although I only took a couple of sips and it'll take an act of parliament to give me permission to carry the cup back to Harry's bedroom.

'No problem. I hope all goes well with Harry.'

Harry is waiting in the bathtub, minus the water. I fill it up and start washing him. I've lost count of the amount of times that I have left Harry in the bathtub on his own, with instructions to bathe himself, only to return half-an-hour later to find him sitting in the exact same position and the soap bar completely dry.

'You could've asked mummy to bathe you. She does it when you stay at her house.'

'When you and mummy are together I want you to bathe me.'

I think that this is just Harry's way of compartmentalising his bath times. All the same, I hope that Laura didn't hear his comment.

'Tomorrow morning one of the staff will be helping you bathe.'

'I don't want them touching my nails. If they do I'll give them a couple of black eyes and pinch their ears.'

Laura has her shower shortly after I finished bathing Harry. I pack our clothes in our overnight bag and we're all ready to go.

'Shall we stay with him while he has his breakfast?' Laura asks me as we approach the dining room.

'No, it's best we go now.'

His main carer, Kevin, is waiting for us.

'First night went OK?' he asks.

'Not bad. He did get up wanting some chocolate at some ungodly hour, but eventually went back to sleep.'

'Yes, I know. I was briefed. He'll realise soon enough that we won't give in if he attempts that again.'

Kevin's arrogant and patronising tone grates with me, but nothing will please me more if they manage to stop Harry seeking out goodies in the middle of the night.

Harry notices his new friend, Chris, leaving the dining-room, with his carer.

'Is the breakfast fucked up?' Harry asks Chris.

'First of all I had cornflakes, which could've been made better, so that was forty-six per cent shit; then I had toast on brown bread which had way too much butter on it, so I'll give that twenty-four per cent shit; and then I finished it all off with eggs and bacon. The eggs looked rather ugly and the bacon was situated on the left hand side of the plate but I like it in the middle, so that's thirty-seven per cent shit.'

I'm not sure how you can mess up cornflakes?

Chris should definitely hook up with Gordon Ramsay. What a team they would make.

'OK, Harry, it's time for breakfast. Why don't you say goodbye to your parents?' Kevin tells my son.

Harry is looking over Kevin's shoulder at all the food laid out in the dining-room.

'Kevin, can you just give us a minute with Harry please?' I ask.

Kevin nods and walks away.

However, Harry then wanders off to the dining-room.

'Harry, can you come back? We're going now.'

My son still has his back to us as he gathers his plate and heads towards the food. I catch up with him.

'Put the plate down and come back outside to say goodbye to us.'

'They haven't got any black pudding.'

'But you've never had any black pudding before.'

'I saw Reg Varney eat some black pudding in *On The Buses* on Saturday and he loved it.'

I wasn't aware that he was watching *On The Buses*, but if it's good enough for Reg Varney...

'You can discuss this with Kevin after we leave, OK?'

That'll give Kevin a nice introduction to Harry.

Laura joins us.

'Remember, Harry, I want you to behave yourself this week and try not to swear,' Laura says.

'But those bastards hate me; I can tell,' Harry proclaims rather loudly, while pointing at all the staff members.

'They don't hate you at all. They don't even know you yet.'

'I don't like the pink flowers on this plate, they make me feel ill,' Harry remarks, as he stares at the flowery pattern on his dinner plate.

'Just ask for another plate.'

'But they've all got flowers on them. What the hell's going on?'

'We'll bring some plain ones down on Friday, OK? In the meantime just ignore the flowers.'

'I'll put food all over the plate so I won't have to see them,' Harry proclaims.

'Good idea. Anyway it's time we left.'

Laura hugs Harry, but his arms never leave his side as he continues to stare at all the breakfast food on display. Tears roll down Laura's cheeks, but Harry doesn't appear to notice. Food takes preference over everything.

'Just be good, OK?' Laura re-iterates.

'I think I'll have some frosties without any milk, and then some toast, eggs and baked beans.'

Laura nods, and then steps back as I approach him.

'We'll be here on Friday to pick you up, and remember you have your job to go to on Saturday. Now give me a hug.'

'Aren't you sleeping with me tonight?'

'No, we've talked about this. You're sleeping on your own tonight; it'll be good for you.'

'No, it'll be a pile of shit for me,' Harry replies with a worried expression.

'You're sixteen now. You've got to learn to sleep on your own.'

'Why?'

'Because teenagers don't sleep with their parents.'

'Why?'

'You're too old.'

'That's silly.'

'Look, Kevin's waiting for you, now give me a hug and we'll see you soon enough.'

Harry stands motionless, so I embrace him and kiss his forehead. Kevin then leads him towards the food.

'This plate is bollocks,' I hear him tell Kevin as I leave the dining-room. I don't turn around; that'll be too painful.

Laura and I walk towards our car without uttering a word. She's still wiping the tears from her eyes. I feel like the worst parent ever. What must Harry think of us? I just hope that he doesn't hate us for sending him there.

After many lengthy discussions, Laura and I decided that this residential placement was the only long-term option for Harry. She was initially reluctant, but as Harry lives with me I'm more affected by his behaviour. I'm getting older and finding it increasingly difficult coping with him. However, there have been many times where I've laid awake at night questioning our decision.

Right now all I can visualise is Harry's concerned expression when it finally dawned on him that we were leaving and not coming back tonight.

There was complete silence for the first fifteen minutes in the car journey back. Even though I'd discussed with Harry countless times about what was going to happen today he still seemed confused and surprised.

'Is he going to be OK?' Laura asks.

'I hope so.'

'When we first visited there I felt confident about everything, but now I'm not. The staff all seem so serious and Kevin is a bit of a prick,' Laura adds.

I wander how long it'll be before Harry calls him that?

'Yeah I agree with you, but we don't have to be their best friends.'

'Shall we ring them to find out how he's getting on?'

'No, we only left half an hour ago. I'll ring them tomorrow, and they did say that they'll contact us if there's any issues.'

'That whole walkie-talkie thing is just nonsense. What's all that about?'

'It does seem a bit strange, but I suppose they're just being overly cautious.'

I tried to lighten the mood by putting on a Sinatra CD, but thirty seconds into *I've Got You Under My Skin* Laura turns it off. I thought that she wanted to tell me something but the rest of the journey back to Streatham was spent in silence.

Laura decides against going for a coffee and instead heads straight to Sean's office. I'm surprised at her determination as she's not exactly in the best frame of mind. Her departing words were 'I'm going to nip this in the bud once and for all. I want to get on with my life.'

I spend the next hour in the garden just staring impassively at nothing in particular. I try to convince myself that it'll only be another four days before I see him again, but unfortunately I don't have the mind over matter skills that Derren Brown possesses and I'm more tense than ever.

As I'm feeling worked up I take my blood pressure with my own kit. It's very high, so I take deep breaths and take it again – it's still high, but has decreased a little. As I'm on blood pressure medication I regularly monitor this. Given today's circumstances these high readings are not a surprise.

A short time later I find myself standing in Harry's bedroom. There is a blank space on the shelves where he keeps all his Thomas The Tank Engine DVDs, as they're all in Hastings. Although I have no desire to play any Thomas DVDs their absence makes me cry.

I take out his pyjamas from his drawer, and smell his odour. Rather than giving me any comfort it makes me miss him even more.

I then notice his missing toys, clothes and books. The room reflects my mood; empty.

I'm rarely in the house on my own. It seems so quiet without Harry, and of course Kerry and Niall. There have been so many times in the past where I've longed to have some time on my own; but not now.

As I'm having my second cup of tea in the kitchen I hear Kerry and Niall arrive. I quickly retrieve my cricket box from the kitchen drawer and just manage to put it on before they enter the kitchen.

Kerry comes straight over to me and gives me a hug.

'How did it go? Your text yesterday didn't give too much away.'

'I'm not sure about this place. His main carer seems like an arsehole, but maybe I'm judging him too soon.'

'How was Harry when you left him?'

'Confused and worried. It wasn't good.'

Niall then brushes past Kerry and punches my testicles. When he sees that there's no reaction he gives me a couple of hefty pinches on my arm, which really hurt. I've already got a number of bruises on my arm and I think I'll soon have a couple more to join them. Can I now develop a bruise sleeve?

'Niall, will you please stop doing that? Be nice to David.'

Niall looks at me for a few seconds. I've no idea if I'm going to get another pinch, head-butt or an apology. Fortunately it's the latter, as he gently strokes my arm. He then picks up his Spider-Man toy and wanders off.

'I'm sorry…'

'Kerry, there's no need to apologise.'

'He's out of control. What the fuck am I going to do with him?'

I can't find the words to re-assure her.

'I need to get out and have a drink. Do you fancy going to that new Italian restaurant on the high street?' Kerry asks.

'I'd love to, but I'm seeing Ian. Maybe tomorrow?'

Kerry nods her reply, obviously disappointed.

The home situation with Niall is fraught. I'm not sure how much more of Niall's onslaughts I can take. Kerry still has her flat and she has suggested on a couple of occasions that it might be best all round if they go back, mainly because of Niall's unsettled behaviour.

I always feel so guilty whenever I have negative thoughts about Niall as he simply can't help himself.

However my testicles, arms and forehead do need a break from the constant assaults. As Harry won't be in the house during the week I'll be able to sleep more, so consequently I should be in a better frame of mind to deal with everything. Although I've got used to a lack of sleep over the years, it does affect my mood.

A couple of hours later I walk the short distance to the Greyhound pub to meet Ian. I keep checking my mobile in case I miss any calls from Harry's new 'home', or from Laura. I'm not sure if it's a good or bad sign that I haven't heard from Laura. I'm tempted to ring her, but I'm a little afraid to do so.

There's no sign of Ian inside the pub, so I order a much needed pint of lager.

Without the risk of sounding voyeuristic I like observing people and wondering what their lives are like. There's a group of men and women nearby; they all look in their mid to late twenties. They're all laughing and joking with each other, as if they haven't got a care in the world, but I'm sure they all have their own problems. Nobody has the perfect life. I notice a chap sitting in the far corner of the pub on his own. He's sipping his beer and looks reflective. I wonder what's on his mind?

I used to think what it would be like to lead a more carefree life. How different would my life be if Harry was normal? But that's not fair on my son. He had no say in the autistic hand that he's been dealt.

My wistful thoughts are interrupted by the sound of a text on my mobile. It's from Ian.

'Really sorry about the late notice, but in hospital with mum. She had a fall. Looks like broken ankle. I'll ring tomorrow.'

'Sorry to hear that. Give Cathy my best wishes. Take care.'

I finish off my pint and then ring Kerry.

'Is that meal invitation still on?'

'Of course. No Ian?'

I explain about Cathy's fall and then make my way home. I actually walk past the Italian restaurant knowing that I'll be returning there soon, but rather than waiting at the restaurant for Kerry and Niall I need to go back to the house and accompany them back. Even a ten minute walk with Niall is a two person job.

Although Niall doesn't attack me when I get to the house I can see that he's edgy. On the walk to the restaurant he's running ahead of us. As he has no sense of road safety either Kerry or me have to chase after him.

I notice two women walking towards us as we approach the restaurant, but I fail to stop Niall rushing towards them to gently head-butt one of the woman's arms and then grabbing her breasts. She's understandably frightened and starts screaming, while the other woman gives Niall a kick on his shins. I manage to prise Niall away and try to explain about Niall, but they're almost hysterical and are not listening to me.

The other woman dials the police and within a few minutes two police cars screech to a halt in front of us.

Both the women are now crying and are shouting obscenities at Niall. They inform the policemen that Niall is the culprit, and one of the police officers immediately grabs his arms behind his back and handcuffs him. Niall doesn't struggle.

'Don't you dare handcuff my son,' Kerry shouts at the policeman.

'There's been an assault. We're taking him to the station.'

'No, you're fucking not. He's severely autistic. He didn't hurt the lady, he just wanted to say hello,' Kerry screams at the policeman.

'By touching my breasts?' the woman shouts back at Kerry.

'I'm really sorry about that. I know it's totally inappropriate, but he has a lot of OCD issues, and I'm afraid that's one of them. It's the first time that he's done that to a stranger. He doesn't get any sexual gratification out of it, it could've been a leg or arm, it makes no difference to him – that's been confirmed by several medical professionals if you don't believe me.'

The police officers glance at each other. It's clear that this type of incident isn't in the police training manual.

'He head-butted my arm as well.'

'Again I can't apologise enough, but that's another one of his OCD behaviours that he *does* do to strangers. I know this must be so distressing for you but you can clearly see that he can't help it and there's no malice involved.'

The attacked woman looks over at Niall, who is staring at a KFC advert poster, clearly oblivious to the chaos that he has caused.

Kerry starts crying as the enormity of the situation catches up with her. I put my arms around her, but cannot find any words to comfort her.

One of the police officers starts to take down all the details of the incident from the two women. The lady attacked is called Emma. She looks in her late twenties and dressed in smart office attire.

Kerry approaches Emma.

'My life's so difficult with Niall, if you pursue this he'll probably be sent to an assessment centre and his life will be hell, and that'll finish me off. I know what he did was wrong, but I beg of you not to take this any further.'

'If you don't press charges we'll have to let him go,' the police officer tells Emma.

Everyone is now looking at Emma, with the exception of Niall, who is still focused on the KFC advert.

'Maybe I overreacted; I've had a couple of drinks…'

Suddenly Niall makes a grunting noise, which is his normal form of communication. He turns his back to the KFC advert and points his handcuffed fingers to it, indicating that he wants that for his dinner. I'm moved by his simple gesture.

Emma, who now seems calmer, looks at her friend and then at Niall.

'I'm not going to press charges; it's obvious he didn't mean any harm.'

'Are you sure?' the police officer asks.

'Absolutely positive.'

'Thanks so much, I can't tell you how relieved I am. I'm just sorry that you had to go through this,' Kerry says.

Emma smiles for the first time.

'No problem. It was just such a shock. I didn't know what was happening.'

A still tearful Kerry then gives Emma a hug.

One of the policemen frees Niall from his handcuffs.

'Niall, come here and say sorry to Emma,' Kerry tells her son.

'There's really no need…'

I can tell that Emma's nervous, but Kerry and I are holding onto him tightly. He doesn't resist.

Niall strokes Emma's elbow gently.

'Thanks, Niall,' a more relaxed Emma responds.

'Come on, Emma, let's go and get pissed,' the other woman proclaims.

'Sounds like a plan.'

The two women say their goodbyes. That was the longest twenty minutes ever.

'I don't begin to understand the complexities of autism, and I can see that it must be difficult going out and about with Niall, but you have to be more careful. Emma relented, but there'll be others who won't, and then it can get very serious,' one of the policemen tells Kerry.

'Don't you think I don't know that? What am I supposed to do just lock him up in the house?'

'I know your situation's hard, but I'm just telling you to be more cautious,' the policeman adds.

The policemen then takes down our details and a few minutes later go on their merry way.

'That was yet another lucky escape,' Kerry remarks.

'I know that I've mentioned this to you before, but you need to take him to the doctor as soon as possible to review his medication. His OCD behaviour needs controlling.'

'He touches my breasts all the time, but never random strangers. How the hell are we going to stop this?'

'A trip to the doctors is the first step.'

Niall is making the grunting noise again as he's pointing at the KFC chicken nuggets.

'I guess it's KFC for dinner tonight?' I say.

'Yeah, but wait outside with him and I'll get us a bargain bucket. It looks crowded in there and the last thing I need right now is for him to approach anyone else. We'll bring it home.'

We manage to arrive back at the house without any further incident.

Kerry is quiet throughout the journey back. Niall is also more subdued than usual during the meal. I wonder if he's thinking about the earlier incident? Who knows if he ever reflects on his behaviour or anything else for that matter? He certainly didn't seem bothered when the woman kicked him or when they both were shouting at him.

'I feel responsible for what happened earlier,' Kerry blurts out.

'What do you mean?'

'He's clearly not on the right OCD medication and I've been slow to react to it.'

'You can't blame yourself; it's only recently that he's taken it to another level.'

'But all the signs were there. He's constantly attacking you and he's been inappropriately touching his teachers more and more recently. And of course there was the incident in Hyde Park yesterday.'

The sound of my mobile text interrupts our conversation. It's from Laura.

'Had talk with Sean. He insists that it's just work that's keeping him away. Still not sure he's telling me everything. No news from Harry? Had one too many drinks – never good on your own. Will ring tomorrow.'

'Sean's a good guy, have faith in him. I'll ring you after speaking to Kevin,' I text her back.

Kerry is busy putting the dishes away so I pop up to Niall's bedroom. He's in bed, just staring at the ceiling.

'Have a good night's sleep,' I say, as I kiss his forehead.

He doesn't react and continues to stare at the ceiling. I look up to see if there's anything unusual that he's focusing on, but it's just a ceiling that could do with a lick of paint.

A couple of hours later Kerry joins me in bed. She seems restless.

'Things will look better in the morning,' I say.

'Actually, I think they'll look worse.'

'Booking a doctor's appointment will make you feel better. At least you know you're doing something about it.'

'So you're saying that I've been ignoring everything up to now?'

'You know I don't mean that, now try to get some sleep,' I say as I cuddle up to her, but she turns her back on me.

'He's got so much worse since we've moved here,' I hear her mutter.

'Do you regret it?'

'Sometimes.'

'Have you ever thought about splitting up with me?' I blurt out.

'No.' Notably there was a few seconds hesitation before her reply.

'Why, have you?'

'Never,' I respond with more conviction than I actually feel.

It's been a stressful twenty-four hours and I'm now more worried than ever about my future with Kerry.

Am I reading too much into her responses just now?

I'm contemplating going downstairs to read a book or watch TV as I've also got too many things on my mind. Our brief conversation has unsettled me. Tonight's incident with Niall has got Kerry very nervous. As one of the police officers mentioned, if he continues to do this with strangers then it's only a matter of time before it could lead to very serious consequences.

It's just after ten and the bedroom lights will now be switched off in Harry's new bedroom. What is he thinking about right at this moment? This is the first time since Kerry moved in that I'm in bed with her at this time in the evening. Normally I'm cuddled next to Harry, telling him to turn off his portable DVD player as he's watching his Thomas DVDs. He's usually informing me of the latest Thomas and Percy antics, which normally bore me to death, but tonight I long to hear these stories.

Understandably, Kerry and I are having difficulty getting off to sleep. We're just replicating Niall by staring at the ceiling in the dark.

'Shall we go downstairs and watch TV?' Kerry asks.

'Yeah, what's on?'

'Anything that will send us to sleep.'

'There must be something with Miranda Hart in it.'

She doesn't react to my joke; is she a closet Miranda fan?

As stressful as the last few hours have been it's taken my mind off Harry; until now.

'I'm having serious doubts about Harry's home.'

'David, it's too early to make such a judgement. Give it time.'

'I wasn't impressed with what I saw yesterday. Have I just made a big mistake?'

'It's your first night away from Harry and you're feeling fragile. Don't jump to too many conclusions right now.'

'Is that your best advice?'

'What do you mean?'

'It sounds like you're just paying me lip service. I don't think you'd be so blasé if it was Niall.'

'Fuck off,' she shouts, as she storms out of the bedroom.

I immediately regret making such comments. Kerry was just trying to reassure me. After the incident with Niall earlier she must be on edge herself; she didn't deserve that. But without making any excuses it's nearly two in the morning and I haven't slept a wink. My emotions are raw.

I follow her up to Niall's bedroom.

'I'm sorry, Kerry. I didn't mean that.'

'Whatever. Now if you don't mind I need to get some sleep before work,' she says as she climbs into Niall's bed.

I realise that pursuing this conversation wouldn't be my wisest move, so I make my way downstairs.

DUCK

Even though I'm feeling exhausted I've got too much on my mind to go to sleep, so I make myself a coffee and watch a bit of TV. *Only Fools And Horses* is on again (is it ever off?) and I immediately think of Harry, as it's one of his favourite programmes. For the umpteenth time in the last twenty-four hours I start to cry. The last time I shed this amount of tears was when my father passed away. I knew that this would be hard, but right now I'm finding it unbearable. I just can't seem to concentrate on anything and am constantly thinking about Harry and how's he coping.

I know for my own sake that I've got to get a grip. Am I going to break down every time I see something that reminds me of Harry?

I need to keep myself occupied and I suppose work and a more active social life will help in that respect. For the last few years I've been consistently dropping out of social events, mainly because of Harry. Consequently my circle of friends has slowly decreased. Now I don't have any excuses.

Perhaps I should renew my gym membership? Getting fit is something I've been meaning to do for the past couple of decades (at least). The last run that I went on was four years ago. Harry and I 'ran' on Streatham Common. My son was so far ahead of me I managed to lose him. I had to get in my car and drive on the outskirts of the common to locate him, however I almost got arrested for speeding (in my car, not for my running).

I should also make more of an effort to go out socially with Kerry. Because of our commitments with Harry and Niall we've never been out together, without the boys in tow. Getting any respite from social services has been non-existent. We can't even ask your average teenager to baby-sit; it has to be an autistic carer.

Now I've instigated the Harry move I'm going to help Kerry with getting Niall some respite care. This has to happen. It'll provide Kerry and me with some much needed time alone, if she still wants to, and it'll give her a break from Niall, which she desperately needs.

Maybe Kerry was right when she said that it was too soon to judge Harry's new 'home'. It's a big adjustment, so I suppose it's only natural that I'm feeling nervous and over critical.

Although it's only two o'clock in the morning I suspect that Harry will be awake. I don't think he'll sleep much tonight.

The restricted movement in Harry's home would probably mean that he'll be confined to his bedroom until a respectable hour. He's not going to like that. However, if I'm adopting the glass half- full approach it may help him understand the need for self-control and privacy. I just hope that he doesn't get too upset or angry.

What will he be doing today? Off the top of my head I can't recall the daily schedule, but it'll involve lessons and outings. Some of the lessons lined up for him are Art, IT, Mathematics, English and a book club.

'What sort of books does Harry like to read?' the residential manager, Philip, asked me a couple of weeks ago.

'Thomas The Tank Engine.'

'What else?'

'Nothing, apart from telephone directories.'

'I don't think there's too much of a plot in the telephone directories, so the first Harry book that we'll review in the book club will be a Thomas book then,' Philip replies.

No shit, Sherlock.

My friends, Sarah and Nigel, have a 'normal' teenage daughter called Andrea. They're always telling me how much they worry about her, especially when she goes out at night. They never go to sleep until she returns home safely. I don't have such worries with Harry as he's never out on his own. In fact he doesn't like going out at night at all. If we go to the local pub he wants to leave after one drink and even if I order a second drink he'll pester me constantly to leave, so there is zero chance of a third. On the rare occasions I take him to watch an Arsenal night game we always leave at half-time as he's obsessed with being home early. But getting back to Andrea, at some point she will leave home and live an independent life and I am guessing that as she gets older Sarah and Nigel will worry less and less about her. Unfortunately that's not the case with Harry. I will constantly worry about him until my dying day.

I have spent many sleepless nights thinking about Harry's future and my anxiety levels have increased even further with the Hastings move.

This household is not a calm place to be in right now; but was it ever?

I lie down on the couch and flick through the channels, but as usual I can't find anything of interest to watch. Am I getting more selective in my TV choices as I get older? Conversely, Harry will watch a nineteen thirty-five black and white western that the BBC probably purchased for one pound and twelve pence. I've just got to get some sleep otherwise I won't be able to function at work. I settle for *Only Fools and Horses* and the last thing I remember before nodding off is Del Boy telling someone that 'you're a twenty-four carat plonker'.

'David, it's eight-fifty-five. You better get ready for work,' Kerry tells me.

'How long have you been up?' I say, still half asleep.

'About an hour.'

'Why didn't you wake me up earlier?' I gently ask.

'I locked the living-room door as I wanted to get Niall ready without disturbing you. Here's your cricket box.'

'Oh, OK; thanks for that.'

Before I have a chance to repair the damage from last night Kerry and Niall are out of the door. That's not the ideal start to the day but at least I didn't get my balls crunched.

I immediately dial the Hastings number and I'm put through to Kevin.

'How did it go yesterday?'

'It took a lot of persuasion to get Harry to the Art class. He kept telling me we're interrupting him watching *Thomas And The Magic Railroad*, but eventually he came and drew some nice train pictures.'

'No surprise there,' I say, which doesn't get a reaction.

'He did tell Mister Porter that he looked like a duck, which we've put down as an incident.'

'What do you mean?'

'Any behaviour that we deem as disruptive or inappropriate will be reported.'

'You're joking, right?'

'No, I'm most certainly not.'

'But the whole reason Harry's in your place is because he's different from your normal child, therefore every day he's bound to say or do things that are inappropriate.'

'But he shouldn't be saying these things. How would you like it if someone called you a duck?'

'I've been called a lot worse.'

'We draw up graphs at the end of each week and this'll give us a good indication on how we'll approach his behavioural management.'

'How did he get on last night?' I say, not wishing to pursue 'duckgate', as I might say something that I'll regret.

'He didn't sleep much and had to be reminded several times to turn off his DVD player, as he refused to do so. In the end we had to take it away from him.'

'How did he react to that?'

'He said that he'll sue us.'

Despite the ever present knot in my stomach I can't help but smile.

'I've got to go as I've got to supervise Harry and co with their breakfasts.'

Yes, the whole infrastructure will collapse if you're not there. My conversation with Kevin hasn't exactly eased my worries. I know that it's early days and there's bound to be some teething problems but reporting Harry over that duck remark is disturbing. He makes similar comments many times during the course of the day. These incidents are going to mount up.

I feel bad that they took away his DVD player, but I suppose they have their rules and maybe it might teach Harry some self-discipline. However, Kevin's superior attitude really pisses me off. Is it too early to ask if Harry can have a different carer?

But work beckons. I quickly shower and within an hour I'm sitting at my desk. I again make my apologies to Lucy, on Harry's behalf (not that he gives a toss), which she half accepts even though she does then tell me that 'I don't know why you or your son think I'm the office tart'.

'I know that your son has special needs, but I really didn't deserve the fat fuck remark,' Mark also tells me.

'Yes, I know and again I must apologise,' as I watch him tuck into a jam doughnut.

'And I was a little offended when he implied that I couldn't pull a bird. If I put my mind to it I can get any chick in this office.'

'You're having a laugh, aren't you? Maybe Gladys in HR, who's about ninety-seven and practically blind, but that's your lot, mate,' is what I feel like saying to him, but instead I nod my agreement.

Ray, on the other hand, seems to have forgotten my prick remark, which he knows I made, but instead asks how Harry is getting on 'in his new home.'

'He's doing OK, thanks,' is all I can say. I'm not in the mood to get into a detailed discussion.

For once being at work served its purpose as I was extremely busy and for periods of the day it took my mind off Harry.

At lunchtime I went for a long walk and tried to contact Kerry, but it kept going to voicemail.

Just before I leave the office I ring Hastings again.

'Hi, it's David; Harry's dad. How did he do today?'

'Hello, David. It's Kevin here. I'm afraid there's been a couple more incidents. He told me that I was 'a ninety-two per cent wanker' because I wouldn't let him have his DVD player back until midday and he then told Helen that she was a shitbag for making the breakfast sausage medium rare when he told her he wanted it well done. He also said that she should be sacked immediately.'

'I can only apologise on both counts, but unfortunately that's one of Harry's problems; he just says what he feels; he has no filter. I don't think that'll ever change.'

'I hate to contradict you, but I think it will. We'll make sure of that.'

Again I have to resist from saying what I'm really thinking right now. Nothing would please me more if Harry somehow refrained from making such harsh comments, but I've tried to stop him for so many years without success, and by the sounds of it Kevin thinks he can solve this problem in a relatively short time span. Well good luck with that.

Instead I thank Kevin for the update and make my way home feeling more depressed than ever.

Kerry's in the kitchen cooking, with Niall watching over her shoulder. As soon as Niall sees me he rushes over and instead of attacking my testicles he gives me a couple of hefty pinches on my second chin. I find this very intimidating as he's effectively grabbing hold of my neck. Needless to say this really hurts. Given the effectiveness of the cricket box he's now moving onto other parts of my body. Does this mean I'll now have to invest in a neck brace?

As usual Kerry ushers Niall into the living-room and puts on a Gordon Ramsay TV programme. Through the kitchen hatch I can see Niall walking up and down, holding his Spider-Man toy and occasionally glancing at the screen. Harry just loves Gordon Ramsay – no prizes for guessing why – yes, the excessive swearing.

'David, I'm sorry...'

I glance at myself in the mirror and notice that there's already a couple of red marks on my neck.

'Why does he keep on fucking doing that?' Kerry shouts.

'Don't worry; it's OK.' Actually it isn't.

She sits on the sofa and stares blankly at the wall in front of her, just shaking her head.

'Anyway, it's me who should be apologising after yesterday,' I say.

'There's no need. Maybe I over-reacted.'

'No, you were right. I've been feeling crap since our argument. You've got enough on your plate right now.'

We hug each other tightly.

'I know that it's not easy, but we need to support each other,' she adds.

I nod my reply.

Before I have a chance to update Kerry on Harry, my mobile rings; it's Laura.

'I'm just about to ring Hastings and I thought I'd better check with you first,' she tells me.

'There's no need. I've spoken to them a little earlier. Harry called Kevin a wanker, which I felt was richly deserved, and the cook a shitbag for cocking up his sausage. That's two more incidents for their graphs.'

I hear Laura breath heavily before speaking.

'It hasn't got off to a good start, has it?'

'No, but we've got to persevere. It's too early to be making any decisions.'

'What decisions are you talking about?'

'I thought that you were going to question the placement.'

'Why, do you think it isn't the right place?'

'I don't know; I really don't know.'

MOVING OUT

The next three days pass by slowly. For once, my work is a blessing and even Mark informing me of his latest software problems doesn't bore me rigid.

On Friday I leave work at three o'clock and head straight to Hastings. I'm so excited at the prospect of seeing my son again. Will I always feel like this when picking him up, and then equally depressed when I have to drop him back on Sunday?

I'm greeted at the Hastings home by Philip and Kevin.

'Before you see Harry, can we have a quick word?' Philip asks, as he leads me into his office.

Philip sits down and Kevin stands alongside him.

'This doesn't look good,' I say.

'No, it's not like that. It's just a quick review on how things have gone this week.' Philip replies.

'OK, give me the worst.'

Philip hands me a piece of paper with pretty colours on it.

'What's this?'

'It's a graph on the number of incidents this week and colour coded on the severity of the incidents.'

'Twenty-four incidents. Really?'

'It is one hundred per cent accurate, Mister McCarthy. You already know about calling Mister Porter a duck, and making even worse comments to myself and Helen, but there are many more of these. It's all detailed on page two,' Kevin chips in.

'Refusing to go to the gym because it's for arseholes with big bellies; telling Mrs Dudley that she had yellow teeth; and calling Kevin a short arse,' I read back to Philip and Kevin.

'Should Harry have said these things? Of course not, but it's a bit much to formally document them all as incidents,' I add.

'As I mentioned previously we're documenting them to formalise a behavioural management plan, so we can work on modifying and eventually eliminating such behaviours,' Kevin proclaims.

'I did go through this when you first visited us,' Philip announces.

'Yes, but I really didn't expect you to report such trivial incidents.'

'With all due respects, these are not trivial. They're all part of a bigger ADHD issue which we have to tackle head on. At some point we want to be in a position to reduce his dependency on Ritalin,' Kevin states, with an air of formality.

'Who's seeing these graphs?'

'The local authority, who are funding his placement,' Kevin replies.

It's Kevin who's answering all my questions and there I was thinking that Philip was in charge of this joint.

'We've many students here who physically attack both their fellow students and teachers. Harry does this mentally,' Kevin proclaims.

'But at the risk of repeating myself, that's why he's here in the first place. That's his autism and ADHD,' I reply.

'We're never going to cure his autism or ADHD, but the plan we'll come up with will definitely help Harry with his most severe behaviours,' Philip proclaims.

Oh, you *do* work here.

'Of course I'm all for modifying his behaviours, and if you manage to get on top of that it'll improve the quality of his life, but I'm a bit concerned about sending such negative information to the local authorities on such a regular basis. What do they do with this information?'

'Over a period of time they'll assess whether there's been any improvement in his behaviour and if not they'll consider whether this placement is the correct choice for him,' Kevin says.

'You mean they could move him elsewhere?'

'That's a possibility. They would recommend a more suitable placement, but it's way too early to be discussing alternative homes. He's only been here five days and new pupils always have difficulties settling in,' Kevin reassures me.

'Can I keep a copy?' I ask, holding up the offending graph.

'Of course, but please don't be too disheartened; we'll work through this,' Philip adds.

I nod my reply, but I'm still not happy. If their behavioural plan will help Harry in any way then I applaud them, but sending these extremely minor incidents to the local authorities could jeopardise any possible future placement.

Kevin leads me to Harry's bedroom, where my son is sitting on a chair clutching a weekend holdall bag.

'About fucking time. You said five o'clock; it's now sixteen minutes past five. This is totally unacceptable. Now let's get out of this shithole,' Harry tells me.

If they could eliminate Harry's swearing I'll recommend Kevin for a knighthood.

'I was talking to Philip and Kevin,' I inform my son.

'What's the point of that? They're fucking useless.'

That's at least another two incidents to be added.

'We'll see you on Sunday night, Harry,' a cheerful Philip proclaims.

Harry just brushes past him and runs down the corridor.

'He's anxious to see his mum,' I say, even though the truth is he just wants to get the hell out of here.

'So how was your first week at the Hastings home?' I ask, as we drive off.

'I don't like the floor tiles in my bathroom. They're way too big.'

'OK, apart from the floor tiles did you have a nice time?'

'Nah.'

'What's the matter with it?'

'All the adults hate Thomas and Percy.'

'I'm sure they don't.'

'That simpleton, Kevin, told me that I'm too old for Thomas and said I should start getting interested in other things. Nobody is going to take my Thomas stuff away from me. I'll break their big toes if they do.'

'Don't worry, they won't take away your Thomas toys or DVDs. Kevin was just trying to say that you should also be watching other TV programmes that most sixteen-year-olds look at.'

'Not interested.'

'OK, what did you like about the Hastings home?' I ask.

'The pizza dinner on Thursday.'

'That's all?'

'I also liked the Hastings flies. They're much friendlier than the Streatham flies, and they tickle me.'

Pizza and the Hastings flies - that's two positives from the week. I'll talk to Kevin concerning his comments about Harry being too old for Thomas, if that's what he did say. Although nothing would please me more if they could get Harry to diversify his interests, especially with more age appropriate stuff, implying that he should ditch Thomas will not exactly endear Harry to Kevin. That's dangerous territory.

'Is Niall and that Irish broad with the big knockers still at our house?' Harry asks.

'I don't know how many times I have to tell you, my girlfriend's name is Kerry; please address her by her name and don't ever mention again the size of her...'

'Tits,' Harry quickly responds.

'Quite. Do I make myself clear?'

'Is Niall speaking now?'

'No, he may never speak.'

'He's another con artist.'

'What do you mean?'

'He's just pretending that he can't speak, so he doesn't have to take exams, or do the washing up.'

'Again, I'll tell you the umpteenth time, Niall is not pretending; he simply can't speak. Can you imagine how difficult life is for him not being able to say anything? Please be more patient with him, OK?'

'I don't like con artists.'

'What do you want to do tonight?' I ask my son.

'I want to see my house again and all the outside bricks.'

'OK, done,' I reply.

I telephoned Laura just before leaving Hastings and she's standing outside my house as I pull into the drive. She rushes forward and gives Harry a tight hug. Harry is looking over her shoulder at the house.

'And how's my boy keeping?' a smiling Laura asks, but Harry gently brushes her aside and feels the bricks at the front of the house.

'They're the same. You didn't change them,' a delighted Harry announces.

Laura looks disappointed that Harry seems to prefer the house bricks to her.

Kerry and Niall also come out to greet Harry.

'I'm so pleased to see you, Harry,' Kerry cheerfully proclaims.

'Oh, I thought that dad was winding me up.'

'What do you mean?'

'He said that you were still here, but I thought that he was joking and that you really pissed off.'

'No, I'm still here,' a more despondent Kerry responds.

'But have you got a date when you're going back to your own gaff?' Harry asks.

'That's enough, Harry. Now let's get in the house,' I tell my son.

Laura follows Harry in, but Kerry waits outside while I'm fetching Harry's bag from the car. As I get nearer the house Kerry approaches me and says 'we need to have a chat later.'

I nod my reply, but my euphoria of seeing Harry again is immediately replaced by a nervous feeling.

'Harry, what's in your bag? It's really heavy.'

'A tee-shirt and eighteen Thomas DVDs.'

'Why did you bring all your DVDs back?'

'Because the prison staff will nick them and sell them all on the black market.'

I wasn't aware that Harry knew that a black market existed.

'The prison… I mean the Hastings staff won't take any of your DVDs; it's safe to leave them there. I'll buy some of your favourite DVDs tomorrow so you can keep them in both places, OK?'

'My favourite Thomas DVDs are *Thomas And The Magic Railroad, The Great Race, Team Up With Thomas, Hero Of The Rails…*'

'OK, I'll get you three or four to start with and we'll build it up from there.'

Laura approaches Harry.

'So tell me all about your Hastings home,' she asks.

'It's like having a shit in a bucket.'

'Have you made any new friends? You seem to be getting along well with Chris.'

'Chris is three-quarters of an inch taller than me and wears size eight shoes.'

'What do you talk to Chris about?'

'Books.'

'What books does he like?'

'Don't care, but he lines them up by the date that they were written and I line them up by the number of pages in each book.'

'What other boys have you made friends with?'

'Doug likes music. He can play the drums, but he told me that he only plays them for ninety seconds cos the sound makes him go a bit crazy. We want to get a band together. We're going to be called the Shittyheads.'

That's encouraging that he's bonded over music, as Harry loves playing the piano. Four years ago Harry sang, along with four of his classmates, the Beatles song *Let It Be* at the Royal Festival Hall. It was one of the proudest moments of my life. What made it extra special was that the only music accomplishment was Harry, playing the piano. His music teacher, Edward, said straight after the gig that Paul McCartney himself couldn't have played that song any better, and he was dead serious. I've always suspected that Edward's exuberant personality was enhanced by well-known substances, so I think that he must have been slipped something back stage to come out with such a statement. Nevertheless, high or otherwise, it was kind of him to say so.

Unfortunately no further gigs have happened since, and I'll be a tad annoyed if I paid fifty quid to see the Shittyheads and they only played for ninety seconds.

'I've got an idea. After Harry finishes work tomorrow why don't we all go to a restaurant? We can invite Bernadette, as well as Robert,' I say.

'Sounds like a good idea to me,' Laura replies.

'As long as it's not the pizza restaurant,' Harry stipulates.

'I thought you liked their pizzas?' I ask.

'I do, but the cooks and the waiters make too much noise. They keep talking all the time and they laugh too much.'

'Ok, then, what about the Wheatsheaf? They do good burgers,' I inquire.

'Alright, but the burgers have to be well done and if they stick any cheese, lettuce or tomatoes in it I'll squash the burger in the waiter's face.'

That's what you call honest customer feedback.

Notably the only person not voicing an opinion is Kerry.

The rest of the evening just flies past. Earlier Laura said that she felt despondent that Harry hadn't greeted her with more enthusiasm, but when I told her that at least she didn't get the same verbal abuse that I received she seemed to put it into perspective. She also told me that Sean has been in constant contact, pleading with her to not to end their relationship, but she has yet to make her mind up on that.

After Laura left I laid down in bed with Harry. Although Harry slept alone in Hastings he seems more keen than ever for me to join him. I know that this situation has to be resolved long-term, but for tonight I'm delighted to be with him.

'Did you have a good day?' I ask my son.

'Before five-sixteen it was full of pigeons shit.'

'Harry, I know it's difficult settling into a new place, but give it time and I'm sure you'll like it.'

'How long do I have to stay in that building?' Harry asks me once more.

'I don't know yet, but I do know that it'll make your life a lot easier if you abide by their rules.'

'I don't like rules.'

'We all have to live by rules, including me and your mum.'

'That's just ridiculous.'

'OK, Harry, let's go to sleep. You have work tomorrow.'

'Good, I can't wait to see all the lovely KitKats, Bounties, Twirls, Mars Bars, Starbursts, McCoy's crisps...'

'OK, I understand. I'm glad that you're looking forward to it. Goodnight,' I say as I kiss his forehead. I've missed doing that.

I wake up at five minutes past midnight. Harry's fast asleep. I amble into Niall's bedroom and see he's also asleep and on his own. I notice that the living-room light is on so I venture downstairs where Kerry is sitting on the sofa holding a glass of red wine.

'Is everything OK?' I ask.

'We're moving out tomorrow.'

FRIDGE KITKATS

'Is this all because of the Harry remark earlier?' I ask Kerry.

'It's very clear that Harry doesn't want me or my son living here. He's mentioned that to me on numerous occasions, but it's not just that. The last couple of months have been really stressful for everyone, what with Niall constantly attacking you and you being on edge the whole time about Harry's move. I just think it's best that we take a break from each other.'

'Yes, I've been stressed for weeks about Harry going away, but what parent of a special needs child wouldn't be?'

'I know, but it's Niall that I'm concerned about. For whatever reason his behaviour has got so much worse since moving here and that's nothing against you or Harry, I just think it's all a different set up for him and he's struggling. I've got to think of him.'

'Of course, but Harry being away for five out of the seven days must surely help with that?'

'David, this is something that I've been thinking about for a while. Niall needs to get back into his old routine as soon as possible. I'm really worried about him. His aggression towards you is so intense and completely unwarranted. You've shown nothing but kindness and patience with him, which makes this decision even harder for me. I just don't know what to do with him. The attacks on the old man in the park and the woman yesterday have frightened me. On Monday I've booked a doctor's appointment to discuss his OCD behaviour, so at least that's the first step I've taken to help matters.'

'And ending our relationship is the second step?'

'I do this with a heavy heart, but it's the right decision.'

'Why don't you sleep on it and we can discuss this again in the morning?'

'No, I won't change my mind. I'm really sorry, David.'

'So what happens now? Is this a temporary break up? Do we give it a few weeks to see how we both feel?'

'Something like that. I know I've just dropped this bombshell on you but can we talk about this later? I'm tired and worn out. I'll be sleeping in Niall's bed tonight.'

'So the break up starts from now?'

Kerry walks towards me and kisses me gently on my cheek. 'I'm so sorry,' she whispers, before going upstairs.

Now it's my turn to pour myself a glass of wine.

I suppose anyone looking at our relationship objectively could have seen this coming. Two autistic teenagers with different parents and with very specific needs, living under the same roof is bound to be problematic and put a strain on an adult relationship. I do understand Kerry's logic in deciding to get Niall back into his old routine, but I still feel that she should have given it a bit longer, especially given Harry's new living circumstances. However, I know that she's been hurt by Harry's tactless remarks towards her. Although she always tried to underplay it, I could see it all in her face.

I polish off the glass of wine quickly and pour myself another.

So what does the future now hold for me and Kerry? I've no idea. I'll try to meet her at lunchtime so we could discuss everything without the obvious distractions, but as I work in Central London and she in South London our lunchtime chat will be limited, but I've got to make this happen.

In no time at all I finish off the second glass and consider pouring a third, but decide against it as I've a full day at Harry's work tomorrow and the last thing I need is to be nursing a hangover.

I slowly make my way upstairs and to my bed; alone.

'Wake up, dad, its three minutes past seven and that lady from Ireland has buggered off at last.'

I immediately sit up.

'Did you say Kerry's gone?'

'Yep, she left with her kid, you know the one who pretends he can't speak, at five fifty-three and she wrote you this letter,' Harry replies, as he hands me an envelope. I open it.

'David, I couldn't sleep at all last night and thought it was best to leave before you wake up. I couldn't bear saying goodbye to you. I've gathered all of Niall's clothes and managed to get most of mine. I'll ring you to arrange to collect the rest. I'm so sorry about this, David, but it's for the best. I'll be in touch. Apologies for missing the dinner tonight. I love you. Kerry xxx'

'Are you pleased now?' Harry asks me.

'What do you mean?'

'You won't have to listen to that stupid voice of hers any more. She sounds like she's lost her brain.'

'Now that's the sort of hurtful remark that made her want to leave.'

Harry simply stares at me, looking confused.

'You never said anything nice to her, did you?'

'On Saturday December the eighth two thousand and eighteen I told her that the black dress she was wearing made her look like a whore.'

'And that's a compliment?'

'Of course. All men love whores,' Harry replies before literally skipping out of the room singing that Katrina and the Waves song *I'm Walking On Sunshine*. If that song reflects his mood I'll have to dig out Leonard Cohen's Greatest Hits for the car journey to *PriceLess*.

I walk over to the bedroom cupboard and notice that only a very small handful of Kerry's clothes are now left. I feel like I've been robbed; which in a way I have.

After having breakfast I'm sitting at the kitchen table trying to come to terms with Kerry leaving. My emotions change from trying to understand the reasoning behind her decision to sheer anger. It hasn't been easy for me either – I've been physically abused by Niall for the past few months, but tried to never hold that against him. How could I? I take a sip of coffee but spill it onto my newly ironed shirt. I throw the cup against the wall and it smashes into pieces. It's only when I'm clearing it up I realise that it's an Irish mug that I bought Kerry. The notation on it reads '*There are only two kinds of people in the world, the Irish and those who wish they were*' – she always drank out of it, but as she's no longer around it doesn't matter.

I throw my stained shirt into the laundry basket and blankly stare out of the kitchen window. The events of the past few hours catch up on me and I start to cry.

Harry enters the kitchen.

'Why are you crying?' he asks.

I shake my head, unable to answer.

'Is it because Susanna Reid won't be on *Good Morning Britain* for the next two weeks? I know I'll miss her.'

'It's not that.'

'It must be because that Irish broad's a whore in her spare time?'

'I've just hurt my big toe, that's all.'

What will today bring? Somehow I've got to lift my spirits to help Harry through his working day and then tonight is the restaurant, which I suggested last night as I was feeling happy having Harry back. Now I wish I could cancel it.

On arrival at *PriceLess* we head straight to Steve's office.

'Good to see you again, Harry,' Steve cheerfully proclaims.

'Yeah, whatever,' is the sullen reply.

Harry, I fear, still suspects Steve of stealing his wages.

'Shall we have another stint on the check-out?' Steve asks.

'Don't care, as long as you don't make me sort out those stinky, useless cheeses; they're gross.'

'Do you think that we should give Harry a couple more weeks' experience before going back on the check out?' I ask Steve.

'No, my philosophy is if you fall off a horse it's best to get straight back on it again.'

'I have to ride a horse?' Harry asks.

'No, that's what's just an expression,' Steve replies.

'So you're lying again?'

'Harry, Steve was trying to say that if you don't succeed in something the first time don't be scared to try it again straight away.'

'I don't know what you two are banging on about, but I'd love to ride a horse down the aisles. Can I wear a cowboy hat?'

'Shall we forget about horses now, Harry?' I say.

'But Steve said...'

'Forget what Steve said, OK,' I reply a little too loudly.

'Sorry, Steve, I didn't mean to sound...'

'No worries, David, I should've made myself clearer.'

'Well, there's no time like the present. Let's go,' Steve cheerfully announces.

I do admire Steve's optimism, but I've no idea what it's based on.

For thirty minutes Harry serves the customers without any issues. Under the watchful eye of myself and Steve he scans the items correctly and hands out the right change.

'Shall we quit while we're ahead?' I ask in a jokey manner, but I actually mean it.

'No, I'm confident he'll last the full hour,' came the reply.

A middle-aged lady is the next customer. Her last item is a four pack of Cox's apples. Harry successfully scans them, but then quickly opens it up and takes a bite out of one of the apples.

'What the hell are you doing?' the customer asks, to which Harry responses by spitting the apple back out at her, hitting her in the face.

'Fucking hell, bitch, that's shit, you should've got Golden Delicious.'

Sometimes even in moments like this I wish I could take a photo of the lady, as she looks totally dumbfounded, but I'll resist the temptation.

The lady looks around her several times.

'Is this some sort of prank reality show?' she asks.

'No, it isn't. Let me apologise. Harry is a new member of staff and has special needs, so this is a bit of a learning curve for him,' Steve replies.

'Is calling customer's bitches part of your training program?' she asks.

'No, that was just a slip of the tongue. Let me give you a gift voucher for your inconvenience, and we'll replace your apples,' Steve says.

This immediately seems to pacify the lady. Money talks.

The next customer is an elderly woman.

'You can call me a bitch as many times as you want as long as I end up getting a voucher,' she says with a wicked smile.

Harry looks confused.

'Harry, what the hell did you do that for?' I say, keeping my voice as quiet as possible as there's a queue of customers ahead of us.

'She must be really thick. Those apples taste like Gorilla's shit.'

And when was the last time you eat any Gorilla shit?

'That's irrelevant. The customers can buy whatever they want, and you must never eat any of their food again; is that clear?'

'But I was doing the bitch a favour by tasting it. She should be grateful.'

A lot of Harry conversations go back and forth without any sensible conclusion, and this is no exception, so I don't pursue it.

Harry continues to serve the customers and I'm keeping an even closer eye on him in case he decides to sample the merchandise again.

I'm concerned about this latest incident as Harry's still on probation and this could seriously put his job at risk.

Ten minutes later Steve returns.

'I'm really sorry about that. It won't happen again,' I tell Steve, sounding more confident than I actually feel.

Steve nods and smiles, which is re-assuring.

'Now, Harry, it's your turn to apologise,' I say.

'What for?'

'For eating that lady's apples of course.'

'How many times must I tell you; they were repulsive.'

'But you shouldn't have eaten them. They belong to the customer.'

'I was just testing the apples for her. What's wrong with that?'

'Harry, your father's right. You must never eat the customer's food,' Steve tells my son.

'What about their drinks?'

'No.'

'You're making my job much, much harder,' Harry informs Steve.

'Harry, I think we've discussed this in full. You know what *not* to do,' I intervene.

My son looks fed up, but continues to serve the customers, with me and Steve in extremely close attendance. He gets through the rest of his stint without any further incidents.

'Harry, overall you've done really well. You show great potential. If you can just avoid eating the customer's food then you'll be OK,' Steve tells my son.

I am truly blessed to have Steve as Harry's manager. Anyone else would probably have Harry on a disciplinary by now; special needs or not.

'Can't I throw away all the shit food that they give me to scan?'

'Absolutely not. The customer can buy whatever they want. You don't throw away anything or advise them on their choices. Now would you like to work in the confectionary aisle?' Steve asks.

'What the hell's that?'

'Sweets.'

'Are you fucking kidding me? This is my dream come true. Let's go old man,' Harry tells Steve.

Steve leads me and Harry to the confectionary aisle and gets a new basket of chocolates and savoury snacks for Harry to put out. He then leaves me in charge of Harry. My son is thrilled to bits to be working amongst all the sweets and for the next couple of hours he's happily singing various Thomas The Tank Engine songs, which does get a few double takes from some of the customers.

Just before lunchtime a lady picks up a KitKat.

'What time are you going to put that in the fridge?' Harry asks her.

'Sorry, I don't understand.'

'Oh, I forgot – old trollop's can't hear a damn thing,' Harry tells her before shouting the same question directing into her right ear.

'For Christ's sake, you frightened the life out of me. Are you crazy?'

'I'm sorry, my son's autistic. He's just started working here.'

'Does he know that he should respect the customers, rather than insulting them? I'm only sixty-eight you know.'

'Yeah, right. You look ninety-eight and a half,' Harry kindly tells her.

'That's it. I want to speak to your manager,' she demands.

Before I have a chance to reply a man walks towards us.

'What's happening?' the man asks.

'That boy shouted at me and called me an old trollop. I want to see the manager.'

'My son's autistic,' I explain again to the man, who smiles back at me.

'There's no need to speak to anyone, Audrey. This was just a misunderstanding, and we'll leave it at that,' the man says.

'By the way my name's Roy, I'm Audrey's husband,' he tells me.

'But what time are you going to put that fucking KitKat in the fridge?' Harry asks again.

'Harry, please stop that swearing, OK?' I tell my son

'But they're deliberately not telling me about their KitKat policy.'

'Harry likes to put his chocolates in the fridge for several hours before eating them,' I explain.

'Oh I see. We don't put our chocolate bars in the fridge. We'll probably eat this KitKat on the way home,' Roy replies to Harry.

'That's mental, and so risky. Why don't you follow the chocolate rules?'

'And what are they?' Roy asks.

'Always put chocolate in the fridge for a minimum of two hours and fifty-three minutes before eating it. I leave all my chocolate bars in the fridge for seven hours and four minutes because it's safer; you should do the same. The only chocolate bars that you don't need to put in the fridge are Twirls.'

'Why's that?'

'Because that's in the rules.'

'Oh, OK, thanks for your advice,' Roy replies.

'And thank you both for your patience; it's much appreciated,' I say.

Roy smiles in return, but Audrey still looks annoyed as they both go about their shopping. Without Roy's intervention yet another complaint would have been forthcoming, so that's another lucky escape. I won't bother to inform Steve about this latest customer encounter, but I don't feel guilty as I'm sure another similar incident is just around the corner.

At lunchtime I re-iterate to Harry several times about not advising the customers on his chocolate rules, but his only response was 'they need educating.' However he must have taken note because he didn't pass on his chocolate eating concepts to anyone else for the rest of the afternoon.

Although it's somewhat nerve wracking being around Harry all day in a working environment, not knowing what he'll do or say next, I'm also enjoying my time with him and despite the two incidents today I'm so proud of the way he has approached his work.

A lot of the *PriceLess* staff popped over to Harry during the course of the day to ask how he's getting on, which was touching.

Steve again re-iterates that Harry needs to work on his 'customer service approach', which was a polite way of saying that he mustn't call the customers bitches or eat their food that they've just paid for. However, he also praised Harry for his work ethic, which was absolutely wonderful to hear.

'Can you come back next week? We'll pay for your lunch and travelling expenses,' Steve asks me as we're leaving the building.

'Of course, I'll be here.'

We left without Harry asking Steve for his wages. Is he beginning to soften his attitude towards his boss? I hope so.

We make a quick pit stop back at the house for Harry to get changed from his *PriceLess* uniform and shortly afterwards we arrive at the pub. My sister, Fiona, is already there.

'How was your day at *PriceLess*?' Fiona asks Harry.

'I loved spending the day with the Mars Bars, KitKats, Twirls, Bounties, Crunchies...'

'OK, Harry, we get the idea,' I intervene.

'A really thick couple were going to eat their KitKat raw, but they were both decrepit and probably didn't even know if they were wearing any clothes,' Harry tells my sister.

'I'll explain later,' I inform Fiona.

'And what about your Hastings home?' Fiona asks.

'The sea makes too much noise, it's too windy and all the prison staff wear black socks.'

Fiona looks over at me, but I shake my head to indicate not to pursue this conversation. She picks up on it straight away.

'Where's Kerry?' Fiona asks me.

Just as I'm about to answer Laura arrives. We hug each other and she gives Harry a big kiss before settling into her seat.

'Is Kerry not coming?' Laura inquires.

I hesitate to answer as I'm feeling extremely emotional about it, but Harry has no such qualms.

'That Irish bird fucked off,' he declares.

That wasn't quite the words I would have expressed, but he's got the point across.

'What happened?' Laura asks, looking concerned.

'She told me last night that she wanted to move out and left before I got up this morning. I suppose it's been coming. She thinks that living with us has really affected Niall and wants to get him back to his normal routine. He's approaching strangers more and more recently and it doesn't always go down well. His attacks on me have been relentless, and that's influenced her decision. Niall's well-being obviously has to come first; I get that. It's been a very stressful couple of months.'

'Is there any chance of getting back together?' Laura asks.

'I'm not sure. We've got to meet up to discuss everything. But I do know that the four of us can't live under the same roof and that doesn't bode well for the future, does it?'

'I'm so sorry, David,' my ex-wife says.

'That's another relationship fucked up.'

'Don't give up hope yet,' Laura replies.

'I just can't see how it'll all work out; can you?'

'Once Niall's OCD medication is sorted, things might change,' Laura adds.

'I was so happy when they moved in. Of course I knew that it wasn't going to be easy, but I thought that over time things would've settled down. Well they haven't.'

'Any time you need to talk just pick up the phone.'

I nod, but feel too upset to respond.

THIRTY-ONE CHIPS

Stephanie and her son, Robert arrive soon after. Like Harry, Robert is on the more able end of the autistic spectrum. He has been friends with Harry for a few years as they were in the same class together. Robert walks straight up to Harry.

'How's Thomas and Percy?' he asks my son.

'Well, Thomas is angry because Percy was late coming into the station and Thomas couldn't leave until Percy arrived.'

'That's typical Percy, he can be a prick.'

'You got that right.'

They speak about Thomas and Percy as if they're friends.

Stephanie comes over and gives me a tight hug.

'How are you keeping?' she asks with a fretful expression, almost as if she's aware that I've split up with Kerry, but she can't possibly know.

'I'm OK. How about you? Are you still with that gymnasium chap?'

'Oh no, that only lasted about ten days, but it was a very enjoyable and intense period if you know what I mean.'

I smile and nod. I'd say that Stephanie is a sex addict and has no issues about going into great detail about what she gets up to in the bedroom, living-room, kitchen or any other room in the house that she can pursue her romantic interest.

'David, is it OK if I leave Robert with you? I met someone on the train this afternoon; he was really cute and he's asked me out for a meal tonight. How lucky was that?'

They say that you make your own luck, and if she was wearing that same extremely low cut dress earlier I'm guessing that the odds were heavily in her favour.

'No problem, Stephanie, I'll drop him home. If you're going to be late just let me know. Have a great night.'

'Thanks, David, you're a sweetie.'

With that Stephanie rushes out of the restaurant, heading towards her rendezvous with the train man.

'Mister McCarthy, what sort of chips do they have here?' Robert asks me.

'What do you mean?'

'I always thought that you were a bit thick, but my mum told me you weren't.'

Thank you, Stephanie.

'She said that you just *looked* a bit thick.'

Laura and Fiona both laugh at this, but Robert just stares at them.

'Are the chips like the chips you get in the fish and chips shop? Or are they like the McDonalds chips? Or are they curly fries, garlic fries, cottage fries, potato wedges, steak fries...'

'OK, Robert, we understand.'

'Do you?'

'Yes, but I'm not sure what type of chips they have.'

'You're fucking clueless, and I don't like your ears.'

'What's wrong with my ears?' I ask.

'There's too much skin on them. They're way too fat.'

'I've told him that before but he doesn't do anything about it,' Harry tells Robert.

So now I've got to lose weight on my ears?

The next to arrive are Bernadette and her mum, Alice. Bernadette heads straight to Harry.

'How's prison life?' she asks.

'The driveway to the prison is full of little stones and it makes a crunchy noise when a car comes along. Why don't they just put that grey cement on top of it?'

'They must be idiots.'

'Oh yeah, and my prison officer is called Kevin and his shoes squeak every time he walks. I told him to take his shoes off because it makes my head explode, but he just ignores me.'

'Why don't you just set fire to his shoes?' Bernadette asks.

'That's genius.'

'Harry, you're not going to set fire to Kevin's shoes, OK?' I tell my son.

'But they make too much noise.'

'Bernadette, that really wasn't a helpful suggestion,' Alice adds.

'But the prison man is a tosser.'

'Please don't use language like that,' Alice tells her daughter.

'I bet Philip Schofield would've punched him up his nose,' Bernadette proclaims.

'Ok, can we drop this conversation and look at the menu?' I say a little too loudly.

Laura looks over at me, a little surprised at my abrupt manner.

'Where's that alien lady?' Bernadette asks.

'Kerry's gone back to live in her own house,' I reply before Harry has a chance to respond in his typically blunt manner.

'Did she leave because you're a crap lover?'

'That's enough, Bernadette,' Alice sternly informs her daughter.

In the short time I've been at the restaurant I've been told I'm thick, clueless, need to lose weight on my ears and discovered I'm a crap lover. Still the night is young; I'm sure there's more to come.

'Excuse me, Mister,' Harry says to one of the waiters walking past our table, 'what colour are the toilet seats in this joint?'

'I'm not sure, why don't you go and find out yourself?' he replied, thinking that Harry was taking the piss (no pun intended).

'Why don't you?' Harry responds.

'I'm sorry, my son's autistic, don't worry, I'll find out,' I say to the waiter, who smiles in return.

'What difference does it make what colour the toilet seats are?' I ask my son.

'If they're not white then I'm going home to have a shit.'

I venture out to the gents toilets and to my relief all the toilet seats are white. If they weren't it would've have been a twenty minute all round journey back to the house.

A short time later a different waiter arrives at our table.

'Are you ready to order?' he asks.

'Are you ready to take our order?' Robert replies.

The waiter nods, but looks confused.

'What sort of chips do you have?' Harry asks, picking up on Robert's earlier inquiry.

'Harry, forget it; whatever chips they have you'll eat them, OK?' I tell my son.

'How many chips do I get?' Harry asks the waiter.

'I've never really counted them.'

'That's so weird. What happens if Bernadette or Robert gets more chips than me?'

The waiter must have thought that he's just walked onto the set of *One Flew Over The Cuckoo's Nest*.

'Can I have thirty-one chips and a burger that's well done, without any shit on top of it?' Harry demands.

'Yeah, give me thirty-one chips, with a medium rare burger, but don't give me one of those buns that has seeds on it, OK? The seeds get stuck in my teeth and I can't sleep at night knowing that they're still in my mouth,' Bernadette tells the waiter.

'OK, no problem.'

'What sort of toast do you have?' Robert asks.

'Do you mean what sort of bread do we have?'

'I don't give a monkey's arse about the bread, I just want to know how you make the toast.'

'We just put the bread in the toaster and it automatically pops up when it's ready.'

'So no-one's actually watching it?' Robert inquires.

'Not really.'

'That's unacceptable. Cancel my toast order.'

'What would you like for your meal?'

'What have you got?' Robert asks.

'It's all there in the menu,' the waiter patiently explains.

'That's way too complicated. Just tell me.'

'Well, we have burgers, steak, chicken, fish, pasta, sausages, chips, peas, beans…'

'Do you recommend the sausages?'

'Yes, I suppose.'

'Can I have seven sausages, with a whole tin of beans?'

'OK.'

The waiter smiles, no doubt aching to get back to his colleagues to tell them about his encounter with table eighteen.

The rest of us order our meal, without detailing the exact number of chips that we require.

While we're waiting for our meal to arrive I'm constantly glancing at my mobile in case I miss a text from Kerry. I'm also thinking a lot about Niall. He would've loved being in this restaurant. I know that being with Niall in this type of situation would be stressful, but if I'm going to have a future with Kerry I have to come to terms with that.

'A penny for your thoughts?' Alice says.

'Sorry, my mind was elsewhere.'

'I hope it all works out for you and Kerry. You're well suited.'

'Thanks,' is my only reply. I'm touched by her kind words, but I really can't see how it will all work out. The combination of Harry and Niall has put an unbearable strain on our relationship, and as Kerry has rightly told me Niall comes first, and of course so does Harry.

Alice has been through a lot as well. She's divorced from Francis and virtually brought up Bernadette on her own, especially in the last few years.

'Dad, what do you think of Drew Edwards?' Harry asks me.

'To be honest I don't think about him an awful lot.'

'You've really got to get out more. Edwards is an amazing man. He was born on the first of June nineteen sixty-one and is six foot exactly.'

'Thanks for that update.'

'He never blinks when he looks at the camera.'

'I know, I always watch the news to see if he blinks, but he never does; he's remarkable,' Bernadette adds.

'I never knew that you were both interested in the news,' I say.

'I don't know what the hell he's talking about and I don't think he does too, I just want to see if he...'

'Blinks, yes, I know.'

'Harry, shall we go up to the BBC to get Edwards' autograph? We can have a McDonalds as well,' Bernadette adds.

'That's a fantastic idea. Maybe we could invite Edwards to go to McDonalds with us?' Harry replies.

Laura, Alice and me all look at each other and instantly smile. Harry and Bernadette have such a sweet relationship. I'm pretty sure it's a platonic relationship as I've never seen them even holding hands, but they've been seeing each other for four years now, so who knows where it will lead?

'If you want I'll take you both up to the BBC next Sunday? I know which building they film the news as I had to do some IT work there last year,' I say.

'Alright, Dad, but I don't want you embarrassing us in front of Edwards, OK?'

'I'll try not to.'

'If we can get into the studios we can throw stones at him to see if he blinks when he's reading the news, that'll be a great test,' Bernadette remarks.

'You're just amazing, Bernadette,' Harry replies.

Bernadette responds with a smile. I look over at Alice who is also smiling at her daughter. It's just wonderful to see the loving interaction between them, albeit in a conversation about throwing stones at a BBC newscaster.

'Don't worry, I'll check their bags next Sunday,' I say to Laura and Alice.

'What do you think of this table?' Bernadette asks Harry.

'It's repulsive. Mahogany is absolute shit.'

That's the most passionate statement on mahogany I've heard all year.

'Yeah, I agree; it's way too dark. What's the wood like at the prison?'

'All the breakfast tables are beech wood, which is too light. What the hell were they thinking of? I told the headmaster that I'm pissed off about that, but he just smiled. He looks like a village idiot.'

'Didn't your mum or dad notice that before they sentenced you to that jail?'

'Yeah, they did, but they didn't give a shit.'

'That's strange.'

'Tell me about it.'

Their conversation then inevitably drifts onto Thomas The Tank Engine, so I switch off.

'What do you want to do tomorrow?' I ask Harry.

'I want to play the piano at Heathrow airport.'

'But you have a keyboard at home.'

'But all those people with suitcases are going to love my beautiful music.'

No lack of confidence there.

'That's a stupendous idea, Harry. I can dance to your music,' Bernadette adds.

I look over at Laura and Alice, who both smile back.

'I'm sure they have pianos at some of the train stations; wouldn't you prefer doing that?' I ask, only because it'll be easier to travel to a London train station.

'Nah, because they make too many announcements at the train stations and I want everyone to listen to my music instead.'

He obviously thought this through and given that he'll be anxious going back to his 'home' later I'm willing to do anything to at least make him happier in the morning.

'OK, sounds like a plan, but we'll have to be up there early as Harry has to go to Hastings in the afternoon,' I say to the newly acquired dancer.

'I'm not bothered about that, I don't sleep anyway,' she replies.

Sounds familiar.

'David, can you video it please? I'd love to be there, but Sean can only make tomorrow lunchtime and it's important that I see him.'

'Yeah of course, but I suspect it'll be a YouTube hit before the day is done.'

'Do you mind if I tag along?' Alice asks me.

'Of course not. This could turn out to be the musical event of the year.'

'I'm going to wear my sparkling dress that mum got me for Christmas,' Bernadette announces.

Alice grins at her daughter and then looks away. She discreetly wipes away a tear or two.

'Harry, please do not play *There ain't half been some clever bastards*, OK?' I tell my son.

'But that was going to be my encore.'

I'm impressed that he's already got a set list.

'There'll be a lot of police at the airport, so you mustn't swear, OK?'

'But the pigs will love the bastard song. The zombies at Grandma's house thought it was amazing.'

The 'zombies' are so far gone right now that they'll happily sing along to *The Wheels On The Bus* if need be.

'Harry, for the last time there'll be no swearing, otherwise we're not going, OK?'

He doesn't acknowledge me, so I've no idea if he's going to take my advice. Although it's an unusual activity for a Sunday morning it could be a lot of fun.

I make arrangements with Alice to pick them up at nine o'clock and I notice the look of disappointment on Laura's face, as I know that she would love to be there.

'Harry, I want you to stay close to your dad tomorrow, OK?' Laura says.

'But he walks like a man who's just about to die.'

Charming.

'Heathrow airport is very busy, so you can't wander off on your own,' she re-iterates.

Laura leaves shortly afterwards and I drop Robert off at his house. I wait until Stephanie arrives and she immediately informs me that she's already arranged a second date with the train man and mentions that he has very tight buttocks. It sounds like an interesting first date.

Half-an-hour later I'm lying in bed with Harry. It's been a long and emotional day. There's still no further communication from Kerry. I thought that she would text me to find out how the evening went, but disappointingly she didn't.

Everyone seemed to enjoy their meal at the restaurant. Harry and Bernadette confirmed to the waiter that he delivered the correct number of chips; as requested.

'Are you looking forward to going to Heathrow airport?' I ask my son.

'Six hundred and fifty planes leave Heathrow every day and there are seventy-six thousand and six hundred people who work there.'

'Did you just google that?'

'Fuck off,' everyone knows that.'

'What did I say about the swearing?'

'But it makes me happy.'

'OK, it's time you went to sleep,' I say, as I kiss his forehead.

'Bernadette's a cracking bird, isn't she, dad?'

'Yes, she is.'

Harry then turns his back on me to read his Thomas book.

Is there a hint of romance in the air? Nothing would please me more if their relationship developed beyond just friendship.

My day ended on that happy thought.

HEATHROW AIRPORT

'Are you up?' I text Kerry at twelve minutes past four.

'Yeah, are you?' came the reply. At least she hasn't lost her sense of humour.

'How's Niall?'

'Can I ring U?'

'Yes, give me a couple of mins. Just popping downstairs.'

Just as I'm walking into the living-room my mobile rings.

'Niall's doing fine. I think he's glad to be home, but of course it's difficult to tell,' Kerry tells me.

'That's good to hear.'

There's an awkward silence before Kerry speaks again.

'I'm so sorry for the abrupt way I left yesterday.'

'When can I see you again?' I ask.

'I don't know, David; I need some time to think.'

'Are we talking days, weeks?'

'Please don't pressurise me.'

'So you don't want me to contact you for a while?'

'I think it's best.'

'Doesn't sound too encouraging.'

'I'm as confused as you,' she adds.

'OK, I'll leave you be,' I reply, before hanging up the phone. Perhaps I shouldn't have done that so brusquely but it's clear that she's not in the mood to discuss anything, so why prolong the agony?

An hour later I text her.

'Apologies for hanging up, but I'm also hurting.'

She didn't reply.

I miss her so much. How am I going to get her to come back to me?

'Does Father Christmas shit in the toilet?' Harry asks me, as he enters the living-room.

'Harry, it's just after four – go back to bed.'

'Or because he's Father Christmas he doesn't need to have a shit?'

'He goes to the toilet like everyone else.'

'So how come I've never seen any Christmas films of him having a shit?'

'Well, that's not exactly family viewing.'

'What do you mean?'

'I don't think kids really want to see Father Christmas going to the toilet.'

'I would.'

'Ok, now why don't you go back to bed?'

'Does Father Christmas still have a dick?'

'Of course he does. Why are you asking me all these questions? Christmas is four months away.'

'I just want to be prepared for when December the twenty-fifth comes around.'

I'm not quite sure that knowing Father Christmas has a penis and goes to the toilet is any sort of preparation for Christmas, but what do I know?

'Does Figaro like Christmas?'

'I'm pretty sure she's unaware of it.'

'She's a lazy fuck. She just sleeps all day and never smiles. Can't we sell her on eBay?'

'No, we're not selling Figaro; now are you going back to bed?' I repeat.

'Nah, I want to rehearse for my gig.'

'Harry, you're not playing the piano at four o'clock in the morning.'

'But the neighbours can all sing along.'

At this hour? I think not.

'Just wait and play the piano at Heathrow, OK?'

'Can I get the air stewardesses as my backing singers?'

'Harry, this isn't a Las Vegas spectacular, you're just going to be playing a few tunes on the piano and that's it.'

Harry looks disappointed but wanders into the living-room and plays one of his *My Little Pony: Friendship Is Magic* DVDs. I give up asking him to go back to bed.

I don't know whether to pursue the brief conversation we had in bed last night about Bernadette. That's the first time he's openly expressed his affections for her, even though it's clear that he likes her as they spend so much time together. However for the time being I won't instigate any such discussions.

At eight-thirty we head off to Bernadette's. Harry has brought with him several of his piano sheet music books.

'So what songs are you going to play?' I ask my son.

'Just songs on the Heathrow piano.'

'What's the name of the songs?'

'Piano tunes.'

His set list still remains firmly under wraps.

Even though I told Harry on Friday about returning to Hastings today I haven't mentioned it again. I've been debating whether to bring the subject up as it'll inevitably get a negative reaction, but I decide to go for it.

'Harry after our trip to the airport we're going home for a short time and then heading back to Hastings.'

'Fucking shit pigs.'

'There's no need for that reaction. You knew that you were going back, didn't you?'

'But Thomas is definitely happier in Streatham and the DVD episodes are so much better.'

'The Thomas episodes are the same in Streatham and Hastings.'

'No they're not.'

It's pointless to pursue this discussion so I try a different approach.

'On Monday all your class are going to the London Eye, that'll be fantastic, won't it?'

'No.'

'You'll be able to take great photos of Big Ben and the Houses of Parliament.'

'Is that where all those bastards piss around?' Harry asks.

Despite his language I'm impressed that he knows that the bastards, I mean politicians, frequent the Houses of Parliament.

'Yes, the politicians work there, doing their best for the country,' I say, trying to present a positive image.

'Why do all those morons always wear suits?'

'It's important they look smart.'

'They look like a bunch of dickheads, who shout too much. And why are they always talking bollocks?'

All fair observations, I have to say.

'The longer you're at the Hastings home the better it'll be for you,' I remark in a reassuring manner.

He doesn't acknowledge me, so I drop the subject.

Shortly afterwards we arrive at Bernadette's. She's wearing her sparkling dress and looks very pretty.

'I reckon loads of passengers won't be bothered going on their holidays cos they'll all be too busy listening to us,' Harry proclaims.

'You better believe it,' Bernadette replies, giving Harry a high five.

Expectations are high.

Bernadette sits next to Harry in the car, while Alice settles in the front seat.

'She seems excited,' I say to Alice.

'Yeah, she's been up since three.'

'Hey, it's not every day you get to play at Heathrow airport. Even Paul McCartney and Elton John haven't done that yet.'

'Good point, but I really think that Bernadette's expecting a similar audience size to those guys. I hope she's not too disappointed.'

'It'll be fine. At least it's a change in routine. Normally on a Sunday morning the four of us go for a walk around Streatham and usually end up in Neros.'

'Any new developments with Kerry?'

'No, still the same.'

There's an awkward silence before I speak again.

'Can Bernadette dance?'

'Not at all, so it should be an interesting experience,' Alice replies smiling, but I can tell that she's nervous. Then again so am I. Harry can play the piano well and can hold a tune, but believe it or not he can get carried away and that's usually when the swearing starts.

We arrive at Heathrow airport and park in the short-term car park.

When we reach the check-in area a middle-aged man is quietly playing the piano. Harry approaches him and immediately puts his sheet music on the piano holder. The guy looks surprised but before he has a chance to speak Harry gets in first.

'You're playing a load of old crap.'

'Excuse me?'

'Your music is drivel. Is this the first time you've played the piano?'

'No, I teach music.'

'So you're another con artist?'

'I'm sorry about that, my son's autistic,' I say to the confused pianist, who smiles before quietly vacating the piano stool.

Harry immediately sits down and takes his cordless microphone and microphone holder out of his bag. I've forgotten that I'd bought him these after his Royal Festival Hall performance. He sets them up and lays his *My Little Pony* baseball hat on top of the piano.

'Are you ready, Bernadette?' he asks.

'Yeah, I'm going to dance till my ears turn red.'

Harry turns on the microphone.

'Heathrow people, I'm going to play some amazing music, you lucky, lucky bunch of arseholes and I really want you to give me loads of dosh, so I can hop on a plane this afternoon to LA to meet the American voice actress, Tara Strong; OK? She's in the *Powderpuff Girls* and *My Little Pony: Friendship Is Magic* TV series and was born on the twelfth of February nineteen seventy-three; which was a Monday.'

'And she played Dil Pickles in the *Rugrats* series,' Bernadette shouts into the microphone.

A few people stop and look over. At least Harry and Bernadette have got their attention. I wasn't aware that Harry was going to ask for money, I'll have to put a stop to that.

'Anyway the first song that I'm going to sing is *Crocodile Rock*. Some John bloke sang this song a couple of centuries ago, but I'm going to sing it much better.'

He then proceeds to enthusiastically launch into the song, with Bernadette kicking her legs in the air and waving her hands in a figure of eight movement. I don't remember ever seeing this style of dancing before, but it definitely catches the eye. I've heard Harry play *Crocodile Rock* before so my nerves reduce somewhat. He does a great job and when he finishes he gets a warm round of applause from the group of onlookers. He then holds his baseball hat in their direction and a good portion of the group put coins in it and even a five pound note. Have they picked up that he's special needs?

Harry looks at the amount in the hat and seems a little annoyed.

'Harry, you shouldn't be asking for money, OK?' I tell my son.

'Does John get more than that when he plays?' he replies, as he waves the baseball hat in my direction.

'I'm not sure, but please don't collect anymore.'

He places the baseball hat back on the piano and addresses the audience.

'You should've given me some more fifty pound notes, but you will after the next song,' Harry says, ignoring my advice.

The ever increasing audience laugh out loudly at this remark while Harry starts singing the *Thomas The Tank*

Engine song *Engine Roll Call*. The song details the roles that Thomas, Percy, Gordon, James, Toby and Emily play. Bernadette sits on the piano stool with Harry and sings with him. It's a lovely, sweet moment. Bernadette has a nice voice and they complement each other perfectly. I thought that he would follow up *Crocodile Rock* with another well-known song to keep the audience on board, but they are all seemingly just as enchanted as me, and give Harry and Bernadette an even bigger cheer when they complete the song. Before I could take away his baseball hat more money is put into it, but then an airport security man comes over to tell us that we have to stop using the microphone as it drowns out the announcements and there shouldn't be any exchange of money unless a licence was shown. I explain this to Harry who promptly calls the security guy a 'bald piece of shit.' I say the 'my son's autistic' line for the umpteenth time in the past twenty-four hours. The security man smiles at me, but gets a hostile reception as he walks through the newly acquired Harry and Bernadette fan club.

But Harry is resourceful and turns off the microphone and starts to play the Beatles song *Lady Madonna*. Bernadette starts dancing again, which this time involves jumping in the air and then doing press ups. I've never heard Harry sing this song before and I am overwhelmed at how good his singing and piano playing is. At the end of the song the thirty or so audience members clap fervently. Harry picks up his baseball hat and gestures for more donations but I stop him as I can see the security chap standing nearby, keeping a close eye on us; however Harry doesn't protest. He then goes over to Bernadette, takes her hand and together they bow to their adoring public. They look so much in sync that I'm wondering if they've rehearsed this?

Alice gives Bernadette and Harry affectionate hugs.

'You were both just incredible,' she says.

A few of the holidaymakers come over to Harry and Bernadette to offer their congratulations.

'Where are you going?' Harry asks one of them.

'Geneva.'

'Where the hell's that?'

'Switzerland.'

'Sounds like a shithole.'

The man laughs and then approaches me.

'Hi, my name's Greg. Are these your children, if you don't mind me asking?'

'Well, Harry's my boy and Bernadette is Alice's daughter; the lady over there,' I say, pointing to Alice.

'Am I right in saying that they're autistic?'

'Yeah, they both have Asperger's. Why do you ask?'

'My sister has a severely autistic son, so I know how difficult life can be. I'd just like to make a small donation to them both if that's OK?'

'There's really no need, but thanks anyway.'

'I felt quite emotional watching them both. You must feel very proud right now.'

'Yes I am.'

'I know that we've only just met but can I have your contact details? That performance brought a tear to my eye, and I noticed it did the same to a couple of others as well. I just want to reward their efforts.'

'Yeah, no problem.'

He writes down my mobile number and then hands me his business card.

'I have to catch my flight now. It's been a great pleasure meeting you and your son. I'll be in touch when I get back.'

He shakes my hand and quickly dashes off.

'Who was that?' Alice asks.

'Some guy called Greg. He said something about giving a donation to Harry and Bernadette.'

'Rather dishy,' she replies, still looking at him making his way through check-in.

'Is he? I wouldn't really know.'

'Trust me, he is. Can I have his business card?'

'I'll give you all his details later, OK?'

'Spoilsport.'

It's at this point that I realise that I'm still recording everything.

'You know that this conversation's on video?'

'I'm a free woman with nothing to hide,' she smiles back at me.

She's obviously in a good mood having just seen her daughter perform her dance routines so well, if a little unorthodox; and Bernadette's singing was delightful.

'Where did she learn to sing like that?' I ask.

'Whenever Harry comes over they nearly always sing together, so I suppose it's just practice.'

I feel guilty not knowing that.

'I've got twenty-one pounds and forty pence, can I go to LA now rather than shitty Hastings?' Harry asks.

'No, that's not enough, but it's a generous amount considering you were only singing for ten minutes.'

Harry then approaches Bernadette and hands over some of the money. Bernadette immediately passes it all to her mother.

'He's given Bernadette sixteen pounds and thirty pence – that's too much, please take some back,' Alice tells me.

'Harry, do you know how much you've given Bernadette?' I ask my son.

'Yep; sixteen pounds and thirty pence. She was the cat's whiskers,' Harry replies.

'But, Harry, that only leaves you with five pounds and ten pence. Are you sure about this?' Alice asks.

'Now that Dad has buggered up my trip to LA I want Bernadette to get another sparkling dress cos she told me on Monday the eighth of April that she wanted another one and I can now buy four original Krispy Kreme doughnuts.'

'That's so nice of you, Harry. It's much appreciated,' Alice tells my son.

I'm in shock. A common autistic character trait is that they are extremely self-centred, just focusing on their own needs. I've never known Harry to share anything with me or anyone else. I walk a few feet away as I start to well up. It may seem strange to others to get so emotional over something so relatively trivial, but living with an autistic child or adult brings so many challenges that anything remotely positive is greeted with great joy. Most autistic parents that I know feel exactly the same. I wipe away the tears and return to the group.

'Harry, you were amazing, and well done for giving Bernadette that money,' I tell my son.

'Gotcha; now can we play Wembley stadium next weekend?'

'Let's keep it a little more low-key. I promise to look into any local events for you both to play.'

Harry smiles at this. It's clearly something that he enjoys and I now feel guilty that I haven't arranged any music events for him after his Royal Festival Hall performance. He certainly feels confident in front of a crowd and seemingly loves the applause.

I approach Bernadette.

'You were wonderful. Where did you learn to dance like that?'

'I watched that old black and white bloke on the telly. I think his name is Fred Astaire. I dance just like him.'

Well if there's any dancer you wish to model yourself on then Fred's your man. However I didn't quite see the connection between Fred and Bernadette, but I'm no dancing expert.

'I feel like opening a bottle of champagne to celebrate,' Alice proclaims.

'So do I, but it's a little early and besides I have to drive Harry back to Hastings.'

'Of course, but if you feel like popping over afterwards you're more than welcome. It's been a very special day.'

'Thanks for the invite; I may very well take you up on it.'

We head back to the car and make our way back to Streatham.

'Dad, can you contact the BBC to get me and Bernadette on that Graham Norton show?'

'I thought you didn't like him?'

'He smiles too much and throws people out of chairs, but we won't have to talk to him cos we'll be too busy playing all of our greatest hits.'

'I don't think that's possible.'

'OK, if you won't help me I'll just ask Drew.'

Good luck with that.

'I want to go to LA cos I want to climb up on the H in the Hollywood sign and then jump onto the O. When I'm on the O I want to jump onto the L, and then onto the other L. When I'm on the second L I want to jump onto the Y. When I'm on the Y...' Bernadette says.

'Ok, we get the idea,' Alice tells her daughter.

'The pressure to go to Los Angeles is building up,' I quietly mention to Alice.

She smiles and nods.

An hour later I park outside Bernadette's house.

'Do you want to come in for a coffee?' Alice asks.

'No, thanks. I've got to get back and then shoot off to Hastings.'

'Good luck, and don't forget my invite.'

'I'll text you one way or another on the way home.'

'Harry, I can't wait to meet Drew Edwards next Sunday. I want to congratulate him on not smiling and never blinking,' Bernadette says.

'Yeah, I'm looking forward to having a big mac with him. We can ask him if he's going to get any taller.'

Bernadette and Harry give each other a high five before Alice and her daughter get out of the car. Just before Bernadette steps into her house she turns around and gives Harry a wave and my son reciprocates.

I'm more convinced than ever that romance is in the air.

Harry's in a good frame of mind on the short journey back to my house as he happily sings several Thomas The Tank Engine songs to himself.

A few minutes after getting back, Laura rings.

'How did it go?' she asks.

I relay to her all the set list details. She was amazed when I told her that Harry gave most of his earnings to Bernadette.

'Can I come to Hastings with you?'

'Of course. I'm going in about half an hour.'

'Ok, I'll leave now.'

I didn't get the chance to ask about her latest meeting with Sean, but I'll find out soon enough.

SEVEN THOUSAND, TWO HUNDRED AND TWELVE MINUTES

The excitement at Heathrow airport has had the benefit of taking my mind off Kerry for a while. Our last telephone conversation didn't exactly end on a positive note and our future together looks more uncertain than ever before. When I get back from Hastings I'll text her about today's events in the hope that at least we can have a semi-positive dialogue.

'I'm staying with Sean,' Laura tells me five minutes into our Hastings-bound journey.

'Wow, that's a change of heart.'

'I'm still not sure I'm doing the right thing, but I've invested too much time in this relationship to give up now.'

'Has he made any promises?'

'Yeah, he said he's going to cut down on his work schedule. We'll see.'

'You don't sound too convinced?'

'I've heard it all before, so I can't get too excited just yet.'

'Well I wish you the best of luck.'

'Thanks, David,' Laura smiles at me. She looks nervous, which is understandable. Is this Sean's last chance?

Laura is quiet for the rest of the journey, but the atmosphere is lifted as Harry sings *Crocodile Rock* over and over again.

'What time are you picking me up on Friday?' Harry asks when we arrive at his Hastings 'home.'

'About four,' I reply.

'OK, I'll see you in seven thousand, two hundred and twelve minutes,' Harry replies.

'Well it'll be slightly less than that as we're coming in with you for a bit,' I reply, impressed with his mental arithmetic, but sad that he's counting down the minutes.

Kevin greets us in the sitting room area. I fill him in on the weekend's activities, including his impromptu Heathrow airport gig.

'That's great news, Harry. Perhaps you'll like to play a concert here?' Kevin asks my son.

'OK, but only if you pay me a grand in fifty pound notes.'

'That's a little too high; how about I get Helen to bake you a blueberry pie?'

'Done.'

'I admire your negotiation skills,' I say to Kevin.

'Yeah, I'm pretty good at getting inside peoples heads'.

My brief moment of admiration for Kevin has quickly evaporated. His arrogance has no limits.

One of the housemates, Chris, approaches Harry.

'Do you like tying shoelaces?' Chris asks Harry.

'Oh yeah, I love it. It's one of the best moments of the day.'

'Do you double knot the shoelaces?'

'No fucking way. My feet would explode into pieces if they were squashed by a double knot.'

Chris nods his response.

'What are your thoughts on toe nails?'

'They make me feel a bit queasy. My dad cuts them. I hate it and always give him a whack across the head when he's doing it.'

That I can confirm.

'But my socks are pleased afterwards because there's more room for them,' Harry adds.

'At what time do you have a shit?' Chris asks.

'About four in the morning. It's the best time to do it as it's so quiet, but I hate touching the toilet paper after my nails have been cut.'

Chris again nods his agreement.

'Ok, Harry, let's get all your stuff up to your bedroom,' Kevin says.

Laura and I stay in the living-room, awaiting Harry's return.

'How many times a week do you two shag each other?' Chris asks us.

'We're not together, so we'd rather not talk about that,' Laura replies.

'So you must shag other blokes that you meet in the supermarket, or on the street?' he asks Laura.

'I really don't think you should be asking these questions.'

'My understanding is that women just love willies. Did I get that wrong?'

Laura looks away, hoping that one of the staff will come to her rescue.

'Chris, can we talk about something else please?' I inquire.

'I saw another chick of yours a couple of weeks ago, and she's got a smashing pair of knockers. You must be a deliriously happy man,' he informs me.

That must have been when Kerry came with us on one of our initial visits.

'Do you like Thomas The Tank Engine?' I ask, in a deliberate attempt to get him off the sex, willies and breasts topics of conversation.

'Of course I do; he's a genius. This afternoon I watched an episode where Percy crashed into Thomas and this got Thomas really pissed off. But to be fair, Thomas didn't swear but I would've done. Anyway, James had to help out...'

'Ok, Chris, can we discuss Thomas another time? Harry's parents are leaving now,' Kevin says, upon his arrival. I've never been so pleased to see the shy and humble Kevin.

'But Harry's dad just loves Thomas, and his mum always wants to shag lots of men,' Chris states.

'Actually that's not quite true,' a slightly embarrassed Laura tells Kevin.

'Don't worry, I understand,' came Kevin's ambiguous reply.

Kevin leads Chris back to the sitting-room sofa, where he immediately puts on a Thomas The Tank Engine DVD.

'We're going now, Harry,' Laura says.

'So you're definitely leaving me in this hellhole?'

'It's a lovely place and you're going to have a fun week,' Laura replies.

'But they still haven't got the right soaps in the toilets.'

'What do you mean?'

'It's that liquid shit. When I squeeze it out it always falls through my fingers. Who the hell decided on bringing that crap in here? Why can't they have the normal bars of soap?'

'Don't worry, the liquid soap is fine,' I try to reassure my son.

'No it's not.'

'Anyway we better get going,' I say.

'You're lucky, you'll spend the whole week in a house that has proper bars of soap and white toilet paper.'

'OK, Harry, give me a hug,' Laura proclaims.

Harry just stands motionless, with his hands down his side while Laura embraces him. He does the same to me.

As we're leaving he shouts after us.

'That's seven thousand, one hundred and ninety-seven minutes to go.'

We turn around and see Harry standing against the living-room wall and just staring down at the carpet. He has a painfully sad expression.

Laura looks on the verge of tears so I quickly usher her out of the building. We cannot show any sign of weakness in front of Harry.

'That was just horrific,' Laura says as we get into the car.

'It's not getting any better, is it?' I say.

'No, quite the reverse.'

'I keep telling myself that there's bound to be teething problems. Hopefully in time he'll get used to everything.'

Laura nods, but doesn't look convinced.

The rest of the journey home was completed in silence.

Back at the house I offer Laura a cup of tea or a glass of wine, but she's keen to leave.

'Do you think Harry's going to be OK?' she asks, as she gets into the car.

'He'll be fine,' I reply, sounding more confident than I actually feel.

Laura smiles before driving off.

It's early days for Harry but he's obviously not happy. Is that the fault of the home? I do think that he'll be having similar issues no matter where he's staying. However, it was very distressing leaving him today; he just looked so down. What a difference from this morning when he was on such a high after his success at Heathrow airport.

My mobile bleeps from a text – 'The champers is on ice – why not pop over?'

Although I'm feeling tired after another long day this will be a welcome distraction and Alice seems keen for me to celebrate with her.

'Sounds good. I'm on my way.'

Due to my forthcoming alcoholic consumption I decide to walk to Alice's house. When Harry was younger we all used to do a lot of walking, mainly to wear Harry out so that he'd sleep better, which rarely worked, but now I take car journeys everywhere, even to the local shops. Twenty minutes later I arrive at Alice's. She greets me at the door, offering me a chilled glass of champagne.

'Wow, that's what I call a welcome,' I say as I take a sip of my champagne before stepping into her house.

'Is this your normal tipple on a Sunday night?' I ask, as we enter the living-room.

'Unfortunately not. It's been in the fridge for a couple of years, just waiting for a special occasion and I'd say this morning's gig is a good enough reason to open it.'

'I couldn't agree more. It's just so lovely to see something positive happening to them both.'

'What was it like dropping Harry off?' Alice asks.

'Not good. As we're leaving Harry informed us that it's seven thousand, one hundred and ninety-seven minutes before we come back for him.'

'That must've hurt.'

'Yeah, it's tough.'

'I've got all of that to come yet.'

'When is Bernadette starting her residential placement in Croydon?'

'In two weeks. I was so lucky to find this one. I think it's going to work out.'

'Really? You have to give me the details.'

'The Hastings placement still not working out?'

'He just seems so unhappy there.'

I take another sip of champagne.

'Lovely champers, it's going down well,' I say.

'I'm glad. I was a bit stressed this morning, but I can't tell you how relieved I feel right now. Bernadette was thrilled.'

'Where is she?'

'She's watching TV in her bedroom.'

With perfect timing I hear Bernadette come thundering down the stairs and into the living-room. She's still in her sparkling dress.

'Have they put the handcuffs on Harry yet?' she asks.

'No, they don't have any handcuffs,' I reply.

'Do they hang him up from the ceiling?'

'No, it's not a prison; it's a nice house and the staff really like Harry.'

'Harry's the best pianist in the world. I just love it when he puts his fingers on those white and black rectangle pieces.'

'That's nice of you to say. You sing beautifully too.'

'Can I go to that pathetic town to see Harry this week without you guys? Whenever I turn around you lot are always there. Why don't you play chess, or go swimming in the English Channel?'

Swimming is another activity I should take up again, but perhaps I'll stick to the local pool in Streatham and then progress to the English Channel.

'They don't allow guests at his home, but if it's OK with your mother you can come with me on Friday to pick Harry up?' I say, looking at Alice who nods her agreement.

'What time do we leave?'

'I'll pick you up from school at three,' Alice replies.

'I can't wait to see my pianist again,' Bernadette proclaims before skipping out of the living-room.

'Do you think Bernadette and Harry are getting even closer recently?' Alice asks.

'I was thinking the very same thing. When we were lying in bed last night Harry said that Bernadette was a cracking bird.'

'Really? Wow, that's great.'

'So where do we hold the engagement party?' I inquire.

'I think The Ritz in Piccadilly would be just fine.'

'Sounds like a plan.'

For the next couple of hours we exchange our own stories about Harry and Bernadette. Some are happy and funny recollections, whilst others are sad. Two hours and a belly full of alcohol later I'm ready to leave.

'Thanks so much for the champagne and wine, but most of all for your company; it was a lovely evening,' I tell Alice, as I give her a hug.

'You're more than welcome. It was a nice way to end the week.'

As I leave the house Alice calls after me.

'Aren't you forgetting something?' she asks.

'I don't think so,' I reply, checking that I still have my wallet.

'Greg's number?'

'You're really going to call him?'

'Yeah, why not? I noticed that he didn't have a wedding ring, but if he's married or in a relationship I'll soon find out. What have I got to lose? Well apart from my pride.'

I hand over his business card to her.

'Do you need to take down his details?' Alice asks.

'No, it's OK; he probably won't get back to me anyway. Good luck.'

'Thanks,' she replies, proudly holding up his business card.

As I make my way through the residential streets of Streatham I realise that this is one of my rare nights out on my own. I can't deny that it's a sense of freedom without Harry informing me that he has to get home by a certain hour at all costs, but I'm lonely without my son alongside me telling me stories about Thomas The Tank Engine, Father Christmas, Figaro or Harry Hill.

I wonder how many minutes there are until I see him again?

CREEPY AND SCARY

The week passes slowly. Far from embracing all this spare time I go straight home from work, eat my dinner, have a beer (or two!) in the garden and spend most of the evening just thinking about Harry. The quiet unnerves me. It's been a painful few days.

Following on from my last conversation with Kerry I have not contacted her this week, but she's never far from my thoughts. I was tempted to text her to find out the outcome of her visit to the doctors regarding Niall's OCD medication. I hope and pray that it went well.

But Friday has now arrived and my mood has picked up, because in a few hours I'm going to see my son.

'Did you manage to resolve that registry problem?' my work colleague, Mark, asks me.

'Yes, I did. Thanks for your help on that.'

'And the rebuild on your PC was successful?'

'Yeah, no problem.'

'What are your plans for the weekend?' I ask.

'I'm rebuilding Cyril.'

'I'm sorry, I don't understand.'

'I've named my four home PCs. They're Cyril, Rupert, Annabel and Maria.'

How comes that doesn't surprise me?

'Are you doing anything else?'

'There's an excellent BBC documentary on Saturday about glass-making in the nineteen twenties. I'm really looking forward to that.'

'Are you absolutely sure you're not on the autistic spectrum?' I feel like asking, but don't.

The rest of the afternoon drags, but dead on three o'clock I rush out of the office.

'Are you sure you're OK with Bernadette coming along?' Alice asks me, as she hands me a coffee.

'Of course I am. It'll be a nice surprise for Harry.'

Bernadette enters the kitchen.

'You're drinking at a time like this?' she asks me.

'What do you mean?'

'Harry's held up in the slammer and you just don't give a toss.'

'Bernadette, I don't know how many times I have to tell you, but Harry's in a good place; it's not a prison; OK?' Alice tells her daughter.

'Yeah, right. Now come on let's hit the road old man.'

'Bernadette, don't be so rude.'

'But he's really, really old; just look at him. His hair is disappearing every time I see him. Are you selling it on amazon?' Bernadette asks me.

This is unnerving as it's almost the exact same conversation that I have with Harry on a regular basis.

'Who do you like best, Tom Hanks or Adolf Hitler?' Bernadette asks me, on the car journey to Hastings.

'I'd have to say Tom Hanks.'

'Is that because of Hitler's moustache?'

'Not just that.'

'Or is it because Hitler was always pissed off?'

'No, he wasn't always a nice person.'

Slight understatement.

'But Tom Hanks was a load of old tosh in *Big*. He looked stupid dancing on the piano. Harry never does that.'

'Why are you so interested in Hitler?' I ask.

'That bloke in the park just loved him, so when I got home I googled him. I didn't like Hitler's hair.'

That really wasn't quite the worse thing about him.

'What do you like best, knives or forks?' Bernadette inquires again.

'I'd never really thought about it.'

'But you eat every day don't you?'

'Well, yes.'

'So just tell me which one you like and stop pissing me about.'

'I suppose it's a knife.'

'Are you crazy? That doesn't make any sense. With your fork you can easily gather up the chips, beans and mashed potatoes. The knife is shit for doing that.'

'Ok, maybe you're right.'

I was going to give evidence on behalf of the knife, but decide against it.

This type of conversation continued all the way to Hastings.

'What did he do this time?' I ask Kevin and Philip a little impatiently, as we're once again in Philip's office.

'Twenty-nine incidents this week; ranging from calling me a useless fuck, eating the roses in the front lawn and telling one of the overnight staff that his hair looked like a monkey's arse. There's plenty more, as you can see,' Kevin tells me, as he hands me the ever colourful incident graph.

'OK, I do understand that Harry shouldn't have insulted you or eaten the flowers, but surely you've got to see the funny side of the monkey remark?'

'We do not see any humour in that comment whatsoever,' Kevin replies.

'So where do we go from here?' I ask.

'As the incidents are increasing we need to sit down and come up with a strategy to deal with Harry's outbursts,' Philip says.

'You haven't devised a plan yet?'

'We're working on it,' Philip replies.

'Your eyebrows are too close together,' Bernadette tells Kevin.

'Yes, Harry has already mentioned that,' Kevin wearily replies.

'Was that reported as an incident as well?' I inquire.

'David, please don't get too hung up on these incidents. As we've told you previously they'll be used constructively to create a behavioural plan which will help your son. Mark my words, you'll see a massive improvement in him soon enough,' Kevin states.

I do admire his confidence, bordering on arrogance.

'Isn't it a shame that Batman can't fly?' Bernadette tells Kevin and Philip.

Her comment is met with bemused expressions.

'That must really piss him off, especially when he sees his neighbour, Superman, flying all over the place and being able to see through buildings. Still at least he's got a butler.'

'Are you guys finished talking absolute drivel?' Harry announces as he bursts into Philip's office. 'I want to see all the Streatham streets *now*.'

He then spots Bernadette and he breaks into the widest smile. He approaches her and they give each other a high five. Even Philip and Kevin grin in reaction to this.

'What do you think of this joint?' Harry asks Bernadette.

'It's creepy.'

'And scary,' Harry adds.

'Enrol your child into our care home; it's creepy and scary,' is not exactly what Philip and co would be looking for their advertising campaign.

Bernadette and Harry's less than enthusiastic assessment has immediately wiped the smiles off the faces of Philip and Kevin.

'And that's the moron who thinks Thomas is a loser,' Harry remarks, pointing at Kevin.

'His eyebrows are fucked up, his shoes should be sent to the dump and the hair at the back of his head is overgrown; what a simpleton,' Bernadette adds.

'Ok guys, that's enough of the character assassination. I'm sorry, Kevin.'

Kevin looks annoyed, but nods in acknowledgment.

'Well, I think that they're both keen to go, so I hope that you have a good weekend, Harry and we'll see you on Sunday,' Philip says, but Harry's already on his way out with Bernadette walking alongside him.

'I apologise for their comments,' I say as I follow Harry and Bernadette.

They don't respond.

THE DISCO

'Why were you so rude to Kevin?' I ask Harry, although that question could also be directed at Bernadette.

'His noisy shoes make my ears burst.'

'Forget about his shoes. Just be nice to him.'

'But why does his shoes squeak so much?' Harry asks.

'Don't worry about his shoes...'

'He has four different pairs of shoes and they all make thunderstorm noises.'

'Stop talking about his fucking shoes,' I shout at my son.

'But if you had to listen to them every day you'd want to hang yourself,' Bernadette adds.

As with most conversations with Harry and Bernadette, they go around in circles and tend not to reach a satisfactory conclusion, so I decide to put on a Simon and Garfunkel CD in the hope that it'll relax my car passengers; and me.

'But that's just ridiculous,' Harry proclaims.

'What is?'

'That Simon character banging on about being a poor boy when I read on the internet that he's worth forty-five million bucks,' Harry says, in response to listening to *The Boxer*.

'He's not talking about himself; he's referring to a fictional character.'

'What are you blabbering on about?' my son asks.

'Paul Simon's making up a story about someone. Like Thomas The Tank Engine is a fictional character.'

'Has your Dad gone berserk again?' Bernadette asks Harry.

'Yeah, he likes to talk through his arse and his brains are a bit loose.'

I immediately take the CD out in the hope that it'll bring an abrupt end to this conversation.

A few minutes of blissful silence follows before Harry speaks again.

'I'm looking forward to going to the disco tonight.'

'So am I,' Bernadette adds.

'What disco?' I ask.

'The *Specialist Care* disco. It's on at Trinity Hall in Thornton Heath, and starts at seven o'clock.'

'I don't know anything about this.'

'The letter arrived on Friday August the ninth, so I rang up Belinda to tell her that I'm coming and I'm bringing a chick.'

Belinda works for an organisation called *Specialist Care*. They organise social activities for children and adults of special needs.

'I haven't seen this letter.'

'I tore it up thirteen times and threw it in the bin. Letters are completely useless after you've read them.'

'Ok, it's no problem, but I'm coming with you.'

'Really? I don't want an ancient, bald geezer next to me while I'm dancing to *Summer Holiday*.'

'Don't worry, I'll keep my distance,' I say.

'And I'm going to wear my sparkling dress again and dance with Harry until all the birds are saying good morning to each other,' Bernadette adds.

There have been some really stressful days in the past couple of weeks, but there have also been some lovely moments, and this is clearly one of them. I now believe that Harry and Bernadette's relationship has gone up to another level. Surely this disco 'date' is proof of that? Combined with the fact that Harry definitely doesn't want me around to cramp his style is evidence that he needs privacy for his evening with Bernadette.

I can't wait to contact Alice. I'm certain that her daughter also hasn't bothered to tell her yet, as she would've already been in touch. I'll also ring Laura as soon as I get home.

My encounter with Philip and Kevin and their 'discussion' with Harry and Bernadette depressed me, as every time I go to Hastings it seems it's nothing but bad news. However the disco 'date' has now lifted my spirits.

'Are they going to be playing *He's A Really Useful Engine*?' Bernadette asks Harry.

'Fuck yes; if they don't I'll sue them.'

I don't remember *Summer Holiday* or *He's A Really Useful Engine* being played at any disco that I've attended, but maybe they were, as it's been a while since I went to one. In fact I think Showaddywaddy were top of the hit parade the last time I boogied along to the latest hits.

As expected Alice is thrilled when I tell her about the disco.

'Would it be OK if I come along?'

'Of course, there's no need to ask.'

Although there'll be carers at the disco I would still like to be there. I know that this is selfish, but not only would I like to witness the two of them together, I also want to check on Harry to ensure that he doesn't do anything untoward. With special needs children and adults you just have to be extra careful.

I'm also aware that both Harry and Bernadette don't want me and Alice there, and I can perfectly understand that so I'll try to persuade Laura not to come along this time. I don't want to turn up at the disco heavy-handed.

Laura is waiting for us when we get home.

'How was your week?' Laura asks Harry, as she gives him a hug.

'Full of turd.'

'Why?'

'The sun shines right onto my bedroom, so I can't see Batman's face properly in *The Dark Knight Rises* on my DVD player.'

'Was everything else OK?'

'No, it was all shit from sixteen minutes past five on Sunday to five thirty-two today,' Harry replies before dashing up to his bedroom, clutching his *The Dark Knight Rises* DVD. Hopefully he'll able to see Batman's face this time.

'What did Philip have to say?' Laura asks me, with a nervous expression.

'Not good – twenty-nine incidents this week and Harry was a bit mouthy towards Philip and Kevin.'

'How much more can we take? He's obviously very unhappy there,' Laura replies.

'I know, but would it be different anywhere else?'

'I just can't bear to see him so miserable.'

'But I do have some good news. I found out on the journey back that Harry and Bernadette are going to a *Specialist Care* disco tonight. They're both really looking forward to it.'

'Wow, that's a surprise. Are *Specialist Care* picking him up?'

'No, I'm taking him. I'm going with Alice.'

'And I'm excluded from this?'

'I'm sure that *Specialist Care* don't want me or Alice there, so I thought I'd keep it to a minimum. Sorry.'

'And why should you take preference?' she asks with an edge to her voice.

'I've been his main carer for the past twelve years and solely looked after him when you had your breakdown, remember? So I think I'm entitled, don't you?'

That's what I want to say, but I decide not to.

'OK, you can go with Alice,' I tersely respond.

'Oh no, I really don't want to spoil your cosy night out.'

'What's that supposed to mean?'

'You seem to have got very close to Alice recently. It didn't take you long to get over Kerry.'

'You're talking bullshit. It's just a friendship. Her daughter and our son are the ones developing a close relationship, not me and Alice. Now I've got work to catch up on. Let yourself out,' I say as I rush upstairs to my bedroom.

As I'm logging onto my PC I hear Laura go into Harry's bedroom and start reading the latest Thomas The Tank Engine book to him.

Shortly afterwards she lets herself out without saying goodbye to me.

DREW EDWARDS

I'm already feeling guilty about omitting Laura from the disco evening. It's almost like I'm subconsciously punishing her for not being there for Harry when he was growing up. Maybe deep down I do feel some resentment towards her. It was such a stressful time for me to be solely responsible for Harry, and still holding down a full-time job. I'm not quite sure how I managed to pull it off, but somehow I did.

Laura has always been a worrier. When Harry's autistic behaviour began to unravel she just couldn't cope and it destroyed her mentally. Our relationship never recovered.

'Fucking, shitting bollocks head,' Harry proclaims, as he bursts into my bedroom clutching a piece of paper.

'What's up?' I ask.

'The disco's cancelled. Get our lawyer on the phone *now*,' Harry insists as he hands me the piece of paper. It's a letter from *Specialist Care* and reads as follows:

'Due to the lack of response, we regret to inform you that we have to cancel the disco at Trinity Hall on Friday August the ninth. We apologise for any inconvenience caused.'

'Where did you find this?' I ask Harry.

'It was in your pile of letters on the dining-room table. Why didn't you open it? You must always read the letters and then destroy them; OK? The only letters you mustn't demolish are from American cartoon voice actors, Hollywood stars and BBC newscasters.'

Harry is always searching through the post in case he gets a reply from one of his many autograph requests. This probably came on Wednesday as my work phone rang just as I arrived home that day, and I must have picked the letters up and just dropped them on the dining-room table whilst I was concentrating on the work issue.

'That's a shame,' I say, feeling guilty that I didn't see this earlier.

'Can we contact the pigs about this?' Harry asks.

'What do you mean?'

'The police – they can arrest everyone who works for *Specialist Care* for fucking up my night.'

'No, it's just because they couldn't get enough people to make it worthwhile.'

Harry looks confused and disappointed.

I wish I'd seen that second letter as it would've avoided my argument with Laura. I'll ring up Alice to tell her the bad news. Naturally she's disheartened.

'Let's think of an alternative,' she suggests.

At that moment Harry bursts into the living-room.

'Bernadette just told me that Drew Edwards is telling the news *now*. He's banging on about the earth quaking in some shithole. If the earth isn't quaking in Streatham who gives a fuck? Anyway he finishes at seven so let's go to the BBC straight away and hang out with that genius.'

'Did you hear that?' I ask Alice.

'Yeah, weren't we supposed to going to the BBC on Sunday?'

'That's right, but they can't wait that long.'

'What are the chances of actually seeing him though?'

'As I said before I did work for a few weeks at the BBC last year and I saw a lot of the stars and also some of the newscasters come out of the main entrance, so I think there's a good chance that we'll see him if we get there on time.'

'Sounds like a plan. Hardly a conventional date, but it's got to be better than watching the traffic lights changing; surely?'

'Err, yeah. From what I remember the newscasters leave pretty soon after they're on air, so if I pick you up at six would that be OK?'

'OK, I'll see you then.'

'Well, are we going?' Harry asks me.

'Yes, on one condition; you don't bring any stones to throw at him to test his blinking capabilities.'

'But Drew will love that.'

'No he won't. So it's no stones, are we clear on that?'

'Oh OK, but Bernadette's not going to like it.'

I text Alice, just to remind her of the rockery ban.

Within an hour we're outside the BBC main entrance, awaiting Mister Edwards. There's only the four of us; obviously Edwards doesn't have the volume of groupies that once used to gather outside the BBC after his nightly newscast.

Bernadette and Harry are getting increasingly excited at the prospect of meeting their idol.

'I'm going to kiss his neck when he comes out,' Bernadette announces.

'You won't kiss his neck or any other part of his body, OK?' Alice reminds her daughter.

'What about his calves?'

'No, you can get his autograph, have a chat and maybe a photo, but that's it, OK?'

Bernadette doesn't respond and keeps on staring at the main entrance.

'I'm going to pull his hair to make sure he's not wearing one of those wigging hair contraptions that are glued to his head,' Harry proclaims.

'Drew Edwards doesn't wear a wig, so don't pull his hair.'

'I want him to autograph my foot,' Harry says.

'No, that's not going to happen. Just get him to sign your autograph book.'

This is proving to be extremely stressful. Kissing his neck and calves? Pulling his non-existent wig and signing Harry's foot? Drew has no idea what's awaiting him.

Moments later the great man emerges. Harry and Bernadette dash towards him.

'What the fuck were you waffling on about the earth quaking? That's just bullshit. You should be talking about Thomas, Percy and Edward; especially Edward. Also, why don't you tell stories about *My Little Pony*?' Harry asks Drew.

'I'm sorry, I don't understand,' Drew replies.

'And you're still not blinking. You're an amazing man,' Bernadette adds.

'Can you sign my *Thomas & Friends – Calling All Engines* DVD cover and my photo of Tara Strong?' Harry inquires, as he hands Drew the DVD cover and the photo.

'Shall we go for a Big Mac?' my son then asks Drew.

The BBC newscaster now looks totally confused, as he holds a Thomas DVD cover and a photo of an American cartoon voice actress.

Before the BBC security are called in I approach Drew and explain their autism. He immediately relaxes.

'It's encouraging that you watch the news every night. It must be very educational for you,' Drew tells Harry and Bernadette.

'I don't know what the hell you're talking about. I just want to check that you're not blinking and how many times you look at the papers on your desk,' Harry replies.

Drew happily poses for several photos with his most fervent fans, and he also signs both of their autograph books.

'If you write to the BBC I'll send you a signed photo,' Drew tells Harry and Bernadette.

'Nah, you look like you're having a crap in that BBC photo,' Harry replies.

Harry then gives Drew a much more affectionate hug than he ever gives me or Laura, while Bernadette kisses his ear. Drew was extremely gracious and understanding. I'm sure that he'll be recalling this encounter with his work colleagues by tomorrow morning.

Drew waves as he walks away.

'See you next week,' Harry shouts at him.

Drew's grin immediately disappears until I signal to him that we won't be returning. His smile then returns.

'What a nice guy, and so handsome,' Alice remarks.

'I'm afraid that he's already spoken for.'

'Can't a woman make a complementary remark about a guy without anyone thinking there's an ulterior motive? Besides I've already got a date lined up for next week.'

'Anyone I know?'

'Yes, it's Greg.'

'The guy at the airport?'

'Yep. I contacted him yesterday. We had a lovely chat. He's been divorced for about a year and hasn't really been dating since.'

'So he says.'

'He works away a lot, so it kinda makes sense. He seems nice and is keen to see Bernadette again, which is a good sign.'

'How long ago was your last proper date? Before Francis I mean.'

'Probably when kipper ties were the height of fashion.'

'Surely not?'

'No, only joking. Do I look that old? On second thoughts, don't answer that. He also said that he'd like to catch up with you and Harry.'

'That's nice. Good luck.'

'Have you heard from Kerry?'

'No, in our last conversation she basically said not to contact her for now, so I haven't.'

'Sorry to hear that.'

'So am I. I really thought that we had something special. I miss her terribly.'

Kerry has praised me several times over my patience towards Niall but the same could be said of her tolerance with Harry. He insults her on a daily basis and sometimes I know that it hurts her but she never reacts angrily to my son. I love those rare times when it's just the two of us. We have the same sense of humour, which is a blessing given both our circumstances. I love those nights when we put some music on, share a bottle of wine and talk about whatever's on our mind. Will I ever share those moments again?

'Don't despair; I don't think it's over yet,' Alice adds.

'I just hope you're right,' is all I can say.

MARRIAGE PROPOSAL?

'I just love Drew's teeth, especially the four middle ones at the top,' Bernadette claims.

'Yeah, cos on TV his teeth look pink,' Harry adds, to which Bernadette nods in agreement.

'That was amazing. I'm going to watch Drew's news every night until he drops down dead,' Bernadette says.

'It looks like Mister Edwards has made quite an impression,' Alice quietly tells me.

'Who shall we go after next?' Bernadette asks Harry.

'It's got to be Michael Burt. He's a fun guy.'

'I was thinking exactly the same. Mum, can we see Burt tomorrow?' Bernadette asks her mother.

'Let's arrange that for another date, shall we?'

'I'm going to get an eighteen by sixteen photo of me, Bernadette and Drew and frame it in my bedroom,' Harry says.

'Me too, so when you come around to my house, Harry, you can look at my photo and when I come around to yours I can look at your photo,' Bernadette replies.

'That's going to be such a blast,' Harry proclaims.

They're easily pleased.

'Going round to each other's bedrooms? Can I trust Harry?' a smiling Alice asks me.

'Like his father, Harry's the perfect gentleman.'

Alice looks at me and just rolls her eyes.

'They seem so happy together,' I add.

'Harry's the best thing that's ever happened to Bernadette,' Alice replies.

That's got to be one of the nicest things anybody has ever said about my son. I'm too choked up to reply. Most of the comments towards Harry over the years have been negative – his behavioural issues, the overall reaction of the general public, including my own mother, and right up to his residential placement. It's such a welcome change to hear something so beautifully positive about my son.

'Do you fancy popping back to my place for a glass or two of wine? You did the honours after the Heathrow airport gig, so it's only fair that I return the favour,' I ask Alice.

'That sounds perfect,' came the reply.

As we take our first sips of wine back at the house my mobile rings; it's Laura.

'Where are you? I tried ringing earlier,' she asks.

'We've just arrived home. We've been to the BBC to meet Drew Edwards.'

'I thought that was Sunday?'

'Harry and Bernadette were desperate to go. Sorry for not including you again, but it was a spur of the moment decision.'

'Are Alice and Bernadette with you now?' Laura asks.

'Yeah, why?'

'I was thinking of popping over. There's something I need to discuss.'

'Just come. I don't think they'll be staying too long, but anyway we could just grab a quiet moment.'

'OK, I'm on my way.'

Given our previous argument I was a little nervous about telling her about the BBC visit, but she didn't seem bothered about being excluded. I did think about asking her and it would've been an ideal opportunity to make amends, but given our frosty relationship right now I thought it best that I just went with Alice. Laura must have something important on her mind to contact me so soon after our row, coupled with the fact that's she's being so secretive about it.

While waiting for Laura I again ask Alice about Bernadette's residential placement.

'I can't deny that I'm nervous about it. It's such a big step, but I know that it's the only way forward. I don't know how you're coping,' Alice tells me.

'I'm not. I'm really struggling.'

'Then you're an excellent actor.'

We both take another sip of wine.

'Does she know?' I ask.

'Oh yes, and she keeps making those same Hastings prison references.'

'I really believe if the residency's suitable then a lot of the worries are removed. I just don't think Harry's in the right place, but I'm hoping they'll prove me wrong. Laura's popping over shortly, but please don't mention my concerns to her; she's worried enough as it is.'

'No, of course not.'

Shortly afterwards Laura arrives, carrying a bottle of wine.

'Are you celebrating something?' I ask as she enters the living-room.

'Sean's booked a room at the Inter-Continental hotel in Hyde Park for tomorrow. That can only mean one thing; a marriage proposal,' Laura nervously blurts out.

'You'll probably want to discuss this in private; I should go,' Alice says.

'No, please stay. I'm feeling a little anxious and I'd feel much better talking about this with both of you.'

'You sure?'

'Of course, now where's that corkscrew?'

'You're convinced he's going to pop the question?' I ask.

'I'm pretty sure he is. Sean says that he wants to make up for all his late nights recently, but the rooms there are five hundred quid a night. That's a lot of making up. He's also been very coy, which makes me believe I'm right.'

'But it wasn't all that long ago that you were thinking of leaving him,' I say.

'Yeah, and that's why I'm so confused.'

'So what's your answer going to be if he does pop the question?' Alice enquires.

'I don't know, I just don't know...'

NINE O'CLOCK
NEWS EPISODES

Over several glasses of wine we discuss the possible marriage proposal from every conceivable angle, but Laura still left feeling anxious.

Maybe she's misread Sean's gesture, but why would he go to all that trouble and expense of staying in a top London hotel if he didn't have something up his sleeve?

If it is a proposal and she refuses, will that end their relationship?

'Can you post this to the BBC?' Harry asks me, handing me a letter.

The letter reads as follows:

'Dear BBC, my second favourite BBC bloke is Michael Burt. Can you send me all the DVD episodes of the *Nine O'Clock News* from nineteen seventy-six to the year two thousand, but only the ones with Michael Burt in them? The other episodes are crap and those old newscasters are wasting my time. I've seen some clips on YouTube but I want the whole of the Burt series. My dad will give you the dosh.'

I'm pretty certain that the *Nine O'Clock News* 'episodes' are not available on DVD, and if by some remote chance that they are, who the hell would want to watch twenty-four years worth of newscasts, even if they are presented by Michael Burt?

'I'll send it off but I don't think they'll have all those newscasts on DVD.'

'Of course they will,' Harry replies.

'Did you enjoy meeting Drew Edwards?' I ask my son, as we're lying next to each other in bed.

'It was the fourth best moment of my life.'

I wonder if I feature anywhere in the top three?

'Bernadette looked like she enjoyed meeting him as well,' I add.

'Oh yeah, she kissed his ear, which means that she really likes him.'

Does she also do this to Harry?

'Are you looking forward to working at *Priceless* tomorrow?'

'Only if those people stop walking near me.'

'You mean the customers?'

'Yeah, they're all a bunch of bastards and their brains are not with them anymore.'

That's a tad harsh.

'Do you like mum's friend, Sean?'

'He has Sky TV, so he's OK.'

Harry's friendship is easily bought.

'Would you like it if mummy lives all the time with Sean at his house?' I ask, deliberately leaving out the marriage bit.

'As long as he doesn't get rid of the Disney channel.'

As I'm trying to get to sleep my thoughts turn to Kerry. Despite telling Alice earlier that I'm not going to contact Kerry, I think I will tomorrow. I want to get this situation resolved one way or another. I hope and pray that we can get back together and give our relationship another go. I know that there's many obstacles facing us (well two actually – Harry and Niall), but I want so desperately to have a permanent relationship with Kerry and Niall. It can only help the situation now that Niall is on OCD medication. I've just got to find out where I stand; I hate being in limbo over this.

I've made up my mind. I will definitely contact her after my stint at *PriceLess* tomorrow.

PAINTBALLING

'It's team-building day,' Steve cheerfully announces, as we enter the *PriceLess* store.

'What the hell are you talking about?' Harry asks.

'It's all about working alongside your colleagues to make us all more efficient and boosting team morale,' Steve replies.

'Dad, is he going mad again?' Harry inquiries, pointing his thumb in Steve's direction.

'No, Steve's just telling us that we'll be doing a different job today.'

'Does that mean I won't get to see the KitKats or the Curly Wurlys?'

'Not today.'

'Then we should go home *now*.'

'I'm afraid that it's mandatory,' Steve says.

'Are you speaking English?' Harry enquires.

'That means that you *have* to do it,' I explain.

'It'll be a fantastic opportunity to get to know your work colleagues,' Steve remarks.

'What, even the fat ones?'

'Yes, the big boned employees will also be involved.'

'But they're all imbeciles?'

'Not *all* of them are imbec... I mean they're not imbeciles. They're great people, who work hard for this company.'

Good recovery.

'Is that fat fuck, Malcolm going to be there?'

'Harry, please do not swear or insult your colleagues; OK?' I say.

My son has a thing about overweight people and has no qualms letting them know, whether they're relatives, friends, work colleagues or strangers.

'I realise Malcolm could lose a few pounds, but none of us are perfect,' Steve declares.

'I know you're not,' Harry replies.

'Harry, that's enough. My apologies, Steve.'

'Don't worry; I understand.'

Steve's a remarkably patient man. Harry's lucky having him as the store manager. Would my son still be in a job if it wasn't for Steve?

'We're going to do paintballing,' Steve excitingly announces.

'That sounds a load of old shit,' my son replies.

I agree.

'No, you're going to love it. The staff are already on the coach, so let's join them. I'll explain the rules on the way there.'

As Steve can't afford to lose too many of his staff there are only five other people on the coach. Steve tells us it'll be two teams of four.

'When I blast these idiots with my gun will they spend the rest of the year in hospital?' Harry asks Steve.

'I certainly hope not,' Steve replies. He's smiling but I notice a slightly nervous expression.

'Malcolm, you're so humongous that you'll be the easiest one to hit. How can I miss?'

'Harry, please stop insulting Malcolm,' I remind my son.

'Apologies, Malcolm, he doesn't mean to be offensive,' I say.

That's questionable.

'No problem,' Malcolm replies. However judging from his reaction I'm guessing that he's a little sensitive about his weight.

We arrive at our destination and get all geared up. A couple of paintballing guys go through all the health and safety instructions to us, but Harry's not interested.

'Cut the crap and let's start killing each other,' Harry announces a few minutes into their talk.

'He doesn't mean that,' I explain.

Actually I think he does.

Our team includes Alexander, who is a rather posh chap in his mid-forties. He's short, has a receding hairline and wears glasses. Which one of those three will Harry mention first? Our other team member is Hilary, who is very masculine – very short hair and tattoos. The opposite team consists of Steve, Malcolm and two other chaps who I haven't seen before.

As we gather in our groups, Harry approaches Alexander.

'Have you got a car?' Harry asks Alexander.

'Yes, it's a Honda Civic hatchback.'

'You're talking bullocks. How many wheels has it got?'

'Well, four...'

'What's in your glove compartment?'

'Maybe a couple of CDs and some store receipts.'

'There's no gloves?'

'No.'

'Then take that fucking thing back to wherever you found it; it's useless.'

Alexander looks at me for an explanation, but my mind is just focused on this damn paintballing.

Harry then moves towards Hilary.

'Are you a man or a woman?' he asks her.

'That's enough, Harry,' I say.

Despite her physical appearance Hilary looks like she's close to tears, which is not an unusual reaction after a conversation with my son.

As Steve starts to explain the rules in more detail Harry aims fire at Malcolm and gets him right in the neck. Malcolm falls over with the impact. Harry then rushes over to him and fires again, this time he hits him on the forehead.

'That'll teach you for being too fat,' Harry shouts at him.

I immediately take the gun off him.

'Why the hell did you do that? You could've hurt Malcolm.' I shout at Harry.

'Could've?' Malcolm replies, while still on the ground.

'I'm doing him a favour. If he has to go hospital then he'll have to eat that hospital shit food and he'll puke it up, so he'll lose his fat. He should be thanking me.'

'I'm really sorry, Malcolm. Are you OK?' I ask.

Steve is kneeling next to Malcolm and examining him. I remember seeing Steve's photo in the staffroom listing him as one of the first aiders.

''He'll be fine; maybe a couple of bruises in the morning.'

'The instructor told you not to hit anyone around the facial area, didn't he?' I tell Harry.

'That man's a moron. Now can I go back and sort out the KitKats?'

'I think that's best,' Steve replies.

FRISBEES AT
STREATHAM COMMON

The rest of the afternoon at *PriceLess* was notable for only two incidents. When a customer asked Harry where the baked beans were he replied 'how the fuck do I know?' He also approached a guy and straightened his tie as it was 'all over the place'. I managed to pacify both of the customers with my usual 'I'm sorry, my son's autistic' line.

Steve and the rest of the paintballing team returned just before we're about to leave. They were all in good spirits, obviously enjoying their day despite Harry's attempt to ruin it. Malcolm already has red marks on both his forehead and neck, courtesy of Harry. I tried to get Harry to apologise to Malcolm but he just told me 'there's no point'.

At the end of our stint Steve calls us both into his office.

'Please don't get too discouraged by the paintballing incident earlier. Yes, Harry shouldn't have attacked Malcolm or insulted him, but before Harry joined us I briefed all the staff about his situation and I hope that you agree that they've all been very understanding, and that also includes Malcolm.'

'I'm touched by your compassion. I'm not sure if Harry deserves it sometimes; especially today. Some of his comments to you and one or two others have been out of order.'

'I've a confession to make. I've a four-year-old son called Matthew, and three months ago he was diagnosed with Asperger's, so you could say that I greatly sympathise with you. I can't tell you how pleased I am to be giving Harry a chance to prove himself in the work environment. I have to say that as a company *PriceLess* are just superb for hiring special needs employees. Of course there've been a few difficulties with Harry, but that's to be expected. I have great hopes for your son.'

'I didn't know…'

'None of the staff are aware of Matthew's autism, so for the time being can you keep this to yourself please?'

'Of course,' I reply.

I look over at Harry who's engrossed in the two thousand and ten telephone directory.

'When I see Harry I'm looking into my future. I'll be honest, it scares me. You have my fullest respect for the way you deal with him. It must be so difficult,' Steve says.

'Having only one child I don't know any different. At times it's almost unbearable, but I suppose I have to cope; I've no alternative.'

I won't tell him about Laura's breakdown. Seeing Harry in all his glory on a Saturday is enough autism insight to last a lifetime.

'I understand Harry goes to a residential placement during the week. How did you come to that decision, if you don't mind me asking?'

'Many factors. I've sole custody of Harry and as I'm getting older I'm finding it hard coping with some of his behaviours and the endless sleepless nights. My ex-wife can only help out occasionally, so I think it's in Harry's best interests that he has professionals looking after him during the week. They're in the process of devising strategies to cope with, and hopefully improve, some of his behavioural traits. I do find it logistically quite difficult looking after him and working full-time. It provides some much needed respite for me, so by the weekend my batteries are recharged, which obviously helps.'

'Have you noticed a difference in Harry since he's been there?' Steve asks.

'No, but its early days. He's having a really hard time adjusting to everything, but I suppose that's to be expected.'

'My apologies for asking you such personal questions.'

'No problem, it's perfectly understandable,' I reply. 'Do you mind if I mention Matthew to Harry?'

'Of course not.'

'Harry, Steve's son is called Matthew and like yourself he has autism,' I say.

'I want to meet the person who writes the Streatham telephone directories. They must've knocked on every door in Streatham to ask their names and telephone numbers. Whoever did this must be really fit and have a great pen,' Harry remarks, totally ignoring my question.

'I want the author to sign all my Streatham telephone directories,' he adds.

'Were you listening to us?'

'No, my ears weren't working properly.'

Perhaps that's a good thing.

'I think it's great that you try and give Harry the same opportunities as any other kid his age would have. Well as much as you can,' Steve exclaims.

'A couple of our friends have autistic children and they seem to greatly restrict their social activities. They don't go out to restaurants, pubs, or even on holidays, because it'll inevitably be a stressful experience, but as soon as Harry was diagnosed my wife and I made the decision to lead as normal a life as possible. It just wouldn't be fair on Harry and we didn't want to end up resenting him or each other for restricting our lives. Having said that I perfectly understand why parents choose the first option; it's a coping mechanism.'

'Thanks for that; lots to think about.'

'I'm not an autistic expert, but if you need any advice, or just to talk, please ring me; you have my contact details.'

'Thanks, it's much appreciated,' Steve replies. I can see from his facial expression that he's close to tears. Autism does that to you on a regular basis.

'Can we split this joint? I've sorted out the KitKats, Curly Wurlys, Bounties, Mars bars...'

'OK, Harry, that's enough,' I say.

'Those bastard customers better not mess up my displays by putting them into their basket.'

'Harry, customers like to purchase the chocolates that you put out. Your nice displays will encourage them to buy them even more,' Steve tells Harry.

'But when they pick up one of my KitKats some of the other KitKats are then not in line and they never come back to straighten them out. They really are little shits'.

'OK, on that note I think we'll leave,' I say.

'I'll see you both next Saturday and I promise you there'll be no paintballing,' Steve replies.

'Yeah, that was for turds, but at least Malcolm will get rid of that grotesque fat now.'

A short time after our arrival home my mobile rings, it's Laura.

'Hi ya, how's it going?' is my tentative inquiry.

'I'm engaged. Sean asked me ten minutes ago; I'm so excited. You're the first person we've called.'

'That's wonderful news. I couldn't be happier for you.'

'I know that I was indecisive yesterday, but Sean told me again that he was working overtime to catch up on tax returns, but also to save money for an engagement party.'

'So he was confident you'd say yes?'

'That was my exact same question I asked him. He said that he was just hopeful and that the proposal was the one thing that kept him going during the last couple of months.'

'So how did he propose?' I ask.

'It was a little embarrassing. We had some champagne at the hotel bar and in front of loads of people he got down on one knee and popped the question. As you know I half expected it, but the moment itself was a surprise and the ring's absolutely beautiful. I'm so happy.'

She sounds it.

'A couple of women managed to video it on their iPhones and Sean's speaking to them right now.'

'Please send across those videos when you get them, and also a photo of your ring.'

'Of course, but that's not all. Sean's booked a reception hall at the Hamilton Hotel in Thornton Heath tomorrow lunchtime, for the engagement party.'

'Wow, that was quick.'

'He provisionally booked it a few weeks ago. The hotel told him that if he cancelled, even at such late notice, he'd only lose his deposit. He's going to try and get his parents over from Limerick for it.'

'Won't they be suffering too much from jet lag to properly enjoy the occasion?'

'Very funny. He also asked if your mum could come.'

'I'll ask, but she wasn't too good the last time I saw her.'

'Please try and one more request – he wants to know if Kerry and Niall can come too?'

'Funnily enough I was going to ring her today, but I don't think she'll come.'

'It'll be the perfect opportunity to get you both together,' Laura adds.

'Ok, matchmaker, I'll ring her shortly.'

'Thanks, David. Can you put Harry on?'

I hand the phone over to Harry.

'I've got some wonderful news – I'm getting married,' Laura tells her son.

'Back to my father again?'

'No, to Sean.'

'The alien bloke with Sky TV?'

'Yes, and he's Irish, not an alien.'

'Do you have to speak with that alien voice now?'

'No, as I just said Sean's Irish, and speaks with an Irish accent, and I'm English and I'll still be speaking with an English accent.'

'Can he catch a frisbee?' Harry inquires.

'I'm sure he can. Why do you ask?'

'Well, Dad is totally shit at catching frisbees, his arms are always flapping in the air like a monkey, so can the alien catch my frisbees at Streatham Common?'

'Yes, he will, as long as it's OK with Dad.'

'Yeah, he doesn't give a toss about frisbees.'

Although it's been only a few minutes since I heard about Laura and Sean's engagement I'm already jealous about Sean's upgraded involvement in our lives, and particularly with Harry.

Does this now mean that Sean and Laura will have Harry for part of the weekend, or am I jumping the gun?

However, I'm pleased that Harry seems to have accepted Sean into the family, albeit on a frisbee-catching level.

I like Sean, he's a decent guy and I think that Laura and Sean are well suited, but there's a part of me that feels jealous of him. During the time leading up to Laura's breakdown my relationship with Laura was pure torture and consequently our marriage collapsed. Sean's been with Laura when she's been fit and healthy, just like the first few years of my relationship with her. He never had to go through that hell that I experienced, but I suppose that's unfair of me to draw this comparison. I never want Laura to go through that again. I'm genuinely happy for her. After all that she's been through Laura deserves some happiness.

My only reservation is Sean's two teenage siblings – Timothy and Mary. Laura hasn't exactly gelled with either of them and neither has Harry. However, I'm sure that Laura has taken all of that into consideration before accepting Sean's proposal.

'Nip it in the bud' was one of my father's favourite expressions, so straight away I contact mum. She seems pleased for Laura, but is unsure about coming. After telling her that I'll pick her up, and as soon as she wants to leave I'll drive her back, she decides to come along. I'm delighted as it's been a while since she's done anything social.

One down, one to go.

I ring Kerry.

'Hi ya,' I say, not really sure what sort of a mood she'd be in after our last conversation.

'Hello, how are you doing?' Kerry replies, sounding more cheerful than I expected.

'Not bad. I know that you said not to contact you, but I've some good news – Laura's got engaged to Sean about half an hour ago, and she's having an engagement party tomorrow lunchtime at the Hamilton. They want both you and Niall to come. And before you ask, yes Sean was hopeful that Laura would say yes and pre-booked the hotel.'

'Wow, that's a surprise. How nice of them to invite us, but I'm not sure if we'll be going.'

'Why not?'

'I just want the dust to settle between us before making any decision about our future.'

'Kerry, this isn't a date, it's just a gathering to celebrate such happy news. They'll be disappointed if you don't come; and so will I.'

'I really don't know what to do.'

'Do you want some time to think about it?'

'Yeah, I'll contact you later.'

'No problem. Just one more thing; how did Niall's doctor appointment go?'

'Really well. He's prescribed some drug called Sertraline for his OCD. I haven't seen much improvement so far, but he's on the lowest dosage to start with and we're going to build it up over the next few weeks. I was reassured after seeing the doctor. He seems confident it'll help.'

'Sounds encouraging. I'm so pleased for you both.'

'Thanks, David.'

'The party starts at midday tomorrow, just text me one way or another.'

'OK, I will. If I don't make it please pass on my congratulations to them both.'

I suspect that means they're not coming; I hope I'm wrong.

ENGAGEMENT PARTY

The Drew Edwards, paintballing and *PriceLess* excursions left me exhausted, so I went to bed early last night. As usual I fall to sleep before Harry, and I wake up at 3:00am minus my son. I make my way wearily downstairs and find Harry in the living-room watching a *Harry Potter and the Philosopher's Stone* DVD in Dutch. There are empty Starburst wrappers on the sofa. I'm too tired to reprimand him.

'Why are you watching it in Dutch?'

'It's a much better film than the English version and Daniel Radcliffe has a brilliant Dutch accent.'

'Do you understand any of it?'

'No.'

I don't think I'll pursue this conversation.

'I think it's great that they called the orange fruit orange, but why don't they call lemon yellow?' Harry asks.

'I'm not sure.'

'But then if they also called the banana yellow you'd never know if you're eating a lemon or banana.'

'Good point.'

'Are you happy that mummy's marrying Sean?' I ask.

'How tall is he?'

'I dunno – six foot, six foot one.'

'And you're only five foot nine and a quarter?'

'Yes, I suppose.'

'Then it's OK.'

A frisbee catcher and certain height requirements are essential credentials for a would-be husband it seems.

'OK, let's go to bed,' I say.

'Do I have to go to that shithole again today?'

'Are you talking about your care home?'

'Yeah, the shithole by the sea.'

Is that another possible advertising line for the residential home? 'Our special needs professionals will take good care of you in our shithole by the sea.'

'Yes, you're going back there after the engagement party?'

'But the windows in my bedroom are always locked so I can't throw out the toothpaste and the shampoo; what's all that about?'

'It's done to stop you throwing stuff out. They're doing the right thing.'

'And the bedroom ceilings are too high. I can't jump up and touch them.'

'Harry, you'll soon settle there I promise you,' I reply, even though I don't believe that to be true.

Harry looks at me with such a sad expression, which breaks my heart.

'I don't like the wardens there, they're all angry, like the Incredible Hulk.'

I know that it can be extremely stressful looking after Harry, but for Harry to mention that they're enraged is a bit worrying, or is that just Harry's own interpretation? I shall mention this to Philip and Kevin when I drop Harry off later.

I pick up my mobile and notice that there's a text from Kerry – 'good to speak to you earlier, delighted for

Laura, and yes we'll come to the party. See you tomorrow.'

I'm really surprised. That's given me a tremendous boost and it's got to be a good sign, or am I reading too much into it?

'Really pleased you can make it. Look forward to meeting up,' is my reply.

I eventually persuade Harry to go to bed and we both manage to get some extra sleep.

As we're waiting in the reception area at mum's care home a few of the residents approach Harry.

'Can you sing us that bastard song again?' One of them asks.

'I'm afraid we're in a bit of a rush, maybe when we return,' I reply.

They look disappointed, which is endearing. Maybe Harry could take up a concert residency here? They seem to like him and he'll have a captive audience.

Mum walks slowly towards us, accompanied by a staff member. She's well dressed in a lovely summer style green coloured frock, but she looks even frailer than the last time I saw her.

I've a strong grip on Harry's hand to stop him barging into mum again.

'Blimey Grandma, are you walking straight to your funeral?' Harry asks.

'The way I feel right now I could very well be,' mum replies.

'Ah good, will they have chips and pork pies to eat afterwards?'

'That's enough now, Harry. Can't you see that Grandma isn't feeling too good?'

'She looks the same as always; bloody awful.'

'I can always rely on Harry for being brutally honest. He won't be happy until the good Lord takes me,' mum tells me.

'Mum, please don't take his comments seriously,' I reply, although Harry does seem obsessed with my mother's demise.

I look at my mother struggling to walk to my car and I think back to when I was a kid. She ruled the household with an iron fist and if there was any physical punishment to be dished out it was nearly always her who would do it. Dad just let mum get on with it and rarely challenged her. I suppose you could say that this was a weakness of his, but I never thought of it that way; I just adored him.

We're greeted at the hotel by Laura and Sean. Laura hugs me tightly.

When I first met Sean I was secretly hoping that he would look like some nerdy accountant, but he is tall, slim and dare I say it good looking.

'I'm so pleased for you, Laura,' I say to my ex-wife. She already has a tear in her eye and a smile of pure happiness that I haven't seen since for a long, long time. It makes me both happy and a little sad.

'You take good care of her,' I tell Sean with more intensity than I intended.

'Don't worry about that, David. I nearly lost her a couple of weeks ago, but rest assured that's *never* going to happen again. I've loved her from the first day I saw her,' Sean replies, with refreshing honesty. Men don't usually disclose such information so easily to each other.

'Welcome, Mrs McCarthy, I'm delighted you came,' Sean says to my mother.

'Is that a Limerick accent I'm picking up?' mum replies.

'Yes, my folks are over there; I'll introduce you.'

'It's a great shame that you're not from Cork, but at least you're Irish. Just make sure that Laura doesn't go bonkers again, will you?'

'I'll do my best.'

'And how are you today?' Sean asks Harry.

'What Sky package have you got?' Harry replies.

'Not sure, you'll probably have to ask Mary or Timothy.'

'Do you have all the movie channels?'

'I don't think so.'

'Then there's no point you marrying my mum. Can we go *now*?' Harry asks me.

'Don't be so rude. What does it matter if Sean hasn't got the movie channels? We don't,' I say.

'It just proves he's not a proper man.'

What does that say about me?

'Actually, Dad, we do have the Sky movie channels,' Timothy proclaims.

'Does that mean it's OK to marry your mother now?' Sean asks Harry.

'As long as you block any film with John Travolta in it.'

'Why's that?'

'Because he keeps on growing a beard, then shaving it off and then growing it again; it confuses me and gives me a headache.'

'OK, that's a deal, Travolta is banned in Bensham Grove.'

'That's better, now where's the food?'

'The caterers will be coming around with food on trays, you can just pick what you want,' I reply.

'That's a load of old bollocks. I want all my meal on my plate at the same time, so I can eat all the food on the left side of the plate first, then the middle, before finishing off everything on the right. This tray nonsense is wasting my time.'

'I thought you'd say that. Let's go to the kitchen and we'll sort out a plate for you,' a smiling Laura tells Harry.

'Have you split up with Kerry?' mum asks me, not noted for her small talk.

'We're taking a break from each other.'

'She's not another one cracking up on you?'

'No mum. It's been really difficult living with Harry and Niall under the same roof.'

'Now *that* I can understand. But Kerry's a good looking woman and you haven't exactly got a lorry full of models knocking on your door asking for a date.'

'I'm not looking beyond Kerry.'

'You're getting old, your hair's disappearing by the hour and you're a bit chubby, so just shit or get off the pot.'

'What's that supposed to mean?'

'Don't let Kerry go, or she'll be snapped up by someone else in no time and you'll end up with a south London chav, who has a fag dangling out of her mouth.'

I can always rely on mum for a pick-me-up.

Harry returns with a plate full of food.

'I told the chef that he's a bit of a prick because he didn't have any pork pies,' Harry announces.

'Don't worry, I explained everything to him,' Laura re-assures me.

Timothy approaches Harry as he's tucking into his dinner.

'Hi ya, Harry, nice to see you again.'

Harry doesn't acknowledge Timothy and continues to eat his dinner.

'Looks like we're going to be related,' he adds.

'But do you like bathrooms?' Harry asks.

'What do you mean?'

'What's your favourite bathroom?' Harry re-iterates, while still eating his chips.

'Well I suppose I just like a nice clean one.'

'I only rate our bathroom six point two because it has beige tiles on the wall that are too wide and the toilet seat is too hard on my arse. What's your bathroom rating?'

'I'll give it a seven, I suppose.'

'Good, that means I can stay overnight at your gaff more often. That's a relief.'

Timothy looks over at Mary and they both smile, but it's an affectionate smile, rather than at the expense of Harry. I wonder if Sean has given them another talking to?

'You're welcome to stay anytime, Harry,' Timothy offers his hand to Harry, but my son ignores it.

'Harry's not too good with handshakes,' I say to Timothy, who was unaware that I was watching this encounter.

'That's no problem, Mister McCarthy. I know that I haven't always been great with Harry, and I'm really sorry about that, but I aim to make it up.'

'Has your Dad been onto you again?' I ask, attempting a light-hearted tone.

'He's mentioned that we need to be on our best behaviour around Harry, but on this occasion I hope I don't need to be warned. An Asperger's girl called Melanie joined our Maths class a couple of months ago and after spending some time with her I'm beginning to understand more of Harry's typical behaviour. I feel so guilty for the way I've treated him sometimes; I can't apologise enough.'

'Is Laura aware of all of this?' I ask.

'No, I haven't even told Dad yet; but I will.'

This change of attitude is wonderful news – on par with the engagement announcement in my opinion. Laura will be absolutely thrilled, as it now paves the way for her longer term happiness within Sean's family. From what I've seen, Timothy and Mary have a very close relationship – she tends to look up to her older brother, so I'm hoping that she'll also adopt Timothy's new attitude towards Harry.

I notice Laura pouring herself a glass of wine, so I approach her.

'Do you want a glass?' she asks.

'I better not, I'm driving.'

'So what do you think of my ring?' Laura asks, flashing her engagement ring in front of me.

'Very nice, he must've worked a lot of overtime. Any wedding plans?'

'We both want it sooner rather than later. At our age what's the point of a long engagement?'

My mind immediately flashes back to my wedding proposal. I had picked up the engagement ring in the morning and wasn't planning to ask her until the following weekend but I was so nervous thinking that she might say no that on our way to a wine bar I got down on one knee in the middle of the high street and asked her. She was really surprised and immediately said yes. As we were hugging and kissing each other an old bloke walked past us and said 'mate, you could've picked somewhere a bit more romantic' and then said to Laura, 'good luck with Mister Darcy.'

Mum walks over to me.

'Sean's parents are nice people. It's amazing that they've come all this way today; they must be exhausted,' mum tells me.

Yeah, a sixty-minute plane journey is gruelling.

'Do you remember much about your grandparents?' mum asks.

'Of course, but I was still young when they passed away.'

Mum doesn't talk about Dad's parents, as she fell out with them very early in my parent's relationship. Apparently they didn't care too much for mum, saying that their son could do so much better. Consequently I didn't see much of them either, which was a real shame. However, mums' parents, Liam and Bridie, were just lovely. They were so affectionate and would always give me and Fiona sweets every time we met up. Conversely, mum would conceal all her goodies from us, but I always found her hiding places and of course faced the consequences when she found out that her confectionary inventory had decreased. 'You'd always find my chocolate, even if it was stuck up my arse,' was one of her favourite sayings.

'It won't be long till I meet up with them again,' mum announces.

'Don't be silly, you've got a few years left in you yet,' I reply, somewhat unconvincingly, but I really don't want to spend any time talking about death on this day of celebration.

'Grandma, do you shag any of those zombie blokes at that scary home?'

'I beg your pardon?'

'The zombies have to exercise their willies, don't they?'

'Stop talking like that right now,' I say.

'I really don't know what goes on in Harry's mind half the time,' Mum proclaims.

You and me both.

'But they can't only use their willies just for pissing,' Harry adds.

'I'm feeling tired. I want to go home *now*,' mum tells me, ignoring Harry's last remark.

'No problem,' I reply, but I'm anxious to return to the hotel as I don't want to miss Kerry.

Harry stays on at the hotel, while I help mum into the car.

'What's going to become of Harry?' mum asks, on our journey back.

'Sorry, I don't understand?'

'What sort of a life is he going to have?'

'Well, for the time being he's at the residential home and works in the supermarket on Saturday. He's doing OK.'

'Is he? Have you ever thought how his life's going to be like when you're no longer around?'

'Come on, mum, this is a bit heavy for a Sunday afternoon.'

'You've got to think of these things.'

'The long-term plan is for him to stay at the residential home and maybe work longer hours at *PriceLess*.'

'And you're happy with that?'

'Yes, I am. I know he isn't going to the CEO of the Bank of England. Up to a few weeks ago I thought he'd never get a job, so I'm pleased he's in employment.'

'I heard you talking with Laura about the Hastings home. It doesn't sound good.'

'There's teething problems, but that's to be expected. It'll all work out,' I reply, sounding more confident than I feel.

Mum is quiet throughout the rest of the car journey and we're met at the care home by one of the staff.

'Did you enjoy yourself Mrs McCarthy?' she asks mum.

'Yes, it was lovely spending time with my son and grandson.'

I'm surprised at this positive response; most unlike mum.

'OK, mum I better go.'

'Don't go driving like James Bond, OK? If Kerry wants to see you she'll wait,' my mother tells me.

'Yes, I'll drive carefully.'

'Give Harry a kiss for me and tell him to stop talking about men's genitalia.'

Mum then comes up and hugs me. She rarely embraced me when I was a child, but has done so with every visit in the past few months.

Despite my eagerness to leave, I stand in the reception area looking at mum being slowly lead away. I'm still standing there after she's gone from sight.

'Is there anything else we can help you with?' one of the staff asks me.

'Yes; just take good care of my mother.'

CATS ON TRAINS

As I enter the reception hall at the hotel I see Kerry taking to Laura. I feel both excited and nervous as I approach them.

'Hi ya,' is all I manage to utter.

Kerry turns around, smiles at me and gives me a hug. It's an embrace that a friend would give, not a long-term partner.

'How are you keeping?' I ask.

'Fine, just fine,' came the reply.

This is awkward.

'And how are you?' I ask Niall.

Niall doesn't acknowledge me, which is par for the course. He's more interested in pulling off the arms and legs of his ever present Spider-Man toy.

'Say hello to David,' Kerry tells her son, but then Niall spits on my shoes. I presume this is his way of telling me that I'm not welcome?

'Now say sorry to David,' Kerry tells her son.

Niall looks at my shoe and takes off one of his trainers and wipes off the spit with it. He then places his trainer on the top of my head and gently taps it a couple of times.

'Sorry, David,' Kerry says, as she wipes the top of my head with a napkin.

'No problem,' I reply. I quite liked her gentle touch just then. It gives me hope.

A waitress comes around with a tray full of sausages – Niall takes the tray off her and starts tucking in. Kerry then grabs a couple of the sausages and hands the tray back to the confused waitress.

'Let me just fill up his plate, we won't be long,' Kerry tells me.

As Niall is happily scoffing his meal Kerry approaches me.

'I missed your mum, how is she?'

'She's been better…'

A couple of minutes of strained silence follows as we're both staring at Niall. Although it may look as if I'm struggling to hold a conversation, I'm thinking a million thoughts.

'I'm pleased you came,' I say.

Kerry nods her reply.

'So have we got a future together or not?' I blurt out, but before she has a chance to answer Harry interrupts us.

'I never see cats on trains, why's that?'

'It's just easier to bring a dog on a train,' is all I can come up with.

'Then let's get rid of Figaro – just throw her out on Streatham Common and buy a dog on amazon.'

'Figaro's going nowhere; OK?'

'Do you like bras?' Harry asks Kerry, the master at changing the subject.

'I don't mind them,' Kerry replies with a smile.

'If you don't wear a bra do your tits just fall to the ground?'

'No; not yet anyway.'

'Do men wear knickers?' Harry inquires.

'No, men wear underpants and women wear knickers,' I reply.

Although there are some exceptions, which I'm not going to elaborate on right now.

'But knickers and underpants are exactly the same aren't they? If you're out walking and suddenly you piss yourself, or have a crap, they're really useful to catch everything.'

'OK, Harry, why don't you go over to Timothy and have a chat with him?' I say.

'You mean the boy with the fantastic bathroom?'

I nod and Harry then wanders over in Timothy's direction.

'Look, Kerry, just forget I asked that question. You came here for Laura, we can discuss our situation another day.'

Kerry looks at me and smiles.

'David, you've been so patient with me. I know this can't be easy for you. I tell you what, tomorrow I'm going to contact *Specialist Care* and try to get someone to look after Niall for a few hours; if you could take care of Harry we'll arrange a night out; then we can chat.'

'Sounds like a great plan. I'm sure Laura will help me out, if I can tear her away from Sean.'

'Did you know that we've never been out for an evening together; without the boys?' Kerry proclaims.

'I know, and that couldn't have helped.'

'I'm sorry to cut this short, but I'm going to leave now. Niall's been good, but I just want to quit while I'm ahead. I'll ring you as soon as I speak to *Specialist Care*.'

Kerry takes Niall's hand.

'Say goodbye to David,' she instructs her son.

Niall approaches me and then flicks my chin several times before walking away. Compared to some of his previous physical attacks this is relatively harmless.

'Lovely to see you,' I tell Kerry.

'And you too.'

We briefly hug each other before Kerry catches up with her son.

I'm elated. I didn't expect us to walk off together hand-in-hand this afternoon, so this is the best possible outcome. The fact that she wants to meet up has got to be encouraging. I just hope that I haven't misread the situation, but after our evening together I'll have a better idea what the future holds for me and Kerry.

STREATHAM CLOUDS

I spend another hour at the engagement party and then leave for Hastings. Laura offers to come with me, but I tell her to relax and just enjoy her special day. She doesn't need much persuading.

'Did you enjoy the party?' I ask Harry.

'It was OK, but it didn't have a piano or any pork pies.'

'But what *did* you like about it?'

'The chips.'

After our arrival at Harry's 'home' I pull Kevin to one side.

'Harry tells me that the staff are always angry with him, is this true?'

'Harry's a challenging boy and yes there're times when we have to lay down the law, but overall the relationship between the staff and Harry is pretty good.'

'So you think he's exaggerating?'

'Yes, I do.'

I'm really not sure I believe him, but for the time being I'll leave it be.

'OK, Harry, I'll see you on Friday.'

'But the sea is still making a lot of noise, can you stop that?'

'No, the sea will always be there, so don't worry about it,' I reply. Harry seems obsessed about the sea, but there's nothing I can do about that, unless he moves to another residential home.

'Don't you want me sleeping at the Streatham house anymore? Is that finished now?'

'No, Harry, we've been through this so many times – it's best that you stay here during the week, but you'll always come back at the weekends.'

'But I like Mondays in Streatham. The clouds are much nicer, they move too fast in this shitty place.'

'Harry, just enjoy your week; OK? Now give me a hug.'

As usual Harry just stands there with his hands firmly by his sides, making no attempt to meet me halfway. I lift up his arms and put them around my shoulders to endeavour something like an embrace. I kiss Harry on his forehead but he never reciprocates. I've never had a voluntary kiss from my son.

Kevin takes his hand and leads him to his bedroom. Harry just looks so depressed. I wonder how much more I can take of this?

Soon after I arrive home Laura rings.

'How was Harry when you dropped him off?' she asks.

'Not too bad.'

'Better than last week?'

'Oh yes, definitely better.'

If Harry's frame of mind was a zero out of ten last week, today was probably a one, but I really don't want to put a damper on Laura's special day.

Laura excitingly tells me all about her party and praises Sean for arranging it so quickly. I'm genuinely pleased for her and attempt to match her enthusiasm, but simply can't because I'm too down thinking about

Harry. Normally she'd pick up on this but today she is so loved up and for once not worrying about a thing.

I need to find out more about the residential home in Croydon that Bernadette's going to, so I contact Alice and she invites me over.

'Wine or coffee?' she asks as I settle down on the sofa of her living-room.

'I should say coffee, but I could really do with some alcohol right now.'

'Was it painful dropping off Harry again?'

'Yep, he didn't say too much, but just looked so down.'

'Sorry to hear that.'

'Can you tell me a little more about the Croydon home?' I ask.

'The carers all seem so friendly and chilled out. Because of what you went through I did ask some searching questions, and they told me that there wasn't any night curfew and they would only officially document an incident if someone got hurt or there was some physical attack and such like. Of course I won't know for sure how it is until Bernadette's there, but there's a happy atmosphere about the place and I've got a good feeling that it's right for my daughter. It's worth a visit, what have you got to lose? I believe there's still some places available.'

'Thanks for that. I've lost all confidence in my decision-making. I really thought that the Hastings home was right for Harry, but it's not.'

'Have you given it a fair chance? He's only been there a few weeks,' Alice inquires.

'Yeah, I know – me and Laura keeping saying the same thing. It's doing my head in.'

After a couple more glasses of wine I walk home. During the walk I reflect on my conversation with Alice. I feel re-assured that there could be a suitable alternative if the Hastings home goes pear shaped and the fact that Bernadette will be there is an added attraction.

I return to an empty house. There have been so many times that I've longed to be on my own, to come and go as I please, but now I hate it. I'm also missing my 03:00AM conversations with Harry, talking about Danny DeVito's lack of height or Harry Hill's love of pens.

As it's been a long, emotional day it isn't long before I drift off to sleep, but I have disturbing dreams about Harry. He's in a prison and is handcuffed. He's shouting at the prison warden to let him out and is crying relentlessly. I wake up at some ungodly hour, startled and frightened. I immediately check my mobile in case I missed any Hastings calls and then go downstairs, make myself a cup of coffee and aimlessly flick through the TV channels, when I come across a Thomas The Tank Engine episode. As Harry has been banging on about Thomas since he was about two years old, I'm absolutely fed up with this damn train and all of his mates, but this morning I watch the rest of the episode; it's a link to my son.

LEAVING HASTINGS

I arrive at the Hastings home on Friday with a mixture of emotions. I'm excited at the prospect of seeing Harry again, but dread the inevitable downcast meeting with Philip and Kevin, accompanied by those fucking graphs.

As usual I'm called into Philip's office before getting the chance to see my son.

'What's the latest?' I wearily ask Philip, and his faithful sidekick.

'On Tuesday he refused to put away his DVD player after 10:00PM, so Miss Westwood had to confiscate it again. Harry then called her a lesbian cockhead, so to date we haven't returned it to him,' Philip replies.

'Ok, I can understand that. He should obey the rules and not be verbally abusive to the staff. How's he taken it?'

'Initially he was really angry and continued to be aggressive towards the staff, but in the past couple of days he's been quiet and spent most of his time in his room.'

'What's he doing in there if he hasn't got his DVD player?' I ask.

'Nothing much, just lying on his bed, staring at the ceiling.'

'Has he been involved in the daily activities?'

'Very briefly, but then he just retreats to his bedroom. He normally likes the Art session, but this morning he wasn't interested. Here's the list of incidents,' Philip says as he hands me the graphs.

'Forty-two incidents? That can't be right.'

'I'm afraid it is, ' Kevin chips in.

'You know what? These graphs are fucking shit. Harry's in this place for a reason. Unfortunately he's not always going to act appropriately, so why highlight all of his issues, when so far I haven't see any constructive plan to manage these behaviours?'

'We're working on it...' Kevin adds.

'So you keep saying. Can I see what you've got so far?'

'At the moment we've just talked about it at meetings,' Philip replies.

'And what conclusions have you reached?'

'Well for a start, we can't accept abusive behaviour towards the staff, and, like the DVD player incident, he'll be punished accordingly,' Kevin says.

'That's very generic and hardly attempting to get at the root cause, is it?'

Philip and Kevin glance at each other but don't reply.

'Apart from insulting Miss Westwood what else has he done?'

'He's eating some of the flowers as well as parts of the magazines in the dining-room.'

They both look at me for a reaction but I don't respond.

'He also keeps licking the windows.'

'These behaviours are just part of his autism; you can't punish him for that. Reporting him for licking windows, come on.'

'It has to be documented. He also…'

'Hold that thought for a second. I've just got to make a call. I won't be long,' I say, as I leave the room and dial Laura's mobile.

'Hi, what's up?' she asks.

'I've fucking had enough.'

'What happened?'

'I've just been in with the dynamic duo and there's been forty-two incidents this week.'

'That's ridiculous. What did he do?'

'He got his DVD player taken away from him because he insulted one of the helpers. I get that, but he's spent a lot of time in his room on his own doing nothing. That's unacceptable. They're also logging incidents for eating magazines and licking windows; earth shattering stuff. I've had enough of this. This is going nowhere. I don't want him here anymore.'

'I'm with you. I've been so worried about him these past few weeks.'

'I want him to leave *now*.'

'You mean today?'

'Absolutely.'

'But how are we going to look after him?'

'We'll work it out. I'll homework more and when you're not working you can look after him. We've got to get him out of here. I know he's only been here a short time, but this place isn't right for him. I just can't see how this situation will improve. They're not taking his autism into consideration, which I find astonishing. He's so unhappy.'

'OK, go for it,' Laura announces.

'You're definitely with me on this?'

'One hundred per cent. We'll start looking for other places straight away and in the meantime we'll look after him. Do you think you can work things with Ray?'

'Yes, I really do, he's always been so supportive when it comes to Harry.'

'Can you ring him *now* just to make sure?'

'Yeah, OK, I suppose that's wise. I'll ring you back shortly.'

'Good luck.'

I contact Ray and after explaining the situation he told me that although I'll need to come into the office for some meetings, I can homework for the foreseeable future. He reassured me several times that it's not an issue. I'm so lucky to have such a compassionate and understanding manager. I know that it won't be easy homeworking, combined with looking after Harry, but I don't have much choice right now.

I return to Philip's office.

'Guys, thanks for your help but this place clearly isn't the right choice for Harry, so we're out of here and you can stick these fucking graphs up your arse,' I say, and with great satisfaction I tear up the latest print out and let the pieces fall to the floor. My pent-up anger over the past few weeks taking over.

'I'm collecting all his stuff *now*, and then pissing off,' I declare, rushing out of the room, taking two steps at a time up the stairs towards Harry's bedroom. I can vaguely hear a couple of guys on walkie-talkies, detailing my movements. I find Harry sitting on his bed grabbing his holdall. Normally he would reprimand me for being late, but not today.

'Have you got another holdall?' I ask.

Harry walks over to the cupboard and retrieves one. I quickly gather all of Harry's clothes and put as much as I can into the holdall. I grab a couple of his jackets and hand them to Harry. This will probably require another visit, but I'm getting as much as I can now.

'Are we going to that fucking Italy again?' he asks.

'No, just Streatham.'

'Do I have to wear all these clothes on the car journey?' Harry asks.

'No, you don't.'

I think it'll be a bit much to wear all his eight shirts, six pairs of trousers, a dozen socks, two jackets and countless underpants. The mild weather doesn't warrant it.

Philip and Kevin enter Harry's bedroom.

'David, you're not thinking straight. Don't make a rash decision now, talk it over with Laura,' Philip proclaims.

'Laura agrees with me and If we'd been thinking straight in the first place we wouldn't have sent my son here. It may be OK for others, but definitely not for Harry; even you've got to admit that, surely?'

'You're making a big mistake. You'd be hard pushed to find a better residential home,' Kevin chips in.

'The trouble with you, Kevin, is that you lack confidence,' I say.

'What's that supposed to mean?'

'You are one fucking arrogant wanker; it's as simple as that.'

'Am I leaving this dump forever?' Harry asks.

'Yes, we're going now,' I reply.

'This is the best day of my life. I won't have to listen to Kevin's thunderstorm shoes ever again.'

Kevin looks at the both of us and marches out of the room. Being called a wanker is one thing, but he just couldn't handle the criticism of his shoes.

'I'm sorry for losing my cool just now, but I find Kevin's superior attitude hard to take. He's definitely not the right carer for Harry,' I tell Philip.

'David, I know that you're very emotional right now, but please reconsider. The DVD player incident was relatively minor. We can work with Harry,' Philip says.

'I can't tell you how sad it makes me feel thinking about Harry stuck in his bedroom, all alone without anything to do. He's so unhappy here, and yes we could easily face the exact same problem wherever else we end up, but I'm willing to take that chance.'

'Is there anything I can do to make you change your mind?' Philip asks.

'Absolutely nothing. It's a done deal.'

Philip nods, 'OK, I'll leave you to finish packing.'

'You smile way too much and your nose is too big for your eyes, but your shoes are OK,' Harry informs Philip.

Philip smiles at Harry; grateful to finally get a compliment from him, even if it's just a shoe one. He quietly leaves the room.

Harry's fellow resident, Chris, then walks into the bedroom.

'So you're leaving this wonderful establishment then?' Chris asks. I'm not sure if he's being serious, or just taking the piss.

'Oh yeah, we're on our way to the streets of Streatham,' Harry replies.

'Is it because of the crap chips?'

'Nah, although they were always too small and bendy. I did complain to Kevin, but that crackpot did nothing about it.'

'Are you going because they put too much milk in the corn flakes?'

'Nope, but they always cocked that up as well.'

'I know why you're leaving; it's Kevin's eyebrows, isn't it?'

'Yeah, they're way too long and there's no gap between them, so what's the point in me staying here?'

'Does this mean I'll never see you again?' Chris asks.

'Yep.'

'OK,' Chris replies and promptly walks out of the bedroom.

'Come on, Harry, gather up everything and let's get out of here.'

Harry picks up as much clothes as he can and dashes out of the bedroom. He virtually jumps down the stairs and runs to the car.

I'm met at the bottom of the stairs by Philip.

'Do you want me to get the rest of Harry's clothes?' he asks.

'Yes, that'll be really helpful.'

A few minutes later Philip emerges with the remaining clothes.

'Thanks for doing that,' I say.

'You're welcome. I'm sorry it hasn't worked out for Harry,' he replies.

'Harry, say goodbye to Philip.'

Harry approaches Philip.

'The floors are too creaky in this joint, the ceilings are too high, you have liquid soap and your nails are too long.'

'Harry, don't be so rude,' I tell my son.

'Don't worry, David. You take good care of yourself, Harry; OK?'

Harry just turns his back on Philip and gets in the car.

I may not have always agreed with the home's approach to the residents, but I have to say that Philip is a decent bloke. I almost feel sorry for him right now, as he's got some explaining to do to his bosses. I say goodbye to him and as we're passing the front entrance Kevin emerges. He looks a bit shell shocked at this morning's turn of events. Would I be driving away right now if Harry had a different carer? Who knows? But he certainly made my decision easier today.

A few minutes into the journey I ring Laura and put her on loud speaker.

'How did it go?' Laura immediately asks.

'Dad called Kevin a wanker. That was the seventh best moment of my life,' Harry happily proclaims.

'Well of course they both tried to persuade me out of it. Kevin more or less told me that it was the best residential care home on the planet.'

'What a tosser,' Laura adds.

'I told you he was a ...'

'Yes, I think we've established that, Harry,' I say.

'I'm so pleased I don't have to see those mahogany tables in the dining-room ever again. They're repulsive,' Harry chips in.

'For once in my life I acted on impulse. I couldn't stand seeing Harry so unhappy there.'

'David I'm just so relieved that he's out of that shithole.'

'I told you it was a shithole,' Harry proclaims.

'David, I'm just so proud of you for being so brave to take that decisive action. It couldn't have been easy. I still can't take it all in. I feel like a massive weight has just been lifted from me. What an amazing week. But, David, don't worry. I'll help you out. We'll get through this,' Laura says, with a refreshingly positive attitude. I've got Sean to thank for that.

'I'm going to contact the Croydon home tomorrow, you know the one Bernadette's going to. It sounds promising,' I add.

'Yes, Alice was telling me about that the other day. How are you feeling about leaving the Hastings home, Harry?'

'I hated going on the outings to the beach. The sand would always stick to my toes, which made my teeth go on edge. And those fat fucks were always on the beach with their bellies wobbling everywhere; it made me feel like puking up.'

'Harry, can we forget about fat, I mean big, people for one day please?' I ask.

'What will you miss about the Hastings home?' Laura inquires.

'I liked the grass in the garden. It was much shorter than our grass, which made my feet much happier.'

'David, when you get that Croydon appointment I'd like to come along.'

'Of course,' I reply.

Laura did ask me to pop over for a drink, but I declined. It's been another exhausting day and I just want to chill out with my son.

I'm delighted at Laura's immediate response to taking Harry home. I really didn't know how she'd react, but since last weekend she's found this sudden burst of self-belief, which is an absolute joy to see.

Later on I enter Harry's bedroom, ready to settle down with him. He's already in his bed watching a Thomas DVD.

'You can go into your own bedroom now,' Harry informs me.

'You don't want me with you tonight?' I ask.

'Nah, this bed's too small for you now. Your feet are always sticking out at the end and your big toenail on your right foot needs cutting and this keeps me awake.'

'If I cut my toenail can I come in then?'

'Nope, you're too bald now.'

I slowly walk out of Harry's bedroom. I should feel happy that after all these years I don't have to lay down with Harry every night, but I'm not. I've always looked forward to cuddling up to my son at night and I'm sad that this looks like the end of this special bonding. However, I've got to think what's best for Harry and of course at sixteen years of age it's only right that he should go to bed on his own.

Could Harry's new night-time routine be the result of his Hastings stay, or because of my overgrown toenail and receding hairline?

MUM

The first thing I did this morning was to contact the Croydon residential home. I explained what happened yesterday and inquired if there were still some openings. They confirmed that as they have only recently opened up the home that there was some vacancies and to my surprise suggested that I pop up to see them this morning.

I still can't believe I made that decision about Harry yesterday. I've been so worried about him during the past few weeks, and when I found that he'd been lying on his bed for the previous forty-eight hours feeling depressed, I just snapped. I couldn't let that toxic situation fester and although I'm feeling more nervous about Harry's future, than I did yesterday, I know that I did the right thing. The fact that Laura was in complete agreement reassured me.

I arrange to meet up with Laura in Croydon and during the short car journey there I try to explain to Harry that we're going to see a residential home in Croydon.

'That's better. I like East Croydon station cos it has six train platforms and three tram link platforms. It's nicer than the West Croydon and South Croydon stations, but they're OK too.'

Good railway stations are definitely the key to Harry's heart. So far, so good.

Laura meets us outside the home.

'I can't believe you've set up this so quickly,' she tells me.

'Neither can I. How are you feeling?' I ask her.

'Nervous, but excited.'

Meanwhile Harry is staring at the walls outside the main entrance.

'What's up?' I ask him.

'Be patient, I'm concentrating,' came the reply.

Laura looks at me somewhat confused. We leave him be for a few minutes but time's pressing.

'Harry, we're going to be late for our appointment.'

'Ok, I got it.'

'What have you got?'

'There's thirty-seven bricks across the front of this building and forty-two bricks in height. That makes it one thousand, five hundred and fifty-four bricks in total. But of course I need to subtract the number of bricks that would be covering the front door and the windows, but you kept on interrupting me, so I haven't had a chance to do that yet.'

'Ok, that's good; you can finish this off when we leave.'

Just as we're entering the house we spot Rebecca, whose son, Ben, went to Harry's old school.

'Hi ya,' Rebecca greets us both.

'It's been a while since we've talked; how's Ben?' Laura asks.

'He's doing really well. I've just been in to see him.'

'He's living here?'

'Yeah, for nearly three weeks now. He loves it,' Rebecca replies.

'Harry's last placement fell through, so we're looking at alternatives. Can you give us the heads up?'

'I can't recommend it highly enough. The staff are just brilliant, so caring and very laid back. There's loads of activities every day and the facilities are just superb. I've looked at loads of residential homes and this is by far the best. Once you've been given the tour I think you'll agree with me.'

'Wow, that's encouraging,' Laura says.

'Look, I've got to dash. If you've any questions just give me a ring, and let me know how you get on; OK?'

Rebecca gets in her car and drives away.

'It's looking good already, isn't it?' Laura remarks.

'Yeah, but let's find out for ourselves.'

We're greeted inside by Carrie, who's the manager of the home.

'Good to see you all, and especially nice to meet you, Harry,' Carries cheerfully announces.

'What type of soap do you have in the toilets?' Harry asks.

'It's just the normal bars of soap,' Carrie casually replies as if she's been asked this question every day of the week.

'Can I touch the ceilings in the bedrooms?'

'Yes, they're not particularly high.'

'And what colour are the toilet seats?'

'I think they're all white.'

'OK, let's look at this joint.'

Soaps, ceilings and toilet seats are all essential criteria for a suitable residential home it seems.

An hour later we say goodbye to Carrie. We're both extremely impressed. All the points that Rebecca made rang true. They even have a piano in the spacious living-room.

Carrie told us to put in an application as soon as possible. She confided to us that there are a couple of places still open and she will recommend Harry's placement to the powers that be. Although the final decision is out of her hands she felt confident that they would agree with her. This all seems too good to be true.

'What do you think of the place?' I ask Harry, after he informed us that the doors and windows came to two hundred and forty-eight bricks.

'Is there any sea nearby?'

'No, Croydon is a long way from the sea.'

'Do butterflies visit Croydon?'

'Yes, when the weather's nice.'

'Then it's not too bad.'

'But what do you think of the actual home and all of the staff?' Laura asks.

'Carrie's hair is too long. It kept flying over her eyes the whole time, so she had to pull it back over her ears again and again. Why doesn't she just shave it all off like Harry Hill?'

'Some women like long hair.'

'But that's just weird.'

'Did you know that Bernadette is going to the home as well?' I ask.

'Yeah, I did. I'm so excited that I'm going to be living with that lovely chick,' Harry replies, smiling.

'If you do get in you'll be in separate bedrooms,' I say, to warn my son off any hanky-panky thoughts that he may be having.

Maybe I should tell Carrie about the blossoming romance so she'll just keep an eye on things?

'In our lunch hour we'll go to East Croydon station and watch all the trains. I'll check all the arrival and departure times and Bernadette will write them all down in her fantastic notebook. If the trains are late I'll want an explanation from the station manager.'

Does a station manager actually exist? I knew that the inclusion of Bernadette would be a deal clincher. It's such a different reaction compared to when I first told Harry about the Hastings home. It all bodes well.

'You can go to the train station but Carrie or a member of staff will have to be with you,' I say.

'I want to be alone with Bernadette. I don't want that hairy monster with us.'

Laura and I smile at each other in reaction to Harry's comment. It's yet another sign of the deepening relationship between Harry and Bernadette.

I drop Laura off at Sean's and soon after our arrival home Kerry rings. She's managed to get *Specialist Care* to look after Niall for a few hours tonight and wants to meet up. She seems genuinely delighted when I tell her about the turn of events for Harry. Does this make it easier for her to move back in? I'm not sure, as Harry had already started his Hasting residency when she decided to move out. I'm trying to pick up on any signals that'll indicate what her plans are, but I'm just as confused as I was on the day she walked out on me. Regardless, in a few hours I hope to have the answer and I'll be able to move on with my life, one way or another.

'Are you happy now you don't have to go back to Hastings?' I ask Harry.

'The Croydon bricks are shinier than the Hastings ones and there's much more of them. The Croydon windows are nicer too.'

At this point I'd take anything positive about the Croydon home, even brick and window compliments.

Carrie told us that we should get a decision within a couple of weeks of receiving the application. Although I feel euphoric right now I should be more cautious in front of Harry. It's not a certainty that he'll be accepted and if he doesn't Harry will be so disappointed, especially knowing that Bernadette will be there.

'Harry, we don't know for certain that you'll be going to the Croydon home.'

'Yeah, they'll have me. I'll be able to perform a gig every night of the week and they don't have to get that Elton John geezer now. I'm going to save them a few quid and they know it.'

Of course. Why didn't I think of that? All sorted then.

I contact Laura, who is delighted to have Harry for a few hours. It'll be a good test to see how he gets on at Sean's and whether Timothy's new attitude towards my son has any effect.

I make myself a cup of tea and sit out in the garden. These last forty-eight hours have been surreal. To have been given the opportunity to get into the Croydon home almost immediately after leaving Hastings just doesn't seem possible. Dealing with Harry's situation over the past sixteen years has meant a series of setbacks and countless stressful experiences, so it's lovely to have something positive happen to him at last. It's difficult not to get too excited right now.

'Can Bernadette and me go on the tube today?' Harry asks me.

'Where do you want to go?'

'The tube.'

'What is it you want to see?'

'I want to travel on the Victoria and Piccadilly lines from the top to the bottom. We'll give our marks out of ten for every station. Bernadette has already written down all the stations on her spread sheet, so let's go'.

'Hold on, just to clarify things, you want to travel the length of both the Victoria and Piccadilly lines, and not get out once?'

'Only to change onto a different tube line. When it stops at each station we'll have a quick look at it and then we'll write down our ratings. Robert did this on April the twenty-second and he said that it was the best day of his life.'

Robert's easily pleased.

'How long is it going to take?'

'For the Victoria line from Brixton to Walthamstow Central it takes thirty minutes. We'll then travel from Walthamstow Central to Finsbury Park to get on the Piccadilly line; this takes only nine minutes. From Finsbury Park to Cockfosters takes twenty-four minutes and then we start from Cockfosters and end up in Heathrow terminal five, and this takes ninety minutes. Of course the idiot passengers might be daydreaming and not get on and off the trains on time, so it could be longer. But in order to complete the other leg of the Piccadilly line we need to go from Heathrow terminal five to Uxbridge and that takes…'

'Hold on, from what you've told me so far that'll take two and a half hours, that's more than enough, Harry. We'll have to do the Uxbridge line another day,' or perhaps never.

'But that's the best bit.'

'It'll have to wait.'

'I don't know why you hate Uxbridge so much,' Harry tells me.

I don't respond; there's no point.

I'm thinking about the 'dates' that Harry and Bernadette have been on together – watching the traffic lights in Peckham, playing the piano at Heathrow airport, meeting Drew Edwards and now travelling the length and breadth of the London underground without coming up for air. They're not exactly your normal teenager dates, but Harry and Bernadette are not exactly your normal teenagers.

I contact Alice, who's already aware of the tube outing.

'While Harry and Bernadette are waxing lyrical about the tube stations at least it'll give us a bit of time to talk. I want to have a further chat about the Croydon home,' I say.

'David, I won't be coming, I have company right now. Are you OK to look after Bernadette?'

'Yeah, of course. Let me guess is your visitor the most eligible bachelor in London?'

'If you're referring to Greg, yes it is,' Alice replies, almost whispering. 'He was really keen to go on the underground but I wanted some time with him alone, so we're going out for a meal.'

'Oh, I see, you swan off to some expensive restaurant while I'm stuck on a crowded underground for hours on end.'

'You got it in one.'

'Well I hope you have a great time; you deserve it.'

'Thanks, David, I really do appreciate you taking Bernadette. She's going to love spending time with Harry.'

'Yeah I know. I'm moaning but deep down I'm happy to tag along with them.'

Shortly afterwards we arrive at Alice's. She answers the door but Harry brushes right past her.

'Harry, say hello to Alice,' I say.

'No time, I'm going for a crap.'

'Sorry about that.'

'Don't give it a second thought. Come in,' Alice replies.

As I enter the hallway Greg appears.

'Nice to finally meet up again, David. I briefly caught Harry running up the stairs,' a smiling Greg informs me.

'Yes, he's in need of the lavatory, although that wasn't quite the way he put it,' I reply.

Greg laughs at my remark and I notice Alice looking admiringly at him. She's smitten.

'Are you looking forward to your tour of London?' Greg asks me.

'If we were travelling by bus it'll be a little more interesting, but as long as the kids enjoy it.'

'Apologies for not getting back to you but I've been really busy of late, however things are much quieter now so I'm definitely going to reward Harry and Bernadette for their impromptu gig.'

'Really, there's no need.'

We chat in the hallway for a few minutes before Harry comes charging down the stairs.

'Wow, that was a massive shit. And who the hell are you?' He asks Greg.

'I'm Greg; I met you briefly when you played so beautifully at Heathrow airport.'

'Oh yeah, I remember. I held out my hand to you, but you never gave me any dosh.'

Greg starts laughing again, but Harry simply stares at him.

Bernadette strolls into the hallway and welcomes Harry with a high five. This is greeted with smiles all round from the adults.

'Do you know the way to Brixton?' Bernadette asks me.

'Yeah, I've done that journey many times.'

'Do you know where to park?'

'Yes, there's a car park right near the tube.'

'How much will it be for four hours?'

'I'm not sure, but I'll find out when I get there.'

'Unacceptable. If you haven't got the right change we'll be stuck in the car park for the whole day. You should've found out before getting here. This could be a disaster.'

'Ok, Bernadette, I think David's got enough change on him,' Alice tells her daughter.

Bernadette looks at me suspiciously, 'I don't think so.'

Actually I think Bernadette's right, but I'm sure they'll take my visa card.

We say our goodbyes to Alice and Greg and make our way to Brixton. Unfortunately the car park doesn't accept visa cards so Harry and Bernadette accompany me to Boots where I buy a packet of polo's with a twenty pound note in order to get change. The peanut gallery weren't impressed.

'You're wasting my time,' Harry proclaims.

'This is a fucking joke,' Bernadette announces.

Anyone would think that we're going to be late for an appointment with the Queen, nevertheless the mood is brighter as we board the tube at Brixton.

Bernadette and Harry position themselves by the door and given what happened at Clapham Junction, I'm standing right next to them. With every station that passes they pop their heads outside the train doors and have a quick glance around. If there are a lot of passengers Harry and Bernadette will remind them to shake a leg. 'Get on the fucking train you bunch of losers,' and 'stop daydreaming, arseholes', are two typical ditties aimed at the commuters. Amazingly they don't get much of a reaction; maybe the passengers think it's all part of London Transport's new zero tolerance policy?

Harry and Bernadette are pretty much in sync with their individual ratings, and although most of the stations look the same to me they do come up with some odd reasons to differentiate them. They only gave Pimlico station a four point eight-two because there was a man on the platform with a moustache. Highbury and Islington only got a three point six-five because it had a poster advertising hearing aids and they both agreed that hearing aids are only for 'old fuckers' and nobody wants to talk to that lot, so it's a waste of everyone's time, energy and money.'

Nearly three hours later we're finally leaving Brixton station and heading home. I've been standing up throughout this and I'm feeling exhausted.

'Dad, you've got to admit that was the best day ever,' Harry tells me.

To be honest, I'd put my wedding day, Arsenal winning the Premier League and even last night's episode of *The One Show* slightly higher than today's experience, but I nod my reply.

'So which station got the highest score?' I ask my tube fanatics.

'Brixton of course,' Harry replies.

'Which happens to be the first and last station that we were at,' I add with a slight ironic tone.

'Well done, Mister McCarthy. I really thought that you weren't paying any attention,' Bernadette responds.

'And why was it the best?'

'Because it only had seven people on the escalator.'

'But you didn't look at any of the other station's escalators?'

'You're nearly intelligent now; are you going to evening classes?' Bernadette asks me, without a hint of sarcasm.

'And what was the worse station?'

'Green Park, because too many people were standing beyond the yellow line and the station manager didn't give a toss.'

So after three hours of meticulously analysing numerous stations it all comes down to too few people on the escalator and too many people standing over a yellow line. Go figure.

I drop off Bernadette and once home I have a quick shower, splash on some aftershave and drive to Sean's.

Laura and Sean greet us as we pull into Sean's driveway.

'Did they behave themselves?' Laura asks.

'Yeah, no problem. I'll let Harry tell you all the details.'

I've suffered long enough; it's Laura's turn now.

'Be good for mum and Sean,' I tell my son.

'Only if they don't show any John Travolta films.'

I wave goodbye to him, but he's too busy studying Sean's house bricks.

I park my car a few minutes' walk from the restaurant. What will the next couple of hours have in store for me? I desperately want Kerry and Niall to come back to live with us, but I've no idea what Kerry's plans are. I thought that there was still a lot of affection between us at the engagement party, but whether that's strong enough for our relationship to start up all over again is another matter.

As I approach the restaurant I feel like I'm fifteen-years-old again and about to go on my first date with Sheila Poole. We went to the cinema to see a Woody Allen film and then to McDonalds. That was my one and only date with her. She told a mutual friend that the film was not funny and was insulted that I didn't try it on with her. I was being penalised for being a gentleman.

Anyway, what's the point of going out with someone who doesn't think that Woody Allen is funny?

As I enter the restaurant I can see Kerry holding a menu, but looking out of the window. She looks nervous. Is that a good or bad sign?

Just as I'm approaching her table my mobile rings; it's from mum's care home.

'Hi, it's Annabel, I've some bad news. Your mum passed away about thirty minutes ago. I'm so sorry.'

'What happened?' is all I can manage to say.

'She went to sleep around six o'clock and passed away peacefully an hour later.'

'Was it a heart attack?'

'The doctor thinks it was a blood clot.'

'Why does he think that?'

'He's just examined her and can feel the clot in her right leg. Of course this needs to be confirmed, but her deteriorating health in the past year, plus her lack of movement could point to this.'

'Have you told my sister?'

'No, not yet.'

'OK, I'll go and see her now and then I really want to see my mum; is that OK?'

'Of course.'

'I can't believe it, mum's dead,' I say to Kerry.

'Oh my God no. I'm so sorry, David.'

'I've got to see Fiona *now*.'

'I'll drive you,' Kerry says.

'No, it's OK, I'll be fine. I'll ring you.'

'Take care, David,' she replies as I dash out of the restaurant.

THE KISS

I was tense and extremely nervous at the thought of seeing mum again, but as she looked so peaceful and free of pain it gave me some comfort.

Fiona and I did shed a tear or two when we first saw her and we both talked to her for a while, saying things that we probably should have said when she was alive. I kissed her forehead before leaving her alone in her bedroom.

When I told Harry about mum's death he just said 'Does that mean I can't sing to those decrepit zombies anymore?' I re-assured him that I'll arrange a gig (of sorts) for him there and he just nodded and went straight up to his bedroom. There's nearly always noise coming from Harry's bedroom, sometimes it's music, such as Cliff Richard's greatest hits or from one of his DVDs, but for the rest of the evening there was just pure silence.

It's always sad when you lose someone so close to you, but although it was a shock when it happened, I'd been half expecting it, especially after seeing how much her health had gone downhill recently.

She was never the life and soul of the party, but in the past few years she always seemed so sad; mostly since Dad passed away.

Less than forty-eight hours after her death, Fiona and me are sitting in the admin office at the care home, listening to mum's lawyer reading out her will. We're both amazed to hear that we'll receive nearly forty thousand pounds each, which was the profit left over from her house sale. I never really thought about mum's finances; she kept that information pretty much to herself. Once I get over the shock I'll look into investing a huge chunk of it in Harry's savings account.

As my dad is buried in a town called Dunmanway in County Cork, Ireland, it was no surprise to hear the lawyer say that mum wanted to be buried alongside her husband. The funeral will take place at Saint Patrick's church in Dunmanway in three days. The local funeral directors have already arranged for mum's body to be flown over in a couple of days. I do find it amazing how quickly these things are organised so soon after a death. In Ireland the funeral is usually held within two days of death, but this was delayed because of the logistics of the two countries involved.

Fiona has been my life-saver. After seeing mum at the care home she immediately got in touch with the local funeral directors, who themselves contacted the funeral undertakers in Dunmanway and sorted everything out.

'There was one new amendment to the will that your mother made a couple of weeks ago,' the lawyer informs us.

'And what was that?' I ask.

'I'll read her exact words – I want Harry to play at my funeral and it's not going to be that vulgar bastard song that he loves so much. It's the song that my husband, Dunny, used to sing to me when we were courting – *I'll Take You Home Again Kathleen*. I also want Harry to play it on the piano; he's a very talented musician. Harry's had a difficult life and I haven't always been so understanding of his behaviour. But the poor lad can't help it, he was born with autism. I'm proud of my grandson and I just know that he'll sing this song so beautifully.'

I am stunned by this and having difficulty holding my emotions together right now. I glance over at Fiona who wipes away a tear or two.

What a lovely sentiment to leave this world by.

I know some people who call their parents by their Christian names, but mum was always mum to me. Her name is Kathleen and my father always called her that; he never abbreviated it. I'd seen him sing that song to her many times; usually on a Saturday night after a couple of pints of Guinness.

Now all I have to do is tell Harry about singing the song at the funeral service.

'Will he be OK with that?' Fiona asks as we leave the care home.

'I think so; he seems to like an audience. Just as long as he doesn't play his greatest hits.'

'It's quite a lot of pressure to learn that song before Friday.'

'I'll download the music and lyrics. He's a quick learner when it comes to music,' I reply.

Soon after I arrive home Kerry rings me.

'David, is there anything I can do?'

'No thanks, it's all in hand.'

'I know that I'd only met your mum a handful of times, but I liked her. I mean that. She once told me that I'm far too pretty for you and warned me that I'd better not be stringing you along.'

'Yeah, that sounds like mum.'

'Maybe after the funeral we can meet up? There are things we need to discuss.'

'Of course.'

'I hope it all goes well on Friday. I'll be thinking of you.'

'Thanks, Kerry, that's much appreciated.'

I'm still no wiser about our future together.

I enter Harry's bedroom. He's lying on his bed listening to music.

'What song are you playing?' I ask.

'*Living Doll*, by Cliff Richard and the Young Ones. I love it when Ade Edmondson bangs Cliff over the head with a mallet. Can I get a mallet and do that to that bitch next door?'

'No, I'm not going to get you a mallet. What other songs have you got on your ipod?'

'Nothing, only *Living Doll*.'

'Grandma wanted you to sing an Irish song at her funeral. Will you do that?'

'Which song is it?'

'It's called *I'll Take You Home Again Kathleen*.'

'Sounds shit, can't I sing *Bohemian Rhapsody*?'

'No, it'll mean a lot to me if you can do this,' I say.

'How much is my fee?'

'I'll give you a fifty pound amazon voucher,' I reply without hesitation, anticipating Harry's demands.

'Cool, but I also want Bernadette with me.'

'But it's in Ireland, Harry. It's too far for her to come.'

'Bernadette and the amazon voucher; deal or no deal?'

'Let me see what Alice says, but I'm not making any promises.'

Bizarrely, a few minutes later Alice rang and wanted to know all the funeral arrangements as she, Bernadette and Greg are keen to go.

'Are you sure?' I ask.

'We would be honoured to be there. Greg's looking at hotels and flights as we speak, but he wanted to make sure it's OK with you first.'

'I'd be absolutely delighted if you came. In her will mum asked Harry to sing her favourite song at the funeral service and Harry said he'd only do it if Bernadette's there.'

'That's so sweet.'

'I'm really touched by your gesture. Please tell Greg to book the hotel and flights.'

'Yes I will. Take care, David.'

I was going to suggest to Alice that I'd pay for Bernadette's flights, knowing how much it meant to Harry having Bernadette with him. I just didn't want to take any chances of Harry not performing that song. He just has to do it; it was mum's last request.

I've already contacted my cousins, Neave and Finbar, in Dunmanway to inform them of the funeral arrangements and to ensure that the McCarthy cottage, which is owned by half a dozen McCarthy cousins (and me) is free so we could stay there. Thankfully it is.

Laura and Sean are also coming over. I'm so pleased they're making such an effort. I know mum would've been so pleased.

Laura also informed me that Harry's brief stay at Sean's went without incident. She took great delight in telling me that Timothy and Mary went out of their way to engage with Harry.

The next couple of days pass quickly. Fiona and me spend a lot of this time in mum's bedroom sorting out all of her belongings. We gave most of the clothes to the local charity shops, but kept some more personal stuff like jewellery. In her drawers we found her diaries, which she wrote on a regular basis. Apart from the usual mundane stuff like getting a haircut or visiting Sainsbury's, there were a number of entries which revealed a more compassionate side to her – 'Told David that there was no hope for Harry. I'll regret that until the day I die. I should apologise' – she never did. 'Mentioned to David that he had got fat – why the hell did I do that, even though it's true? I could see that I hurt his feelings.' 'How long must I wait until I see my Dunny again?' These were just a few of many such entries. I wished she had conveyed some of these thoughts to me, but mum wasn't one to show that side of her personality to us, which is a shame because she would have felt better for doing so.

I've been extremely impressed at how quickly Harry has learned *I'll Take You Home Again Kathleen*. It took him a little while to master the piano notes, but once he got that down pat, he practised the singing many times to an audience of one - me. To my amazement he didn't complain at all during all of this. It's been quite emotional listening to my son playing my parents' favourite song.

The day before the funeral has arrived. Laura and Sean had taken an early flight to Cork, whilst Harry and me are on the same flight as Alice, Bernadette and Greg.

'You're holdall looks heavy, what have you got in it?' I ask my son as we arrive at Heathrow.

'Eighteen Thomas DVDs.'

'Why did you bring that many?'

'For the flight and to play when the funeral is on.'

'You're not playing your DVDs at the funeral; you'll leave them all at the cottage.'

'But that priest geezer is going to bang on and on about boring shit.'

'Harry, we've been through this a million times. You're going to listen very carefully to the priest and be very quiet in the church.'

'But he always wears that white collar all the time. He should go to Primark and get a psychedelic shirt, then he'll be a lot happier.'

'No DVDs at the church,' I re-iterate.

'OK, I'll play them all during the flight,' Harry replies.

'Harry, the flight is only one hour.'

'But that means I'll only be able to play seventy-five per cent of one DVD. Can't we just ask the pilot to fly the plane to that China place, and then go straight back to Ireland, so I can play more of my Thomas DVDs?'

'No, that isn't going to happen.'

'If I show the pilot the *Tales From The Rails* DVD he'll want to watch all the other Thomas DVDs won't he?'

'No, he won't. He's taking the plane from Heathrow to Cork and not making a detour to China; OK?'

Harry looks disappointed but doesn't respond.

Once we boarded the plane, Harry insisted on sitting next to Bernadette.

'Thomas has never been to Ireland,' Harry proclaims.

'Do the Irish hate him?' Bernadette replies.

'I don't know, but the problem is there's a big sea between England and Ireland. I looked it up on the internet yesterday. So how is Thomas going to get across that sea?'

'So maybe the Irish haven't been given a chance to watch Thomas because of that ocean?' Bernadette replies.

'Yeah, whatever bastard put that fucking ocean there is stopping Thomas from going to Ireland.'

Will there ever be a day when Harry is not obsessed about Thomas The Tank Engine? I seriously doubt it.

While Harry and Bernadette continue their Thomas discussion, my thoughts turn to my parents. Along with thousands of Irish citizens, mum and dad came over to England in the early fifties, mainly to seek work. It must have been hard to leave their parents, brothers and sisters behind.

All of our family holidays were spent in Cork. I have such vivid memories of travelling on the ship across the turbulent Irish sea every summer. We would always spend a couple of weeks at the McCarthy cottage in the beautiful town of Dunmanway. It was an idyllic time. Unfortunately in recent years I've only been back there a handful of times with Harry.

It's a scenic route through the beautiful countryside from the airport to the cottage, passing many familiar towns with their multi-coloured houses that you see everywhere in Ireland.

I feel quite choked up as I approach the cottage. It's been in the McCarthy family for many generations and it's the house that my father lived in for most of his life in Ireland. As I open the front door I immediately catch the familiar smell and again my thoughts are transferred right back to summers many years ago.

'Are you OK?' Alice asks.

'Yeah, it's just this house holds so many happy memories for me.'

Alice smiles and gently rubs my back.

'Where's the Sky box?' Harry asks.

'There's no Sky TV, just the terrestrial TV channels,' I reply.

'What a shithole.'

'Harry, this is the house that my father lived in, so please be respectful.'

'So your dad never had Sky as well?'

'No, and for probably all of his life here he didn't have a television, just the radio.'

'Was he a caveman?'

Alice, Greg and me immediately laugh at this remark. It brings some much needed light relief to us all.

'Harry's quite a character,' Greg tells me.

'That's one way of putting it,' I reply.

'David, I hope you don't mind, but we'll be on our way to the hotel now,' Greg says.

'Yeah, no problem. You know the way?'

'I've got it all on the sat nav. It shouldn't be more than a twenty minute drive.'

As we're bidding our farewells, Bernadette looks concerned.

'I want to stay with Harry,' she tells her mother.

'You'll see him tomorrow; come on, we'd better get going,' Alice replies.

'But I want to have frosties with him in the morning, cos he doesn't like the frosties with milk and neither do I.'

'That's right, although I have to have milk with the corn flakes cos otherwise they taste like plastic,' Harry chips in.

I lead Alice into the living-room, away from Harry and Bernadette.

'Alice, it's OK with me if Bernadette stays.'

'Are you sure?' Alice asks.

'Of course, we don't want the star of the show tomorrow to throw a wobbly because his girlfriend wasn't with him at all times.'

'That's the first time you've referred to Bernadette as Harry's girlfriend. I like it.'

'Well to all intents and purposes they are girlfriend and boyfriend, don't you think?'

'Yes, I do. Thanks again for looking after Bernadette. You've got so much on your plate right now.'

'I've just got to contact the funeral directors, that's all. Having Bernadette will be a welcome distraction.'

'OK, I'll get her clothes together.'

A couple of hours later Harry and Bernadette are in the kitchen watching a Thomas DVD, while I'm sitting on a sofa in the living-room enjoying the wine that Neave and Finbar kindly left for me.

Fiona texted me a short time ago, she's just arrived at the airport and will be staying with some other cousins a few towns away.

All the funeral arrangements are in place; all I have to do is turn up at the undertakers at ten o'clock tomorrow morning.

I find it hard to believe that mum's body is only less than a five minute drive away in the town where she first met my father. My mother was nineteen years of age when she went to a dance in this town. I remember her telling me that all the boys were standing on one side of the hall and the girls on the other. After each dance was finished they would chat for a minute or two before returning to their respective corners. Given that my father had limited time to speak to my mother he must have had some really good chat up lines - but dad had that Irish charm in abundance, so no problem there.

Before I leave I want to visit that dance hall. The last time I came here it was a pub; I hope it's still there.

Harry bursts into the living-room.

'Bernadette wants to go to bed now. She has to have the lights on in the bedroom, hallway and toilet. The window has to be twenty-five per cent open. Her mother always sings Michael Buble songs to her when she settles into bed, so I'm going to sing a couple of his hits when she's ready. She's put on her *My Little Pony* pyjamas on in the toilet while you were getting blotto.'

I've only had two glasses...

'OK, Bernadette, shall I show you to your room?' I ask.

Bernadette rushes into the living-room, goes straight up to Harry and gives him a kiss on the lips.

'Wow, you kiss like a hot, hot chick,' Harry tells her.

'I know,' Bernadette modestly replies.

I show Bernadette to her room and she settles in her bed without any fuss. She's smiling the whole time. I wonder why?

'Do you want me to sing any Buble tunes to you?' I ask, thinking that Harry might be embarrassed to see her again so soon after their sultry encounter.

Her smile immediately vanishes, 'no, no, no, no.'

I think I got the message.

When I arrive downstairs Harry is packing away his DVDs.

'It's time to go to bed, tomorrow's a busy day,' I say, deliberately avoiding saying anything about what just happened.

'Dad, I love Bernadette, so can I marry her tomorrow after we get rid of Grandma?'

'No, you're too young.'

'We've got the church all booked up so why don't you slip that bloke with the white collar some bucks so he can marry us?'

'Harry, I'm delighted that you and Bernadette are getting on so well, but you're not ready to get married right now.'

'OK, but you've got to admit she has some great ears.'

With that Harry makes his way to his bedroom.

I pour myself another glass of wine. Could the town that brought my parents together so many years ago be also responsible for finally uniting Harry and Bernadette? Who knows what the future holds, but my greatest wish is that the girl with lovely ears, and who doesn't like milk on her frosties, becomes Harry's partner for a long, long time; if not forever.

FUNERAL

I wake up at five o'clock. I check on Harry and Bernadette; they're both asleep (in separate bedrooms). That jet lag is a killer!

There's a couple of acres of ground at the back of the cottage so I go outside for a walk. My thoughts immediately turn to Harry and Bernadette. I just couldn't get to sleep last night thinking about their kiss, and Harry's marriage intentions. I just can't wait to tell Laura and Alice.

If Harry and Bernadette were 'normal' teenagers I suppose I'd be more concerned that they would get up to much more than just a kiss, but their love is pure innocence, and it's not often you can say that in this day and age. However, I'll still keep a watchful eye on their relationship just in case.

I look at the stunning countryside surrounding me. At one point after my divorce from Laura I thought about living in Ireland. Most of my relatives are here and I find the people to be extremely friendly and compassionate. Also, they seemed very understanding of Harry during my previous trips here. But it was never going to happen because of Laura. How could I ever separate Harry from his mother?

By the time I'm back in the cottage, Harry and Bernadette are sitting in the kitchen in their pyjamas.

'Oh there you are, we thought you buggered off back to Streatham,' Harry tells me.

'Why would I go back to Streatham on the day of my mother's funeral?'

'Because you thought that she was a pain in the arse?' my son replies.

When someone dies usually only nice things are said about them and during these last few days I'm only remembering all the happy moments that I've spent with my mother, but in many ways she was a difficult person. She was much moodier than my father and had almost a child's mentality in telling me exactly what she was thinking, even though it could be extremely hurtful. So Harry's pain in the arse comment has an element of truth to it.

'So are you confident about singing that song, Harry?' I ask.

'I still haven't seen that amazon voucher,' Harry replies.

'You'll get it as soon as we're home. I've been a bit busy lately.'

'You better not be pissing me around.'

'Don't worry, you'll get your voucher. Now are you looking forward to singing that song for Grandma?'

'The audience are going to fall asleep listening to that tedious crap.'

'No, they won't. The congregation will actually love you singing for Grandma.'

A slight difference of opinion.

'Afterwards can I sing *It's Great To Be An Engine*?'

'Not at the church, maybe at the reception,' I vaguely reply.

'In a few weeks I'm going to be living with Harry,' Bernadette cheerfully announces.

'Maybe, it hasn't been decided yet.'

'Don't be ridiculous. Of course the home will have him. They'll pay a world record transfer fee to get him in.'

Bernadette obviously thinks that Harry is the Messi and Ronaldo of the autistic world.

'I'm going to stroke Harry's ears and ankles every morning while we're having our frosties,' she proclaims.

'With no milk,' Harry adds.

I suppose ears and ankles stroking is innocent enough, isn't it?

Bernadette puts her hand on the table and Harry immediately holds it. I wish I could take a photo of this and send it to Laura and Alice.

'What are you waiting for? Can you make us those frosties now?' Harry impatiently asks me.

I pour the frosties into two bowls, accompanied by two spoons and hand them over to the love birds. Gordon Ramsay would've been so impressed.

A few hours later Alice and Greg arrive. Alice helps Bernadette put on a beautiful dark blue dress.

'But this makes me look like a bit of a tart,' Bernadette complains.

'You look lovely and so smart, just like all those female BBC newscasters,' Alice replies.

'Oh, OK then.'

'I don't want to get hanged,' Harry also protests when I attempt to put his tie on him.

'That won't happen. You have to wear a tie for funerals.'

'Show me that rulebook.'

'There's no official rulebook, it's just the done thing.'

'So you're trying to strangle my neck for no reason?'

'Harry, as soon as the funeral is over you can take it off; OK?'

'That's if I'm still alive at the end of it,' Harry replies, shaking his head.

I drive the short distance to the undertakers where we meet up with Laura, Sean, Fiona, Neave, Finbar and a few cousins. The undertakers take the coffin to the hearse, but before they close the doors Harry dashes over to it and bangs on the coffin.

'Yep, definitely oak,' he remarks.

'Good choice, Mister McCarthy,' Bernadette adds.

The undertakers look at each other in confusion. That must be a first for them. I don't bother with the 'I'm sorry, my son's autistic' explanation.

With the help of my cousins I carry the coffin into the church.

Halfway through the service the priest announces, 'would any of Kathleen's siblings like to say a few words?'

'There's no way I'm standing up there, you'll have to do it,' Fiona whispers in my ear.

I slowly make my way up to the altar. Although I hadn't prepared anything I know exactly what I want to say.

'In the last few years mum's health was poor, so I'm pleased that she's not suffering anymore. She wasn't one to share her personal feelings so easily, but after she had a couple of sherries I would sometimes ask her about her early days with Dad and she would recall with great fondness her first few dates in this town. However, there were other days when she simply didn't want to talk about my father, as the pain of his passing was still evident so many years later. I am so pleased that I got to spend some quality time with her only a few days ago at Laura's engagement party. I shall miss her, but I'm glad that she's finally reunited with her husband and my father.'

With that I walk back to my aisle seat.

'Very well said, David and I believe that Harry will now sing his grandma's favourite song.'

Harry walks up to the piano and puts his sheet music on the holdall.

'I didn't understand any of that Dad; were you talking a load of old bollocks?'

This brings a ripple of laughter from the congregation, but the priest looks far from impressed.

'I thought that grandma was a miserable old bag. She always looks pissed off. And she never liked me singing the *there ain't half been some clever bastards* song. My dad said that I have to sing this boring song for her, but what's the point? She's dead and won't know if I sing it or not, but I don't want to lose my fifty pound amazon voucher that dad promised me, even though he's hasn't given it to me yet.'

The priest looks annoyed, so I make my way to the altar and briefly explain Harry's autism. He immediately relaxes and before I return to my seat Harry starts singing. Even though I've heard him play and sing this song many times over the past few days I'm still moved to tears, as the song is so appropriate, particularly the line when the man promises to bring Kathleen home, where she'll no longer feel any pain.

Despite Harry's criticism of the song he sings it beautifully, and as soon as he finishes, everyone in the church applauds. My mother would have been so very proud.

I turn around and see that Laura is also wiping away some tears. She smiles gently at me.

'And now I'm going to do *Piano Man*, which was sung by Billy Joel. He used to have loads of hair but now he hasn't got any, not even one. Did he sell it all off for charity? You can sing along with me if you like.'

Again the priest looks stressed, so I quickly make my way to Harry and quietly tell him that I'll increase his amazon voucher to one hundred pounds if he stops right now.

'But he's going to love it,' Harry protests, pointing at the priest.

I think not.

Even with doubling his voucher amount Harry reluctantly picks up his sheet music and accompanies me back to our seats.

I look at the sheet music resting on his lap and there is a Billy Joel songbook, left open at the *Piano Man* page. So it seems that Harry did intend to perform a lengthy set list after all.

The rest of the service passes quickly and before long we're carrying the coffin out to the graveyard, which is just outside the church. After the coffin is lowered into the ground I look up and to my astonishment I see Kerry and Niall standing a distance away from the rest of the mourners. How can this be possible? I didn't give her any funeral arrangements. Niall is sitting down, picking up blades of grass and eating them. He does love his grass.

Following tradition I throw a handful of dirt on top of the coffin. Fiona does the same and then everyone else follows suit, with the exception of Harry who throws his tie in.

Some of my cousins approach Fiona and me to offer their condolences, while the rest head straight to Glynn's Bar for some much needed food and drink. Before long it's just me, Harry, Kerry and Niall outside the church.

'Hi, I had no idea you were coming,' I say.

'I always intended on making the trip, so I contacted Laura and she gave me all the details. I only arrived this morning as I didn't want to distract you. I'm so sorry for your loss.'

'Thanks, Kerry. I can't tell you how pleased I am that you're here. And how are you, Niall?'

Niall approaches me and flicks me on the chin. He then sits down and continues his grass meal.

'Dare I say it, but is that OCD medicine now working?' I ask.

'Yes, it's definitely taken the edge off things. He still approaches people but not as much and with less intensity, plus he's now on ADHD medicine for the first time and that's helped,' Kerry replies.

'I can't believe you're here. Today has been surreal.'

'David, I know that this is hardly the time or place to have this conversation but I've been preparing this speech since the restaurant and was going to say the same the other day on the phone, but understandably you've had a lot on your plate. You've always been just amazing with Niall, you've never lost your temper with him, even under the most violent physical assaults. But as I've just said I think that Niall's in a better place now and my son was the main reason why I left you. What I'm trying to say is that I want us to get back together, that's if you'll still have me?'

'This isn't out of sympathy because of mum?'

'No, I made my decision before your mum passed away. I can't tell you how much I've missed you. Will you have me back?'

'Of course, it's what I've always wanted.'

We hug each other tightly.

I look over my shoulder and see Harry sitting next to Niall, also tucking into the grass. Harry looks up.

'Dad, the grass here is better than the Streatham grass cos it's much greener.'

Harry glances at Niall. 'Hey, mate, leave some of that grass for me OK?'

That's the first time Harry has called Niall his mate. Kerry notices this too and smiles at me. Is this a sign that it'll all work out this time around? I approach Harry.

'Harry, Kerry and Niall are moving back in and from now on I don't want you saying anything bad to them both. Do I make myself clear?'

'Bernadette was right, you're acting more and more like that Hitler chap every day.'

We walk the short distance to Glynn's bar and meet up with the others. There's loads of buffet food laid out, but for once Harry doesn't eat any of it.

'That grass is filling,' he remarks.

He never leaves Bernadette's side for the rest of the evening. I catch a couple of their conversations about Thomas (who else?) and debating the different types of toilet paper. They both seem to have strong views on its colour and texture.

Greg approaches Harry and Bernadette.

'You guys are just amazing and I've been meaning to reward you for your superb Heathrow airport gig.'

'About time,' Harry chips in.

'There's a comic con event in New York in October and you are both coming with me, Alice and David. I've already arranged a meet and greet with Tara Strong. How does that sound?'

'We're going to meet the *My Little Pony* actress, Tara Strong?' Harry excitingly asks.

'Yes, the very same one. You're going to have your photo taken with her and you can ask her anything you want, within reason.'

I'm so pleased he added those last two words.

'This is the best day of my life,' Harry proclaims as he hugs Bernadette, not really taking into consideration that it's my mother's funeral today.

'Let's write down twenty-three questions for Tara,' Bernadette tells Harry.

That was an amazing gesture from Greg and just so thoughtful. From what I understand Greg is quite wealthy but I insisted on paying Harry's fare as well as my own. It only seemed right after my newly-acquired inheritance. I can't wait to see their reaction when they finally meet Tara; that's going to be special.

On a day of great sadness there's also a feeling of absolute joy witnessing the deepening relationship between Harry and Bernadette. Laura and Alice have talked about little else all evening.

Of course the icing on the cake was the wonderful surprise seeing Kerry and Niall at the church. I simply can't quite believe that they're both coming back into my life.

As we're about to leave the pub my mobile rings, it's from Carrie.

'David, good news. I've just had a phone conversation with a local authority chap and he says that your application looks fine and you should receive a letter by next week confirming Harry's acceptance. Once it's all official I'll let you know a starting date. It'll probably be a couple of weeks later, but we'll move as quick as we can on this.'

'Carrie, that's amazing. I can't believe it. Thanks so much for letting me know.'

'No problem. I'll be in touch. Enjoy the rest of your evening.'

'I think I will.'

I approach Laura just as she's walking out of the pub.

'That was Carrie. Harry's in.'

'You are kidding?'

'I'm dead serious.'

'It's going to work out this time isn't it?' Laura asks.

'I think so, I've got a good feeling about this move. Harry seems really happy about it as well.'

She starts to cry so I embrace her. Sean looks on concerned but when he sees me smiling he realises that it's good news. Laura then takes off her jacket.

'Now, what's everyone drinking?'

After an evening of eating and drinking everyone has now gone back to their respective homes and hotels, so it's just me and Harry in the cottage that I love so much. Harry's in bed, but I doubt he'll get much sleep tonight. I enter his room and sit on his bed.

'What was your favourite part of the day?' I ask my son.

'In fifth place was eating the grass, fourth was singing that awful song, but I did like it when the twenty-two people clapped afterwards because the clapping wasn't too loud. I like soft clapping. Third was having a piss in the pub because it flushed really quickly, then second was when that bloke with the short fingernails told us we were going to America to meet Tara Strong, who is the best actress in the whole world.'

'So what topped that?'

'Chatting and holding hands with Bernadette,' Harry replies without hesitation. 'I also kissed her on the lips five times and on both of her elbows twice.'

'Why her elbows?'

'Because she's got the most beautiful elbows I've ever seen. Even better than her ears.'

I nod and smile at my son. What can I say to that?

'Why did Bernadette's father fuck off?' Harry suddenly asks me.

'Because he wasn't getting on with Alice. It happens sometimes.'

'Did he crack up like mum did when I was little?'

I'm taken aback at this question as he's never mentioned Laura's illness before.

'No, he just didn't want to be with Alice anymore.'

'Was it because Bernadette's autistic?'

'No, not at all.' This isn't strictly a truthful answer. Francis simply couldn't handle the pressure of bringing up a special needs child. He had an affair and left soon after.

'When mum went berserk you still stayed with me, didn't you?'

'Yes I did. Mum wasn't well then, but she's much better now and loves you with all her heart.'

'You won't leave me, will you?'

'You'll never have to worry about that, Harry. I'll be with you forever and so will your mother,' I reply.

This is probably the most serious conversation I've ever had with my son.

Harry smiles at me. 'Now can I play my Thomas DVDs on my own?'

I kiss his forehead and leave his bedroom.

It may seem a strange thing to say on the day of my mother's funeral but I feel at peace with the world. Of course I feel great sadness that my mother is no longer with us, but she's suffered enough in her later years. I still can't believe that I'm back with Kerry. I'm under no illusions that everything will run smoothly but as Niall's behaviour has improved and Harry will be away during the week this can only help. I am absolutely thrilled that Harry has got a care home so quickly and the fact that Bernadette will be there with him has eased a lot of my worries. I feel euphoric just thinking about Bernadette and Harry's relationship.

'I really don't know how you cope,' is often said to me, but Harry's my son; I have to cope. However, his autism brings so many rewards that most parents of 'normal' children will never experience. His innocence means that he'll forever be my child.

I use to wonder what life would be like if Harry wasn't autistic, but no more.

I will always apologise on Harry's behalf whenever he says or does anything inappropriate, but you know what... I'm not at all sorry that my son is autistic.

THE END